THE
GALLERY
OF
UNFINISHED
GIRLS

THE GALLERY OF UNFINISHED GIRLS

LAUREN KARCZ

An Imprint of HarperCollins*Publishers*

HarperTeen is an imprint of HarperCollins Publishers.

The Gallery of Unfinished Girls
Copyright © 2017 by Lauren Karcz
www.epicreads.com

ISBN 978-0-06-246777-5 (trade bdg.)

Typography by Torborg Davern
17 18 19 20 21 PC/LSCH 10 9 8 7 6 5 4 3 2 1
❖
First Edition

For Tricia
This book exists because of two sisters,
a long summer, and a basement.

one

THE PIANO APPEARS on our lawn the week after our mom left. I am swigging orange juice in the living room, trying to decide whether to take Mom's car to school. Then I pass by the window and there's the piano, sitting on the grass, straight-backed and confident as a Marcel Duchamp sculpture on display at MoMA.

I drag Angela from the kitchen out to the yard.

"Well, you said you wanted to learn to play," I tell her.

"I didn't think it would happen like this," Angela says. She taps the key farthest to the right, and it dings out a little note. It sounds like a shy kid speaking out in class for the first time. She plays a few more, and they're clearer, louder, coming at us in layers. A car drives by and honks at the three of us: the piano, my sister, and me.

"Mercedes, try it," Angela says.

I clunk my hands down in the middle of the piano. A couple of friendly Florida lizards scatter across the driveway in response to the mess of sound.

"Brilliant," Angela says. She looks at the keys again, and I think she's getting ready to stay there and compose a symphony, or maybe a rock opera. I recognize the look on her face as a feeling I had once, and that I wish like hell I could get back: the feeling of being on the brink of creation. It's heady and sweet, a little like love in the way it fills up your chest, but less dangerous. I mean, less dangerous until you know what you've gotten yourself into.

Angela looks at me pleadingly, and really, what are we going to do, tape "lost piano" signs around the neighborhood? No way.

The door to the other half of the duplex creaks open and shut, and we're in the presence of Rex, our neighbor and landlord, a bearded industrial freezer of a man who never likes to be left out of the activity of the neighborhood, whether that's a backyard cookout or the police stopping by the house two doors down again or the admiration of an upright piano.

"Morning, ladies." Rex is wearing his early spring uniform: swim trunks and an FSU T-shirt under a bathrobe. "You need some help with that?"

"Actually, yeah," I say. "Thanks."

Rex steadies himself behind the piano and pushes it off the rough grass and onto the driveway, where it rolls unevenly to our half of the duplex. Angela, with a massive grin on her face, holds the front door open as Rex angles the piano through the doorway. We both know Rex wants to ask—he wants to ask almost as much as we want to tell him, *No, we have no idea where it came from, but it's a nice distraction, isn't it?*

"Just, I guess, anywhere in the living room is fine," I tell him.

Rex surveys the living room from his vantage point as the tallest thing in the house. Angela and I haven't moved anything in the room since our mom's fevered departure for San Juan, and it still holds all the souvenirs of her: mascara-stained tissues on the end tables, a paperback thriller wedged open on the arm of the recliner, her phone charger plugged in and sucking energy from the air. A week ago, all of this was kind of a darkly comic still life about Mom being away for a few days, but last night, she called and told us that Abuela's condition had worsened. I couldn't sleep after that—I sat in this room and stared at every little thing she had left behind. It seemed like the most important thing to do at the time.

"Against the window," I say.

"The window?" Angela and Rex say together.

"Come on, we never look out of it."

"I do," Angela says. "How about on the other wall? We can just move the chair somewhere else."

"Wait! Don't move that chair. I sit in it all the time." I pick up the paperback from the arm of the chair and hold my mother's place on page 153. The hero is trapped in a basement and is trying to figure out how to slip through the one thin window at the top of the wall. There's a twist, isn't there? Oh yes, the wall itself is weak.

He punches at it, then slams a wooden chair into it, and the corners crumble, and he is free.

"Can you please not smoke in Mom's car?" Angela says. "She's going to know."

"She already knows." I hit the button that opens all the windows at once. "And anyway, I might have already quit when she gets back."

We're at that perfect time of year when Florida isn't dressing up in dusty beads of humidity or ten-minute monsoons. The air is weightless and the morning haze that usually hangs over our street has been replaced with a bright, clear picture of what lies ahead. Like a daytime version of an Edward Hopper painting. Like the world cracked open at the horizon and saying, *Oh hey, Mercedes and Angela Moreno, welcome to your day!* And we can try to get to that place, but it will hide from us again and again.

"Time for a Victoria detour?" Angela asks.

"I already texted her. How can we not do a Victoria detour when we've got this sweet ride?" I knock my fist against the plastic body of the gray Ford Focus. Yeah, so Mom's car is nothing much, but it doesn't grumble on start-up like my old Pontiac (Mom's old Pontiac) does, and the stereo system is a thousand times better.

Angela laughs hard, a big laugh that makes me nostalgic for last week, and I pull my hand back in the window and smoke a little so that my cigarette doesn't burn itself out in the perfect air of the day.

Marcel Duchamp, the French artist who famously grabbed a urinal, painted his pseudonym on the side, called it *Fountain,* and displayed it as art, once decided to bottle the air of Paris. *50 cc of Paris Air,* he called it. The first bottle broke—artistically, I'm sure—so he bottled the air again, and displayed it in Philadelphia. Dude could do anything and call it art, or not-art, or anti-art, and people would come to see it. And he could capture a day, a place, a breath.

At a stoplight, I grind out the cigarette and tuck it away in the Ford's clean little ashtray. Angela nods at me.

"I'm surprised Mom didn't suggest we stay at Victoria's house," she says. "We could probably live in the back half of the house and nobody would notice for a week."

Yeah, I've thought of that myself, maybe more than a few times, but I'm not going to say so. Officially, Vic is my best friend, and that's it. "Her house doesn't have a piano, though."

Victoria is quiet, because she knows about Abuela Dolores in the hospital in San Juan, and because she knows our mom's going to be away for a lot longer than planned, and because she probably knows that *we* don't know how to feel about any of this yet. She's good like that, most of the time. And maybe Victoria senses, like I do, that if Angela and I unsettle the air too much, Abuela could die.

Angela is in the back, her biology book yanked up in front of her face. Vic, sitting in the front, hasn't put on her sunglasses yet, and her dark hair is down, settled in still waves on her shoulders. She comes from a small family where the only people who ever die are the tangential ones: the great-great-uncles in Brooklyn, expiring quietly under a blanket of smiles and stories.

"Still alive?" she finally says.

"Who?" Angela asks. "Us, Mom, or Abuela?"

"All of the above," Vic says. She glances at me sideways, our eyes lock, and then the sunglasses go on.

"All accounted for," I tell her.

"I can't even believe you guys are going to school today," Vic says. "You should stay home and work on your painting, Mercedes."

I wanted to see you, that's all. I could tell her this, because the sedan in front of us is taking its sweet time making this left turn— and then, God, if she *liked* that I'm only here because she is, we could take Angela to school and head back to the Moreno half of the duplex for the day. Sure, she would insist on getting to her dance class on time, and I'd still have to sneak back into school later to pick up Angela, but we'd have the whole morning. All that time. And the drive to the dance studio, her bare feet gripping the curve of the glove compartment, her hand lying in that brilliant space between our separate gray seats, her fingers playing at the place I burned the fabric with a long-ago Parliament Light before I understood what it was like to have her in the car with me.

"You always say you paint better at home," she says.

I tug at my hair instead of diving for another cigarette. She's tied tightly into her trench coat, and now her hands curl around the red purse on her lap. I know she wants to say the right thing, the thing that comforts and sympathizes, the thing that cat-nuzzles your leg and then walks confidently away. But if she knew what that was, she would have said it already.

"Yeah, well, I have a German quiz today." I think maybe I do. "And I really do need to go to art class. We're supposed to hear about the county show."

I'm the last one to get out of the car, because I'm double-wrangling my art toolbox and a big sketch pad. Victoria pops up behind me and grabs the toolbox, which is the same red as her purse, and she swings it by her side as though it belonged to her all along. I shut the car doors lightly, as though I'm placing a new piece of pottery into a kiln. Maybe I've kept a little bit of this morning in the car. We'll probably need whatever leftovers we can get by this afternoon.

Angela trundles ahead to the science wing. Vic stops swinging the toolbox and falls into step with me as we head up to Sarasota Central's main entrance.

"You look like you're freaking out." Vic gives me a small smile, like she's not sure I can handle a full one. "Name a place."

"Umm . . . the Hospital del Maestro in San Juan."

"Okay, fine. How many people at the Hospital del Maestro are saying some form of the word *shit* right now?"

My mother is one of them, if I know her at all. "How many people," I begin, "at the Hospital del Maestro are saying some form of the word *shit* because they can't remember how they wound up in the emergency waiting room?"

Vic hands my toolbox to me as she considers this. She unbuttons her trench coat—it's already getting warm. She has a purple dress on underneath. "I pass. Everything I can think of is gross. Start a new one. Same place."

"Okay. How many people at the Hospital del Maestro are having an out-of-body experience right now?"

"Hey, let's not get supernatural here."

"The unwritten bylaws of this game say I can do whatever I want." I try to make a grand gesture, Abuela Dolores–style, with my free hand. "Infinite possibilities!"

"We know them all, don't we?" Vic says.

"We do," I tell her.

two

THE TABLES IN the art room are color-coded, for no reason besides Mrs. Pagonis's keen and pointless interest in organization. Since I started taking studio art at the beginning of junior year, I've been sitting at the Orange Table with Gretchen Grayson—that's almost four hundred school days of not becoming friends with Gretchen Grayson. This semester, we've been joined by a dude with the name of Rider, who is always shooting meaningful glances in my and Gretchen's direction, in some misguided attempt to become the Rebellious Artist Boyfriend of one of us. I kind of want to tell him, *I've tried your kind. Have you ever heard of Bill Stafford, former king of the SCHS unaffiliated Smoking Corner?*

Gretchen doesn't notice Rider's look today, but she is up to her elbows in art mess, as though she's been here since dawn.

I open my sketchbook and try drawing the piano, but the out-line is stubborn about being a misshapen rectangle. I try shading the left side with a light brown, but it starts to look muddy and I let the half-brown rectangle chill out on my sketch pad rather than turn it into something worse. Screw it, I just want the piano to *tell* me how to draw it, to start playing itself at night in a way that says, yes, make me abstract, make my corners rounded, give me snakes as keys.

"Snakes," I whisper at the sketchbook.

"What?" says Gretchen.

"Nothing."

Gretchen doesn't flinch when I drop the brown pencil on the table and lean back in my chair. She has been concentrating hard for the last few weeks on the canvas in front of her. As awful of a day as yesterday was, what with the news about Abuela hitting me like a Ford Focus to the chest, at least I spent first period being proud that I had deciphered the subject of Gretchen's picture, finally. It is: Gretchen Grayson, as a yellow lizard, surrounded by a bunch of anthropomorphic green lizards in some sort of ornate dining room. I figured out the yellow lizard represented the artist herself when a couple of telling details appeared yesterday: Gretch-en's pearl flower-shaped earrings, and one of her ever-present gray cardigans.

I think I hate the picture, especially this almost-finished version of it. I hate how, even with the earrings and the cardigan, the yellow lizard doesn't match Gretchen at all. I hate how the green lizards are staring directly at the viewer. And I hate how I can't put a real word to how it makes me feel.

I have a hard time figuring out the truth of simple things sometimes, like whether I prefer coming to studio art over, say, second-period German, with Herr Franklin and his persistent butchering of my name (I have been "Fräulein Marino" since August). I'm pretty sure art class is the winner, but a couple of months ago I was *pretty sure* I could have completed a shading assignment, too.

Mrs. Pagonis cranks up her favorite nature sounds CD and sits on her paint-splattered stool at the front of the room. She's got one of her half-artsy, half-suburban outfits on again: a bright patchwork jacket on top and mom jeans on the bottom. Once I saw her at the Publix with her two kids in a shopping cart. Once I saw her smoking in her car while she was leaving school. Gretchen adores her.

"I want you to continue your shading projects today and tomorrow," she says. "Also, I want you to think about what you'll want to enter in the juried show held by the county this year. You'll see I've posted the guidelines for the show next to the whiteboard, along with photos of the winning pieces from last year, in case you need some *inspiration*." She shakes her fingers at us, down-came-the-rain-style, I guess to convey the inspiration that some of us hope to get.

I am the first one up to the whiteboard.

The guidelines are the same as last year—basically, art your heart out, kid, and submit your best damn work for display. It can be painting, sculpture, photography, mixed media . . . pretty much anything except performance art.

A photo of *Food Poisoning #1* is taped to the wall under the guidelines.

It's weird seeing it that way. It's a big painting, and here it is reduced to a four-by-six matte photograph. It's a little like the first time I went to the Salvador Dalí museum in St. Pete and discovered that some of the paintings that looked so huge and regal in my Dalí book were actually small enough to fit on the wall of my bathroom.

Food Poisoning #1, I still have at home. I used to have it on my wall, but I got tired of my mom telling me how much it scared her, so I took it down and put it behind the headboard of my bed.

"How's the follow-up piece going, Mercedes?" Mrs. Pagonis asks.

"It's coming along," I say. Whereas *#1* is hiding in my bedroom, *#2* is hanging unfinished in the laundry room.

What's weird about seeing *Food Poisoning #1* again, photograph or not, is that sometimes I don't feel like I created it. It may as well be Rider's work, or Mrs. Pagonis's, for that matter. I don't know how the artist made the seemingly clashing colors work together so well. I can't figure out what sorts of brushstrokes were used to make the paint look so alive. I can't tell what it's *about* exactly, but looking at it makes my stomach churn and makes my feet warm and my knees cold, so I think it's doing whatever it was meant to do.

Whatever I meant it to do.

Back at the Orange Table, Gretchen Grayson is shading, shading, shading the background with hues of brown and yellow, and Rider darkens the lines on an intricate pattern. And on my sketch pad—ugh, I left it open and now Gretchen and Rider have probably sneaked smiles at each other about my ridiculous piano drawing. I flip to a new page because the promise of something else is better than the mess I've left. I sketch and shade easy things: Gretchen's metallic purple water bottle, the pale peach face of the Moreno-McBride duplex, the red purse sitting on my best friend's lap.

If I ever doubt the existence of a higher power, all I have to do is look at my eyeball. My driver's license says my eyes are brown, but really, there are a hundred colors in there, and everything is working in balance to let me see myself in this soap-streaked mirror in the girls' bathroom. I've never been sure if the Creator of the Eyeball has a plan for me, or for Abuela or Vic or anyone else, but I feel like she or he or it gives us our possibilities.

Next to me, Vic pulls back her hair. "Psst," she says. "Ansley Lyman kind of looked at you when she left a minute ago."

But I'm pretty sure she didn't. And even though I appreciate Vic's acceptance of my attraction to guys and girls, I don't know where she gets the idea that I might be interested in someone like Ansley Lyman.

What I want to do, maybe today, maybe now, is see if Vic will come over this weekend. Which is one of those things I've said a hundred times, but it's felt different lately. I feel like I need to be extra careful in the way I ask, or she'll find the secret lurking in the spaces between my words.

"It's showtime, folks!" She pushes away from the mirror. I hope I never get tired of Victoria Caballini's way of leaving a bathroom.

We head to the Dead Guy with our lunches. There is no more peaceful place in school than right here, at the memorial bench and plaque for one Timothy Gelpy, who died in a car accident during his junior year ten years ago. Vic takes the bench, so I sit on the ground, using the cool marble plaque stand as a backrest. When people die suddenly, it seems like everyone around them wants to create something beautiful and good in their honor, and that's exactly what Sarasota Central High School did for Tim (Vic and I can call him that—we've been sitting here long enough), but not for anyone else who died in the years before or after him.

I'll have to ask Vic sometime what she thinks about this one saintly guy being memorialized over all others, but I don't want to spend our measly twenty-two-minute lunch period on that kind of thing.

Vic sets her container of carrot sticks aside. "Have you heard anything from your mom yet?"

I take my phone out of my pocket and click it to life. The main screen flashes its usual photo of Victoria and me at Tall Jon's party back in January. No notifications.

"Nothing today. I guess everything's the same. She would have told me if Abuela had woken up."

"Maybe. Maybe not." Vic's illogical optimism always makes me smile. In her world, there's a chance that Abuela snapped back to consciousness this morning, and now she and Mom are sitting around having coffee and watching novelas.

Vic checks her own phone out of habit. She's got a photo from the same party as her wallpaper, though it's from the beginning of the night, when we were looking less windblown. "How weird is it not having her around for so long?"

"It's weird. It's quiet. She used to always have the TV on, you know? And she would always sort of narrate her life as she went through it."

"I remember one of the first times I came over, she was in the kitchen putting away dishes, and she just kept saying, 'Dishes, dishes, dishes,' the whole time. It was like she created a little theme song for every part of her day." Vic laughs, maybe out of relief that she could fold this funny story into the most serious conversation we've had at the Dead Guy in a long time.

I try to smile. "Dishes, dishes, dishes," I sing.

Abuela's first stroke was two Sundays ago.

That Monday, Mom made the arrangements to go to San Juan, and she left on Tuesday morning.

And then the next Monday, Abuela had the second stroke, and fell into a coma.

Vic crunches through a few more carrot sticks and I coat my fish nuggets with ketchup before digging in. We could sit inside with the other girls from my fifth-period English class, or with Vic's friends from chorus, but it's nicer like this: Vic, me, and the Dead Guy. We've been able to eat outside for most of the school year. We did last year, too, but over at the picnic tables in the stark, sunny center of the courtyard, where everyone could see us and everything moved way too fast. Connor Hagins and his pals on one end of the long table, Bill Stafford and Tall Jon and two other white guys on the other, and Vic and me in the middle. We always sat next to each other and exchanged looks or bumped arms whenever one of the guys did something worth noting, but there was hardly a chance to talk, and we had to find time later to do a lunchtime postmortem.

That part was so critical: we had to replay everything, to dig deep into our then-boyfriends' words and shrugs and try to use them to predict their (and our) futures. I think we forgot sometimes that we were in charge just as much as they were. And we didn't realize until later that the guys weren't doing the same level of English-class analysis that Vic and I were.

That's why I have to be so wary about every word I say to her.

"You should come over this weekend." I stare at her knees while I say this. And when she says nothing for a minute, I drop my gaze to her ankles. "Spend the night on Friday, maybe?"

"Sure," Vic says. "Or we could go to the beach or walk around downtown."

"That's a possibility. Especially since Angela might be playing the piano all weekend."

Vic straightens up on the Dead Guy's bench. "Wait, you have a piano?"

It's already coming true: Angela has pulled a chair from the dining room to use as a piano bench, and I'm marooned on the back porch with the pieces of *Food Poisoning #2*: a sketch pad with the fifteen penciled thumbnails for the painting, and the canvas itself, its blank patches staring me in the face. I've spent the whole fall and winter not getting this picture right, and now, with a month before submissions close for the county show, and two months to be sure I don't flame out as the Sarasota Central High School senior with the most wasted potential, it's like I expect the thumbnails to rearrange themselves into the raw material I need, or the shape of the painting to jump onto the canvas itself.

But everything is still. The thumbnails, the canvas, the other half of the porch, the hairy moss on the backyard trees, and me. Maybe potential is all I have: energy, all held-up and trembling, waiting to be set free.

Inside, Angela taps at the piano, stopping and starting, trying to fit notes together. But if I'm going to wait for her to come up with even five notes in a row that work, I might be out here a long time.

The door to the neighboring porch opens. "Hi there, Mercedes!"

"Hey, Rex." I pick up a brush for show. Yep, I'm totally an artist at work. "If I could paint you a picture of anything in the world, what would it be?"

Rex comes to the screen that separates his porch from ours. "Hmm. It probably wouldn't be something that's *in* the world. I think I'd ask for an imaginary planet, or your perception of dignity . . . something like that."

"Dignity, huh? I'll take that into consideration." I streak purple watercolor across the canvas. It's the most I've painted all day. "Can you hear Angela from your side?"

"Not too much," Rex says. "A note here, a note there."

"That's pretty much all she's playing right now."

Ding-ding-ding-ding-dong! Okay, that's five decent notes. I'm free from the porch and *Food Poisoning #2* if I want to be.

"Listen, Mercedes." Rex scratches his beard. "I don't know if your mom told you, but I've given you all a break on the rent for the next two months. What with, you know, the situation."

"Thanks. The situation hasn't gotten any better or worse, by the way."

"No need to update me," Rex says. "I know it might be rough going for a while. And it's good that you and Angela have each other to depend on."

"Yup."

"So, your dad knows that you and Angela are here by yourselves, right?"

"Mom talked to him. He knows we're fine." I make a broad stroke of purple across one of the patches that's already purple, but the shades aren't the same and it's going to look odd. "Anyway, she's probably coming back soon, so it's not like Dad needs to drive down here from Ohio."

Angela has reverted to notes that are scratching at one another's faces.

Rex's gaze kind of goes in the direction of the notes, but then shifts back to me. "I also wanted to let you know that I'm going to advertise for a renter for my spare bedroom. I'll introduce whoever it is I rent to. No need to be strangers around here."

"Sure. Hey, if you could find someone who's a piano teacher, I think that would make everyone's lives easier."

Rex grins. "I'll see what I can do." He nods toward my canvas. "What are you working on?"

"The second painting in a series." It's still technically true, even if I never finish it.

I stand at the sliding-glass door, from where I can see the left half of Angela and the piano. Maybe she's got the right idea, devoting herself to this thing that shoved itself into our lives. Maybe if I stand on the driveway, a lacrosse stick or some knitting needles will fall out of the sky. I'll give *Food Poisoning #2* one last shot, and if nothing works, then I'll do something else.

Here's how a painting comes together. First, you get an idea. Maybe it's something you see in your head or in real life, or it's an abstract concept you want to turn into color and shape. Whatever it is, you sketch some thumbnails of it. You get to a thumbnail you like, and then you move to the vast white gulf of canvas. You create a pencil outline of your work on the canvas before bringing in color. Color is tricky and joyful and frightening all at the same time: you start with the broadest strokes, and then you come back again and again with layers and details and texture.

Here's how *Food Poisoning #1* happened: During a ridiculous lunchtime conversation, my then-boyfriend Bill pondered out loud whether the word *salmonella* came about because someone got sick from eating salmon. And I pondered—not out loud—if a whole series of artistic works could be made about food poisoning.

Something that's supposed to be nourishing makes you feel worse, I scribbled on a napkin. I went home and got started—no thumbnails, no outlines, just paint splashed at canvas, newspaper crumpled and torn and embedded in the paint. I added layers and birds. I was color and shape and energy. I finished a layer and had to let it dry, and I swear my fingers and eyes and legs twitched until I could come back and add more paint.

And it won *first fucking place.*

So many things were different about my life during the *Food Poisoning #1* days. All the members of my family were in their expected places: Mom and Angela here in Sarasota, Abuela in her little apartment in San Juan, Dad and his girlfriend still unsure if they were going to leave Naples, Florida, for Columbus, Ohio.

I was sixteen. It was a cool, rainy fall. I was still having sex with Bill Stafford.

I didn't think about Victoria the way I do now.

None of these things can be reversed right now. I can't do a single thing to bring my life back to the way it was then.

I scrape at *Food Poisoning #2,* freeing a few crumbs of yellow paint from having to exist in the picture. Maybe there's one unchanged strand of my life I can grab onto. One simple, comforting thing.

Maybe the one relationship from back then that hasn't changed a bit. The one person who's always been good for a night of cigarettes and nonpiano music. I pick up my phone and give Tall Jon a call.

"Moreno!" he yells over background noise that's louder than

Angela's piano. "I can't believe you called. I just had a revelation about you earlier today."

"I need to escape for a while," I tell him. "Where are you?"

I've just mixed a few shades of purple, as if I could recapture that one thing about the first piece. But what am I going to do—repaint *Food Poisoning #1* on a different canvas?

"It's league night. We're three frames away from the end."

Tall Jon is responsible for my understanding bowling-speak. So I'm off to the bowling alley, to hear about a revelation.

three

TALL JON IS ready for me: a lane set up with *TJ* and *Mercy* on the screen, pizza and fries and Cokes on the table. He has even hunted down the six-pound purple ball for me to use.

"Nah, you can play my frames for me," I tell him.

The other guys on his league team are stowing their bowling gear in bags tall enough for a set of golf clubs. Tall Jon is the youngest guy on the team by at least twenty years. It's his dad's old team—Tall Jon took his dad's place last year when the older-but-shorter Jon's AA sponsor advised him to quit bowling. This was, conveniently, around the same time that Tall Jon graduated from SCHS, and so he turned into a college freshman who spends half of his free time in a bowling alley.

"I'm not bowling as 'Mercy,'" Tall Jon says, "because I have none."

"Oh, fine," I say, "but let me have some pizza and a revelation first."

"The revelation rests on the idea that you still have, ah, feelings for that best friend of yours."

"Sure, yes." My face burns a little. "Idea confirmed."

"Okay, then." Tall Jon waves good-bye to the league guys, and we're alone at this end of the alley. The lights flicker—every time I wind up here, it's right around when the black lights and lasers make their appearance.

Tall Jon grins at the darkening bowling alley, as if he timed this transformation with his revelation. "Well, I was thinking about the way Bill told you he liked you. And we both know he's kind of an oaf, but he was pretty brilliant about getting his feelings out there. And I thought— damn, if Mercedes, or even the awesome but reluctant bowler named Mercy, did something like that for her friend Victoria, I bet little pink hearts would be floating up from their love nest in no time."

"Okay. I'm going to bowl now." I grab the six-pound ball and line up my feet and roll it down the lane and do a follow-through flourish like Tall Jon taught me the last time we were here, and of course the ball rolls into the gutter before it gets even halfway to the pins. I whirl around to Tall Jon. "Wait, did you bring me here as some sort of elaborate metaphor where my gutter balls represent my love life?"

"What? Oh my God, I didn't even think of that." He laughs and his hat falls off. "Sorry, Moreno."

My ball is coughed up from the machine, and I roll again. This time, it grazes the pin on the far left enough to tip it over.

"The thing about Vic," I say, sitting back down by the food, "is that she is so far away from me sometimes. And this—this whole *situation*—is one of those times. Think about what she knows. She knows I made out with that girl Callie at your party. She knows I went out with Keema that one time. Of course all this was after I broke up with Bill, when I told her, hey, I liked Bill, but I like girls, too. And we've left it there, just sort of sitting there between us."

"Like this pizza," Tall Jon offers.

"Exactly. So there would need to be, you know, the interim steps of dough rolling and baking and slicing before I could do anything about it. But I'm not, so it doesn't matter."

"And you thought I was the one making elaborate metaphors," Tall Jon says.

He gets up and bowls a strike. I swear he stood in the same place I did and rolled the ball with exactly the same motion, but his pins fell down as though they weighed nothing.

"Why do you do this?" He flops back into the seat and replaces his hat, or as he calls it, his "jaunty cap."

"Do what?"

"Lock yourself up." He clicks his tongue and sticks his thumb through his fist. "Click, click."

"I do it to see you make stupid gestures like that."

24

"Ah, Moreno, if I wasn't so nice, I'd call her up and tell her myself."

"You can't right now. She's at dance."

"Still?"

"Yup. Tuesday's one of her late nights. And anyway, she'd probably think you were joking. That's how far apart we are on this."

As recently as a year ago, I thought I was broken. I envisioned the part of me that liked girls as being separate, an imaginary friend who would sometimes sit next to me and poke me in the thigh. *Hey, M., look at Victoria. She's hot, isn't she?* I thought I could ignore her, that imaginary friend, and for a while, I tried. But it was such a brilliant relief when I realized that this was part of me, internal and real, as vital as anything else.

Tall Jon points a fry at me. "What's the worst that could happen?"

"I could lose my best friend." I shrug. "Isn't that obvious? And I know you're gonna ask, is that worse than not having her know how I really feel about her? Yes, yes, that is much worse. Okay, end of discussion, let me go roll some more gutter balls."

But I don't. I get five pins down the first roll, and the other five on the second roll. The white stripes in my T-shirt glow under the ancient black lights, and Tall Jon stands and applauds me. For a few flickering seconds, I am the greatest version of myself, standing tall and radiating light. Mercy the Bowling Queen.

Really, I appreciate that Tall Jon doesn't think I'm ridiculous. Because I sort of do. Like whenever Callie comes to mind, all I can do is shudder and hope that she doesn't think too often about me. I let her kiss me, that night at Tall Jon's house right after I broke up with Bill, and then I was kissing her and wondering how long I would know her. Would she ever see the mole on my right shoulder, or know about my extensive collection of pencil sharpeners, or ask me why the hell I like Marcel Duchamp?

"What's your favorite movie?" I asked her, between kisses, as we were trying to get comfortable on the old recliner in Tall Jon's bedroom.

"What?" Callie said. She was white, a redhead, and about Tall Jon's age. She had perfect eyeliner, the top and bottom lines meeting in a sharp swoop.

"I just want to know," I said.

"Um." She fell against me, touching her nose to my neck. "I guess it's *But I'm a Cheerleader*."

She didn't ask me what mine was, or ask if she was the first girl I'd ever kissed (maybe because I made it so obvious), but the next time I saw her, again at a Tall Jon shindig, she told me she'd like to hang out somewhere other than our vertically blessed pal's apartment.

And I told her that, well, there was this *friend*.

Callie looked like she was trying to roll her eyes but couldn't quite get the mechanics right. She said, "Let me guess, your best friend?"

"Actually, yeah."

"Oh, drat."

The major realization I had at this moment was not that Callie was imagining me ridiculous for having a crush on my best friend, but rather that she was the type of girl who had loads of signature swear-substitute expressions. "Oh, crabcakes" or the like. I would just say "Oh, shit," but I get the appeal of those alternate sayings. I totally do.

"You'll survive it," Callie said, already beginning to move toward the kitchen and away from me. "You'll come out on the other side a little more cynical, maybe with some awkwardness in your friendship, and a new understanding of heartbreak."

"It doesn't have to be like that," I said.

"It's inevitable." A smile hit both ends of Callie's wide mouth but never made it to the middle. "Have fun."

Tall Jon pats me on the shoulder after beating me in two games. "Well, Moreno, you're a worthy opponent. Consider your strategy for the next time we meet in the alley of battle." We walk together across the parking lot, to where the Ford is parked next to Tall Jon's Mazda coupe.

"That sounds like a good-bye. Do you have time for a smoke?"

He takes off his hat—a bowling hat, apparently—and tosses it into his car. "I'm supposed to text this girl and maybe meet up with her? Angelina. She works at the station with me."

"Angelina ballerina," I say, just to fill the space between our cars. "One smoke and one band won't kill you. Come on, I'm symbolically orphaned right now."

So we sit in Tall Jon's car with all the windows rolled down and start filling the ashtray while Tall Jon sorts through some music he's gotten in at the station. I don't think I want to go to the University of South Florida, and I know I'd be a terrible college radio DJ, but Tall Jon sure runs across some mind-blowing music. I mean, some of it is mind-blowingly awful, but it fuels our running commentary all the same. Like this band he's got playing right now, known as There's Only Three People in This Town. They're a wall of guitar noise, and not in the melodramatic, bombastic way I can sometimes get into. No, this sounds like these guys wanted to play in a band together, but nobody wanted to be the one who *didn't* play the guitar.

My cigarette dies, as does my ability to come up with a fitting description for these dudes. "They sound like . . . a badger being hit by a sack of badgers."

"Badgers?" Tall Jon snickers. "That's all you've got?"

"Do you have a better animal-inspired metaphor?"

"Hmm. I would say they sound like a couple of musk oxes getting it on."

"Wow. Okay. The plural is *oxen*, and they resent your judgment on their sex life."

Tall Jon shakes his head at me. "Moreno, you weird butt." He lights another cigarette for me, which is convenient because I was just about to ask him why he's yet another person in my life who's almost leaving. Talk about fucking *metaphors*: Tall Jon in the car, with the keys in, ready to go were it not for me occupying the passenger seat. In animal-inspired metaphors, he'd be an Arctic tern getting ready to migrate. Or a wildebeest traveling to a new grazing pasture. Angela and I used to watch a lot of Animal Planet before Mom shut off the cable.

"One more band," I say.

"Fine. Ten minutes." He's texting, then cueing up the next song. "Tell me what you think of this one. They're a new band from Alabama. They sound kind of rough, but I think they're on their way. They're called Firing Squad."

It begins. It's one of those slow-burn songs that starts with a single guitar chord and then calls the rest of the instruments to join in. And they do: drums, a saxophone, a bass, and something that sounds kind of like Angela's upright piano. Each one brings its own hum, and then they join hands. The music throws itself at me through Tall Jon's speakers. It wants to be loved, in the best of ways. It wants to be everything to me, and maybe I will let it. The piano bursts in like a mid-July rain shower. The guitar jumps and sways. Controlled chaos, as Tall Jon would say. This guitarist guy—I imagine him to be a tall, skinny white guy like my music criticism and smoking companion here, but with brighter and wilder hair—has obviously found the one thing on this planet that he can do with absolute transcendence.

I tell Tall Jon this.

"Anytime you start spouting off about transcendence, Moreno, I know it's time for you to go." He stops the music. He promises to send me the Firing Squad tracks. And he tosses the rest of his pack of cigarettes at me.

"Enabler," I say.

*   *   *

Along the shore are the condo buildings and hotels that stand uneasily in that space between the street and the water. My favorite one, an old stucco high-rise with iron balconies clinging to each floor, is lit up tonight like I've never seen. It's brilliant, almost blinding, as though all of Sarasota's sun from the day has been bottled inside and finally allowed out. There's no one behind my car, so I slow to a crawl. The light doesn't create a reflection on the water, or even make it down to the empty parking lot. I've always thought that building was abandoned—maybe it's getting a new life.

Whenever I pass these buildings, I imagine no one but women Abuela's age who live there, passing their time teetering above the Gulf. The light on the top floor shines from two bedside lamps for a woman who sleeps in the center of her bed. Two floors below, a woman prepares her daily injection in her bright kitchen. She steadies her arm. When do these women remember their grandmothers? Their mothers? How long have they kept a secret? Do they worry that death has no color at all? Do they feel heavier at high tide? Are they sleepless like regret?

This is the long way home.

Angela has fallen asleep on the couch. She looks uncomfortable— her arms are stuffed under her belly, and she's open-mouth frowning. I sit on the floor and nudge her shoulder.

"Mercedes," she grumbles. "Ugh, Mercy, you smell awful."

"It's the stench of bowling alley."

"Grrrhm." Which means, roughly, *It is not, and don't be silly by acting like I don't understand.* I was born three summers before she was, and sometimes I forget to do the math. Fourteen. She's fourteen. She's damn smart, but she needs me.

"How did the piano go?"

"I suck, and you know it." She sits up. "Why is everything terrible right now? Abuela in the hospital, and Mom being gone, and me not being able to do anything, and you leaving for hours to smoke in a bowling alley?"

"To be fair, they don't allow smoking *in* the bowling alley."

"Oh God, you know what I mean." Angela fumbles to her feet and straightens out this poor faded pair of Tweety Bird pajama pants she's had since she was about eleven. She's gotten plenty of other pajamas since then, but she persists in keeping Tweety alive.

"I'll be around this weekend."

She looks at me as though I've claimed I'm not going to drive the Ford Focus anymore.

"Really. And Victoria's coming over. We can watch movies or something."

Angela goes to bed. And so do I. But something feels wrong about this place. Yes . . . I have stumbled into our mother's room by mistake. I have curled up in her unmade bed, pulled her covers over me, and settled this pillow that smells like her perfume and hair

31

spray under my head. And it feels wrong because it is supposed to, because everything has gone crooked. I need to find a way to stay close to her, though, so that nothing I do makes Abuela's breathing stop. So this is it—I will sleep in my mother's messy bed until she comes home.

four

REX HAS LEFT us a note on the door: *I FOUND A RENTER!* It's signed with a bearded smiley face wearing a party hat. Rex totally knows how to celebrate a Friday afternoon. At the bottom of the note, in tiny letters, he's written, *M—you'll like her. She's a painter!*

Out the front window, everything looks the same. Unless any of our neighbors witnessed Mom running out to the airport shuttle last week, or Tuesday's moment of piano relocation, they'd have no idea that anything has changed at the Moreno-McBride residence. And so far, there's no sign next door that someone else is moving in. An artist, a painter. Maybe she'll be a portrait artist with an abstraction habit on the side. A VW Bug driver with an all-black wardrobe and a Frida Kahlo brow. Maybe she'll also discover that the back porch is simultaneously the coziest and most difficult place to paint in the house, and she'll adopt it as her studio, too.

I lay the note on top of Angela's piano, but she doesn't seem to notice it, or me. She has the lid thing hiding the keys, and she runs her hands down it like she's petting a dog.

"Do you know what I want tonight? More than anything?" I say, flinging her out of her concentration.

"What?"

"Abuela's mofongo."

Angela takes a breath through her nose, as though she might be able to smell it if she pulls in deep enough. "Yes. Yes, absolutely. Why did you *say* that? There's no way we can make it like she does."

"We don't even have the freaking recipe."

"I wish we could call her."

"Even if she was at home, she wouldn't pick up."

Angela gets up from the piano and heads toward the kitchen. "Yeah, she'd call back like four hours later, and she'd say, 'Bueno, I've got that recipe for you!'"

"I wouldn't care." I follow her. The kitchen still smells like Thursday's grilled cheese sandwiches. "I'd go out and buy a crate of plantains from the store. I'd make it at midnight. I'd make it at one a.m."

"I want to do a *Green Eggs and Ham*–style rhyme for you, but I can't think of anything that rhymes with mofongo." Angela opens the dishwasher, probably because it seems more likely to be a successful mission than opening the fridge, but we roll out the racks to find dirty dishes and the sour smell of old ketchup.

"The Dishwasher Lemur," I tell my sister.

It takes her a minute. "Oh man! He's back. He followed us from Naples, and he's been lurking, waiting for us to be alone."

"Sinister and wily, he is." We shut the dishwasher together and look at each other, like we're embarrassed to be remembering that old story. But embarrassed for who? We are so very alone here.

Okay, so maybe our mother's absence has shown that the better housekeepers in this residence are the ones currently occupying it. However, in the *Who goes to the grocery store most often?* challenge, the absent resident is definitely the winner.

"She's made some sort of pasta with peanut sauce before," Angela says. "I'm positive it used peanut butter."

We're seriously about ready to pull the trigger on this. Noodles, peanut butter, and whatever else we can find to put into the sauce. And we are considering serving this to Victoria. Mom, for all her quirks, would find a way to pull this one off—she'd look hopeless, but she'd magically find a way to whip up a dinner that would serve at least ten, and it'd be delicious. I check my phone, thinking I might text Mom and ask for her recipe. But her most recent text to me was asking if I've heard anything about my college applications, and I don't feel like answering that.

There are three loud, ironically ominous knocks at the door. Rex.

"I've got it." I leave Angela to the mess with the pasta.

Rex takes up our whole doorway. When he says he's got someone to introduce, I figure he's going to lead me to his side of the house. But no—he moves aside and there she is, staring out the little circular windows of the foyer between the two halves of the duplex, as though the flat Florida houses lined up on both sides of the street are the most interesting landscape she's ever seen.

"This is my new renter!" Rex announces. "Lilia Solis. And this is my old renter, Mercedes Moreno."

She turns to me. I think she's Latina, too. She has long black hair and brown eyes and her brows are distinct and therefore very non-Kahlo. Her bright pink, gauzy floral dress looks like something she bought at one of the beachwear stores haunted mainly by tourists.

Also, this Lilia Solis is just a year or two older than I am. And she's an artist? Like, a legit, professional one? I want to know, but I don't want to hit her with questions, especially since she doesn't seem to be much of a talker.

"It's great to meet you," I prompt her. "Welcome to the McBride-slash-Moreno Palacio."

She looks dazed, like she really was expecting a palace, but got this duplex with beige walls and no ceiling lights (that was Mom's chief complaint when we moved in: "I just got divorced, and now I have to buy *lamps*?").

But her eyes lock on mine, and her face brightens. "Thanks. It's nice to meet you, too."

Angela pops in with peanut butter all over her hands and introduces herself.

And Rex says he has plenty of casserole for tonight's dinner.

*　*　*

There is something about being inside Rex's place that makes me feel like I'm on vacation. Like, on one of the vacations I dream about taking every summer, where I hop in my grumpy old Pontiac and point it north until I get out of Florida, and then take another highway and see where it leads. How do people end up on those trips where they meet all sorts of interesting strangers along the way—people who always have a spare room furnished with telling details about their past? People who have the right amount of good stories: enough to have mastered telling them, but not to have worn them out.

I'm not sure if Rex is all those things, but his half of the house feels that way. All along the wall in the living room are framed photos and letters from his extended family of burly redheaded folk. And the intended dining room is so packed full of boxes of *stuff* that there's no space in there for a table. So that's why we're all sitting on the floor around the living room coffee table. It's easy to enjoy a visit to Rex's place, but I can't imagine why someone would pay good money to live in a tiny bedroom on the McBride side of the duplex. And yet, Lilia Solis seems quietly excited to be here, looking around at everything on the walls while finishing her helping of casserole. I should have something artsy in mind to say if she catches me watching her. Or I should make some sort of benign conversation about my day at school, but with the words "art class" emphasized and nudged toward Lilia.

"I love this casserole," says Angela, who has scrubbed most of the peanut butter off her hands.

Rex smiles. "I call it Sunday Slop. And I'm well aware that it's Friday. It's how I use my leftovers from the week."

It's almost seven—Victoria will be here soon. I should find a way to join in the discussion, such as it is, but I keep looking out the front window for Mrs. Caballini's car. Angela is right to love the casserole, but I can barely eat. My chest tightens with every breath. Why am I like this tonight? Why does it seem like something out of the ordinary is going to happen, even though I have planted my flag firmly in the "not telling Victoria" camp? What's going to happen beyond the usual Victoria-hangs-out activities of saying we're going to watch a movie but then spending an hour looking at cat videos on her phone, and me sneaking glances at her while she reads and I sketch, and also talking about things that are not how much I want to give her a kiss (messy at first, but turning soft)? And for all the ways that this doesn't sound like a pleasant evening, it is. It really, really is.

"So, Rex, that's a fascinating painting over there." It's Lilia, pointing to a canvas hanging over Rex's couch. I know it well.

"The orange-and-blue one?" Rex says. "Well, you can compliment the artist. You're sitting right next to her."

For the first time since the foyer, we're looking at each other at the same time. "Ah, okay," Lilia says, and then glances away. I thought I heard it before, but I'm sure of it now—she has a Puerto Rican accent.

Lilia goes on, "There's something unexpected about it. The way you mix the colors. At first, they seem like they go together, but when you look at it again, they're definitely angry with each other."

"It's a mood piece," I tell her. I guess maybe it could be. "It's just how the sky looked one night last summer."

"A mood piece? What do you mean by that?"

She wants me to explain it, to set it cozily in the context of my life, to tell her that it was the seminal piece of my Orange Period or whatever. But really, it was a painting I did sort of absentmindedly right after junior year ended. It was a distraction from thinking about Victoria and knowing I was going to break up with Bill.

"I saw Mercedes finishing it on her porch," Rex cuts in. "I asked her if I could buy it, and you should have seen the look on her face!"

"It wasn't actually finished," I say. "It's still not finished. I gave Rex a bargain."

"*That* look, right? That's the look," Angela says.

Rex grins. "That's it. It's the 'please don't everybody talk about my art' look."

"Okay." Lilia has more of her Sunday Slop, and her gaze shifts back to the painting. My painting. "Well, I was just wondering."

Rex and Angela exchange silence, and since I don't say anything either, they think I'm a part of their conversation. I dig for a sausage-heavy bite of the casserole to take at the same time as Lilia, so we can chew in unison and I can buy some time to find the perfect gateway to the artsy chat that maybe we're meant to be having. *Where do you get your art supplies? Do you love the smell of a brand-new canvas? What's your favorite way to get paint out of your hair? Do you paint from real life or memory or a different place entirely?*

"You're a painter, too?" I finally say.

Lilia's long hair is in her face. "On and off," she tells me, brushing her hair away. She looks at me for a minute, and I'm not sure if she's trying to decide whether to trust me, or if she's already made up her mind that she doesn't. I wish I was better at making friends, artist friends especially.

I glance out the window, at the spot where we found the piano. And a car pulls up.

When Victoria Caballini gets out of her mom's car, or does pretty much anything, she has a nice follow-through, as though every action needs an equal reaction, and the first part of that reaction needs to be made by her. That's the effect of being in dance classes and troupes for over half her life—she has control over her every movement, so much that it slides into directing how people see her and feel about her. But not everything about them.

I messaged her that we were all next door. I even made her a plate. Heavy on salad, light on Sunday Slop. I thought about holding her fork to my mouth before placing it on her napkin.

She pushes open the door with enough force to send the doorknob through the wall, but somehow she keeps it from making contact. She whirls around to close the door, but not in a way that would make anyone else call it *whirling around*. It's all part of one motion, and it's still going as she drops her stuff and waves hello and flings her hair behind her shoulders. And it ends as soon as she drops down next to me. Bam. Applause.

Lilia stares at her as though Victoria has done all this while spitting, or carrying snakes, or wearing a garbage bag, or whatever else

Lilia might find bizarre and obscene. I almost want to swoop in and help Vic, grab her by the sleeve of her purple dress and pull her closer to me, but this seems more dangerous than what's happening here. She's Vic: worldly and self-sufficient. Maybe I'm the one who needs the intervention. I lock eyes with Angela, and I think we both have the feeling of things being askew, of Rex's half of the house being less a vacation and more a version of our home where the doorknobs and bathrooms are not in the places we expect. Where dinner is two feet lower than it should be. Where the fans click as they turn, and the lights burn orange, and where we have this new neighbor. And I feel like if I leave and come back, she might not be here at all.

The blue-and-orange painting gives me no answers (not that it was ever going to). Lilia connected to it, though. She really did. And I'm not going to spoil that moment by saying something ridiculous.

I watch Victoria, who's good about living in the real world.

"Hello," she says to her silent critic. "I'm Victoria."

"Lilia Solis," Lilia says, going back to her dinner.

"I slept in the girl's mom's bed at a sleepover once," Victoria says from the bathroom. "It was so late, and I was so tired, and the other girls were taking pictures of their feet. I started crying out of frustration, and the other girls got super concerned, especially when I insisted that I wasn't crying. They decided I was allergic to the family cats, and I slept curled up at the edge of the mom's bed. A lot like a cat, now that I think about it."

She pokes her head out. She's been washing her face and sniffing some of Mom's vast perfume collection. "What about you?"

"Nah, I was always the one the mom was sorry got invited in the first place."

"Aww, that can't be true. You know my parents love you."

"Well, they're the first. Trust me."

"Can we watch something else, or is your delightful new neighbor going to call the police if she hears a peep after eleven p.m.?"

"I don't know what's up with her." And I mean this in the truest way. Vic probably thinks I'm dismissing Lilia, but I'm not. As much as I want to be with Vic, I also want to peer into Rex's house at the moment that Lilia begins working on her art, to be her silent apprentice.

"She reminds me of this awful girl from my ballet company in Brooklyn. I can never forget her evil stare. Ugh, chills."

"Rex told me she's a painter." I peek out the window to see if any lights from the other half of the house are beaming into the backyard. Nothing.

"Probably of, like, creepy religious murals or something," Vic says.

"Hmm, who knows."

I wish that even one of Vic's T-shirts from the American Ballet Theatre's youth summer program would get shrunk by the dryer or stained into oblivion by a wayward pair of black underwear. Do I have to be reminded that last summer's took place in Alabama (the home of Firing Squad!) and lasted from June 9 until July 31? Does she realize what a damned long time that is, especially when one's summer consists of stirring the egg salad at the deli, driving one's sister back and forth to tennis day camp, and taking a weekly painting course at Ringling College that one did not expect to be full of people older than Abuela?

Vic's wearing the stupid shirt with a pair of red cotton shorts with triangle-shaped slits up both sides.

Why does she have to be so ridiculous?

She flips off the bathroom light and gets into bed. Beside me. Well, not really beside me. She always sleeps curled up, so far to the edge of the bed that a hand dangles over. Her back faces me. *The stars fell on Alabama! American Ballet Theatre Summer Intensive.*

"When you go back to Alabama this summer, I'm coming with you. There's this band Tall Jon played for me the other night—they're from there. I'm going to come with you and see one of their shows."

"Hmm, your dream vacation is Alabama, huh? You're funny."

"Yep. We'll bust that place up." I don't know what busting a place up actually entails, but I'm sure Victoria and I can figure it out.

"I'm not going back, though."

"You're not?" I sit up in bed. Victoria's still lying down. The streetlight or moonlight slices through the curtains and settles on her cheek.

"No. There's no way. I liked it, but there's no way. I've got to get to New York as soon as possible after graduation." She's in that murky place between wake and sleep. I'd like to think that she doesn't know what she's talking about, but for me, that's always the place where my ideas are the clearest. "I don't care if Juilliard accepts me or not. I'm leaving. Like, a few weeks after graduation. I'm just leaving."

"When did you decide this?"

"I don't think I ever really did." Vic rolls over so that she could look at the ceiling fan if her eyes weren't closed. "It was always there, you know?"

I could tell her that I'll go with her, but it would be about as real as claiming that *Food Poisoning #2* is going to be finished anytime soon. For all Vic sounds like she's dreaming, she actually has big, sturdy Reasons lined up for this move: money and talent and parental support. A birth certificate naming a Manhattan hospital. An aunt and uncle living in Brooklyn. The ability to hum the approximate musical notes made by a subway leaving the 42nd Street station. And her very specific aspiration to be not a Juilliard graduate, but a Juilliard dropout (one or two years there, max, she says, and then she wants to be working on Broadway).

My only reason is Vic herself. And would she be enough? Would she let herself be enough for me?

She's asleep now, her breaths long and steady. Not me. I'm all charged up, like how my teeth feel before a thunderstorm.

"I could go with you," I whisper, just to know that I have said it.

Light on my eyelids. Orange. Red. It's the time of day and the time of year that sunlight hits the back of the house harshly enough to have texture and sound.

Wait, no—that's a different sound, coming from the living room.

I keep the covers on Victoria while throwing them off myself. I put my ear to the bedroom door.

Out in the living room, the piano's going full blast: notes, chords, lines of music. Angela. It has to be her, doesn't it? Because who would break into our house to play the piano? I wipe the thought away as though erasing it from a chalkboard. It's Angela, hitting more than one key at a time. It's Angela, playing music.

Victoria sleeps through it, probably because she spends her days dancing intensely and all I do is stare at mostly blank canvases. I slip out of Mom's room and try to be quiet about closing the door, which is kind of pointless because Angela's insistent song fills every space in the house and drips down the walls.

"Angela?" I try calling her from the kitchen, as I wipe the microwave clock with a dishtowel. There are stray streaks of peanut butter painted around the kitchen. "Don't you know it's only seven thirty?"

The piano keeps going.

I pour some orange juice and peek around the corner.

It's true—Angela is playing the piano. But she isn't alone in the living room.

A glance of long dark hair. A purple bathrobe. It's Lilia, sitting in the recliner and watching Angela as she plays. She doesn't see me, transfixed as she is, tapping her fingers against her arm, as though Lilia herself is a part of the music. She's relentless, but so is Angela, keeping pace with notes that run toward the beat and then scatter away from it. There's a rush within my cheeks, behind my eyes, like it's taking all my strength not to start singing. I can't see either of their faces, but all of Angela's body looks strained, as though the piano keys are weights, and they're pulling her down.

five

TALL JON HAS come through with the Firing Squad album. Listening to it with my eyes closed in my mom's car, in the school parking lot, the pureness of the music washes over me just like it did at the bowling alley last week, and I'm obsessed all over again. Plus, Tall Jon is amazing: when he got in touch with Firing Squad to be sure he could make a copy to send to his weird friend Mercedes, he asked the perfect music-snob-in-all-the-right-ways questions about their songs, and they wrote back with the answers. So now, when I'm listening to track nine, "Always Something Left to Love," I can picture the way it was recorded: in a barn, with a bunch of senior citizens hired from a Birmingham retirement community to play a whole chorus of pianos.

The passenger door clicks open. "Hey."

"Angela. Are you listening to this? If you keep up what you're doing, you could play on the next Firing Squad album."

"Yeah, it's pretty cool."

I open my eyes. In the passenger seat, Angela has her knees pulled to her chest and is listening intently, a small smile tugging at the corners of her mouth.

"Wait, is this the day I have waited for? The day Angela Moreno declares that she *likes* the same song I do?" I lean out the window. "Hallelujah, my friends! Hallelujah! Angela's a fan of Firing Squad!"

"Not as much as you," Angela says.

"I'll take what I can get," I tell her. "Let's celebrate by going to the grocery store."

We used to go to San Juan for Christmas and New Year's, and during the last twelve seconds of the old year, Abuela Dolores would make us all eat twelve grapes for good luck in the next year. It takes a hell of a lot of coordination to eat that many grapes so quickly, especially if you get stuck with the seeded ones, and especially if you have a ten-year-old's mouth. Our parents would always cram the grapes in and wash them down with champagne. Angela and I would fumble the grapes all over the place, dropping or squishing or spitting out more than one.

"Bad luck! Mala suerte!" our mother would scream out, followed by all sorts of dire warnings in Spanish.

But Abuela Dolores would pick up the grapes and whisper how

we still had time, how it was still the old year in Alaska.

("Well, in part of Alaska," Angela said. "There are a few islands on the other side of the International Date Line.")

And then she'd say, in English, "You can fight your luck."

Which is something I think about a lot.

I toss a bag of grapes into the grocery cart.

It bugs me that Mom keeps telling us on the phone or over email that Abuela has been "so weak" for a long time. The only potentially wimpy thing about my grandmother is that she won't get on a plane and come to visit us in Florida, and she definitely won't come to live with us, even though Mom has pleaded with her to do so. Abuela hasn't left Puerto Rico since she spent a couple of years on the mainland as a teenager, and she doesn't intend to start traveling again at the age of seventy-five. But maybe that's not wimpy at all—it takes a certain kind of conviction to stay on the same 3,500-square-mile hunk of rock for over fifty years. At that point, your transplanted daughter *should* come to you.

And she doesn't want to die. If I couldn't feel that pricking at me, I've got the evidence from the last time I talked to her on the phone. She was still going to her ballroom dancing class twice a week, and her little dogs were following her around the apartment as we spoke, and she laughed when I asked her where Abuelo was. Just sitting at the kitchen table, she told me. His ashes, that is. Last time I saw her, that week in Puerto Rico last June, she switched his ashes from their old urn to a "more portable" one, so that he could go with her from room to room in the house.

She doesn't want to die.

Angela jogs toward me and the cart with a bouquet of flowers. "These are only four bucks."

"And?"

"And I need to get them for Lilia. As a thank-you gift."

"I'm still not sure what she actually *did*," I tell Angela, but it's nice to see her so happy, and I place the flowers in the cart.

Mom has transferred a hundred bucks into my bank account so that we don't have to attempt another pasta-and-peanut-butter creation. But the flowers now sticking out of the cart feel like a pink-and-purple flag heralding Angela and me as impostors in this world. It's four thirty and the Publix is a mix of parents with kids and people in business-type clothes hurrying from aisle to aisle. It's the kids, especially, who look at Angela and me, like they are going to tattle on these two girls who aren't supposed to be pushing and filling the cart. Humming "Interpretation" (Firing Squad album track two), I snap three cans of black beans off the shelf as though I do this all the time.

Angela says, "I'm not sure either. But I could feel it starting before she knocked on our door the other morning. I woke up with my fingers twitching, and with this idea in my head that if I sat at the piano right that moment, I'd be able to play. And then when Lilia came in, it was like, I don't know, I think I could have played any song in the world."

"Uh-huh." I push the cart. She is still my sister, wearing a Star Wars T-shirt and trying to grab the other end of the cart to take a ride. I swerve from one side of the canned veggies aisle to another, not letting her on.

"I bet she could help you, too."

"I doubt it." But I slow down to let Angela on the cart.

"No, seriously. She told me she has a studio space to finish some artwork. What's it called when someone pays you to make something specific?"

"A commission."

"Right. Well, she's got some sort of commission project she's working on. You should talk to her about it."

"Hm." I stare into the cart. "Hey, have you asked her anything about, you know, how she came to be renting Rex's place?"

"I tried," Angela says. "But she told me she didn't have a past."

The keeper of the cigarettes, the lady at the customer service counter, looks pretty friendly today. I doubt she remembers me trying to buy from her before, but I also doubt she'd hand over a pack. It's been a ridiculous couple of days and I've already smoked through what Tall Jon gave me.

Angela says, "Let's speed up this cart! I need to get home and practice."

My sister is amazing.

She can do all her scales now. She can play chords. She can play "Chopsticks." She can play the first half of "Für Elise." It's only been a week since the piano arrived, but it's a part of our lives now. It's an uninvited houseguest that fits with our family (well, the currently fractured version of the Moreno family). And if Angela's not worried about where it came from, then neither am I.

We're home and she bounds out of the car, unlocks the front door, and raps on Rex's door to announce her arrival. I follow with the grocery bags. Angela sits at attention, her hands waiting on the keys. The living room keeps changing: the piano and the repurposed dining room chair have become fixtures. And now, I drop the flowers into a vase and set them on a table beside the piano.

When Lilia arrives, she says hey to Angela and perches on the edge of the recliner. I duck into the kitchen. "Remember what you did yesterday," Lilia tells my sister. "You can do it again. Keep going." Angela nods and begins playing, starting "Für Elise" with the right amount of quiet and then letting it build until it fills my head. She doesn't play notes anymore—she plays songs.

How did she do it?

I open the back door and step out on the porch to escape the music. *Food Poisoning #2* is still hanging out, waiting for me to return with ideas. "You're gonna be waiting a while, buddy," I say, patting the top of the canvas. Aside from those streaks I made the other day, it's looked the same for so long.

On the other side of the porch, though, there's something different. Four canvases. Half-finished ones, drying. It's Lilia's artwork.

She must also be attempting a series, because all four pictures are of the same building. The building in front of a light blue sky, then a dark blue sky, and then an orange sky. The last one doesn't have a sky yet. But the building is recognizable: about ten stories tall, with iron balconies on each level, and light radiating from each window. It is—it's got to be—my favorite condo building from down on the beach.

A couple of months ago in Mrs. Pagonis's class, we talked about Monet's *Haystacks* series. Literally, a series of paintings of the same haystacks. "I know a lot of you might not think you understand the series," Mrs. Pagonis had said, "or maybe you *do* think you understand. That's fine. But it's also fine to look at the paintings and live in them for a minute and not worry too much about why you're doing that."

That wasn't me, though. I squinted hard at the projection of the paintings on the screen in the classroom, my whole body tensing. *I understand it. I do,* I told myself.

I didn't really understand it. But I get *this*: Lilia's series, and her attempts to capture the building and its light. Because to see something amazing like that is to get obsessed with it, to wonder how it works and where it comes from, but not to wonder so hard that the magic drips away.

I lean against the screen. Her paintings aren't done, or even that good, but they're there. They exist.

Back inside, Angela plays "Für Elise" again. The melody crawls up and down my spine as I approach the living room, as I consider what I'm going to say to Lilia. *I saw your paintings,* I could say. Or, like Mrs. Pagonis sometimes says about giving feedback, start with a question: *Why did you paint that building?* That's what I most want to know.

I stop at the recliner. Lilia concentrates on Angela, who gets to the twinkly high part of the song, raises her hands from the keys, and starts it over again.

"Will you *ever* stop playing?" is what comes out of my mouth, over the music.

They both turn and glare at me.

Okay, fine. Maybe I don't get Lilia at all.

In my own bedroom, I switch on Firing Squad to play through the tiny speakers on my laptop. It's Tuesday, and Victoria's dance class doesn't start until six thirty, so I can message her and not get silence.

Me: Angela's making me crazy. She's too good.

Vic: Jealous????

Me: It's not jealousy. I'd rather listen to music than play it. It's just total confusion about how A can play now.

Vic: She always had it in her, I guess

Me: Maybe.

Vic: I think it's so cool that

Vic: someone's discarded piano showed her what she's good at

Vic: It's like when I think about what if the world's greatest violinist has never picked up a violin?????

Me: Well then they're not the greatest violinist, huh?

Vic: You know what I mean

Me: I just want to know what it's like to have an idea in your head for something you want to create . . .

Me: and then to create exactly that.

We could go back and forth like this forever. I shut the door and call her.

"Remember how I told you that Lilia was some sort of painter?" I check my doorway, because it seems like she should be standing there, nodding and holding a symbolic paintbrush with badger bristles. "Angela told me she even does commissioned work."

"Oh yeah? Are you going to ask her to look at some of your paintings?" Vic is probably in her bedroom, satisfied with being alone in that only-child sort of way. "You should make sure Rex is home if you do. I think her stare will hypnotize you."

"I don't know. She'd probably take one look at my stuff and either laugh or scream."

"Hey, that's no worse than your mom's reaction to your food poisoning picture, and look, you're still painting."

"It's not just that." I feel myself diving into all sorts of opinions I may or may not be able to describe to Vic. "It's not just my weird neighbor possibly telling me I suck, or my mom looking all disappointed and frightened about *Food Poisoning #1*. It's the work itself, I think. I love it, but the art doesn't love me back."

Vic is quiet. Quieter. Still quiet. I slump against the stack of pillows on my bed, to where I can see the Picasso posters I hung on the wall in a fit of "needing inspiration" a few days after I won the county show. The tape is coming loose on *Three Musicians,* to the point that it looks like one musician, the guy with the clarinet, is shortly going to be stuck with the task of keeping the other two from falling, falling, falling onto this tired girl's decidedly noncubist bedspread.

"I know that sounds weird, but it's true. I create these things, and they fight back against me."

In the living room, Angela starts a new song. *New* as in I don't recognize it, as in maybe this song is coming into being right here, right now.

"Well," Victoria says slowly, "I've never felt like that."

And I guess that's fine. I mean, if anyone, she would know. Her feet have been chewed up by pointe shoes, and she's spent more than one movie night with ice packs tucked around her ankles and shins. She's told me the various ways that dance teachers have sniped at her, and through it all, she seems most hurt by the time one of the few straight boys at Summer Intensive turned down her hookup request. She loves the struggle of dance, and the struggle loves her, too.

"Keep painting," Vic says. "Let Angela deal with the creepy teachings of Lilia Solis. Go and work on something of your own tonight."

"Yeah, maybe I will."

"Aw, come on, dearie. Promise me you'll do something that seems hard, like painting what smoking feels like, or trying to draw the perfect foot."

"I hate drawing feet."

"I know! So, promise me."

"Fine. I promise." Except I have been lying to Victoria for a long time now, and sometimes I think I'm being struck with a tiny punishment for this, like each of my days ending exactly one second too soon. I won't notice this break in time until a day I try to tell her something important, and she'll be gone before the words slip through space to reach her.

"Ah, success! And for my next trick, I'll get Mercedes Moreno to listen to Broadway show tunes for fifteen solid minutes."

"I'd like to see you try."

"You'll do it for me. You know you will."

She's right, and it's wonderful. I let her go so that she can get ready for her class. I nudge my phone off the bed and slide out of my jeans and underwear and lie back and consider her. That's what I've been calling it lately—*considering her.*

One thing I've held tight in my mind is the day last spring that I realized I liked Victoria. But I wonder if that was really the day, the moment, or was I realizing it a little every day, for months, for years? The day she was the new girl in English class and when I stared at the back of her head and wondered how we could ever get to be friends. The day a few weeks later when she found me at lunch (I was waiting for Bill) and asked what I thought of English, and I tried to be clever and say something like, "The language? It's not so bad," and then Bill interrupted me but Vic stayed anyway. The eight hundred times I've watched her twist her hair into a ballet bun. The phone videos she sneakily took for me at MoMA and PS1 on her last trip to New York. All the little things and all the big things and all this time, time, time. It expands and contracts. It waits for her but not for me. And if I told her, I think it would stop entirely. She will never never never—

She will never know.

six

OH, LOOK—RIDER is absent today. It's just Gretchen Grayson and me having a stare-down here at the Orange Table. As in, she stares at my piece, and I stare at hers, and not a word is spoken. It's not that she doesn't want to ask: the words "Um, Mercedes, what are you making?" are hanging so precariously over the Orange Table that I expect them to come crashing down into my watercolor palette any minute now.

Gretchen has made more progress on her lizard painting since yesterday. It is definitely more than a mood piece. Every time I look at it, I snap away from it, and then glance back. Damn those green lizards staring straight into me, with their creepy black eyes, and everything so bold and well-shaded, brown walls bleeding into yellow Gretchen bleeding into the light- and dark-green lizards. Lizard Gretchen is folded into herself, her chest and head slumping, and her little lizardy arms in front of her.

There's a new detail on lizard Gretchen, one that's not even dry yet. Lizard Gretchen's arms are covered in blood.

Shit.

I glance at actual Gretchen, with the long-sleeved cardigan she wears all the time, and our eyes meet.

"Is this finished?" I point to an inconsequential, lizard-free spot at the top of the painting.

"I think so." Gretchen smiles a little. "Something about the color in the upper corners seems weird, but I'm afraid I might ruin it if I try to change things now."

I shut my sketchbook on top of the aimless lines and shading I've been working on for the past few classes. "So is that what you're going to enter?"

Gretchen nods. "But I'm scared."

There's a perfect sentence to be said to her, but I don't know what it is. I want to tell her I understand, but it's hard when I don't. Luckily, Mrs. Pagonis wanders over and sits in Rider's seat.

"Ladies! I haven't checked on your progress since last week. How are your projects coming along?"

Gretchen and I exchange looks, and I keep my hands on my sketchbook. Mrs. Pagonis has her moment of losing herself in

Gretchen's painting. Oh man—she's about to get the same reaction out of our teacher as she did out of me. I mean, a louder, less resentful communicating of that reaction, sure, but the same in-the-gut feeling that no matter how much you resist being caught in the lizards' stares, you get stuck there anyway.

"It's glorious!" Mrs. Pagonis says.

Then she asks to see my sketchbook.

I want to open it and find something finished, something beautiful. But what would that even be? For the first time ever, I want to find myself totally laid bare on the page. If I could open the book and find that, maybe I'd be okay with holding it up to the whole class. *Look,* I'd say. *Look, this is me.* But for that to be here, I'd need more than one moment of wanting that.

My hands sweat. The moment's gone.

I flip through my sketchbook for Mrs. Pagonis, and apologize for page after page, and promise her that the real stuff is at home.

Here is what's at home.

One ridiculous canvas that I've left sunning on the porch too long.

One ridiculous canvas that I've been trying to forget about, and that I maybe-unconsciously tried to sabotage by way of Florida weather, and even *that* didn't work.

Food Poisoning #2 looks exactly like it did the last time I saw it. Streaks and patches of color, unintended and unbalanced. My mom's pile of blotchy tissues from the night she left is a better work of art than this. Hell, the peanut butter streaks on the microwave tell more of a story.

I dig my X-Acto knife out of my supply box and strike it across the canvas. Once, twice, from corner to corner. I carve a jagged square out of the center, a messy oval out of the top right corner. A zigzag of my initials across the center, punctuated with a *V*, for good measure.

And it's not quite enough.

The canvas is in shreds, so I send it flying off the easel. The clatter I'm expecting is more of a dry *thunk* as it hits the thin carpet of the porch.

It's dark and strange inside the house after being out in the sun. Angela sits at the dining room table with a notebook and calculator, but I can't pick out the details in her face just yet. I brush past her to where I dropped my backpack when we came home from school. In the front pocket, at the bottom, it should be there—yes. My last Emergency Cigarette. I light it in the kitchen.

"Seriously, you promised not to smoke in the house," Angela says.

"Ange, I need your help with something, just for a minute, and I swear I will finish this outside and you can get back to your homework, okay?"

"You're being ridiculous. You promised."

"I'm walking outside right now! Can you bring me a kitchen

knife and my painting from behind my bed? Please?"

She goes. I shoot trails of smoke out my nose, the way Tall Jon and Bill taught me.

"Here you go, Your Majesty." Angela hands me the knife, handle first.

"Gracias."

I take *Food Poisoning #1* in my other hand and place it on the easel. It's a strange piece. Unsettling in some ways. I guess I can see why Mom insisted I take it off my wall. It's layers of thick, dark paint, mixed with bits of the Lifestyle section of the newspaper. I hardly remember how it all came together—I mean, I recall the basic things, like how I bought all this glue, thinking I was going to need it to hold the newspaper shreds on the canvas, but it turned out the paint was sturdy enough. I remember painting birds, from flamingos to geese. Some of them were abstract, some more realistic. And I remember how Tall Jon got me Parliament Menthols instead of Lights when I was working on the last few layers of paint, and how they tasted too clean but I smoked them anyway.

Angela says, "Be careful."

I kneel on the worn gray carpet and stab out the cigarette on the remains of *Food Poisoning #2*. "Do you want to help?"

"I don't really understand what you're doing here."

"There's nothing to understand. Trust me. Take a knife and go." I hand her my X-Acto knife, and I stick with the kitchen knife. The first slice—it is less a clean cut than a rip. It breaks the layer of newspaper bits. It sends paint crumbs to the ground.

When they gave me the award, I was smiling. I was wearing a knee-length blue dress and a silver necklace borrowed from my mother.

Angela stabs through the canvas with the X-Acto knife. An interesting strategy—fill it with holes and let it collapse on its own. I poke a few holes myself, starting with the corners, but then send the knife stripping lines through the layers again.

Angela came to last year's county art show. So did Mom and Victoria and Bill and Tall Jon. Mrs. Pagonis and some of the other studio artists were there, too. After the awards ceremony, my misfit entourage and I walked down the hall to the reception—or, rather, I walked, and the rest of them stopped in the lobby where *Food Poisoning #1* was displayed. They wanted to take a closer look at this piece I'd been hiding for so long. Mom leaned forward, inspecting the layers, sniffing at them. She frowned.

I carve the center out of the painting. The feathery mess falls to the floor.

"Dang, you're brutal," Angela says.

I cough. "Thank you."

"Is this your new project?"

"Something like that." I point to the top right corner with my knife. "Can you slice that part out?"

Angela does. And I destroy the other three corners and, hmm, might as well do some more work on the stuff that already fell out. So I tear the feathery heart of the painting in two, hand half to Angela, and let her pull it apart again and again.

Finally, what remains of both canvases is the wooden backbone frames, with a few ripped flags of fabric still holding on to each. That's good enough. No one will ever know what was there. No one will ever know that I didn't know what I was trying to say.

I flop down on the floor of the porch. Angela and I have both been hit by some of the painted newspaper bits. They are stuck to our hair and clothes.

"I appreciate the help," I say. "I'll clean this up."

"I think I'm gonna shower before I do anything else," Angela says.

Angela never said anything specific about the painting during its brief period of fame last year, but she tolerated its presence, and that was enough. Bill said it was "cool." Tall Jon said, "It looks like a bunch of dead birds, and I swear I mean that in a good way." Victoria congratulated me about a million times and said I was definitely going to get into Ringling or the Savannah College of Art and Design (also known as SCAD, my dream school) or any other art school I applied to.

How did I not notice that when I tore up the Lifestyle section of the newspaper, I was tearing up recipes and ads for restaurants? A slice of one, covered with yellow: *one-half teaspoon vanilla.* The judges surely thought that was on purpose. It wasn't.

"Are you okay out here?" It's startling to hear a girl's voice coming from that side of the porch. Lilia. She emerges from Rex's house with a canvas in each hand.

"Yeah. I was just cleaning up."

Her hair's pulled back and she's wearing a bright green dress dotted with a floral print and paint stains. She places the canvases flat on the floor. Two more paintings in the condo building series, one with a red sky and one with gray. The light from the windows is the same as before. Lilia studies them for a minute, then takes a step back and wipes at her eyes. Nothing I've ever painted has moved me to tears.

"Hey, it's okay," I say, because that's my usual refrain when someone I know is crying.

"Thanks," Lilia says, just as practiced. She moves away from her paintings and surveys the mess I've made, all the strings and feathers of my former pieces of work. "Too bad I didn't get to see your work while it was still intact."

"This was necessary."

"I guess it is sometimes." She smiles, and it's like the first time I saw a Frida Kahlo painting in person—the thud of *is that really what it is?* It was, and it is.

"Can you tell me about your series?" I ask. The destruction of the paintings has made me feel lighter somehow, as though now I can reconstruct myself into whatever type of artist I want to be. "Because I know that building. I saw it all lit up like that the other night."

"Oh yeah?" Lilia stares at me through the screen. She has long eyelashes and a scar on the side of her mouth. "Did it make you want something?"

I step back. "I don't know what you mean."

"I mean," she says, "sometimes you look at a thing, to draw it or sculpt it or paint it, and it becomes more than just your subject. It compels you in some way. You want it, you need it. ¿Entiendes?"

"Um, I guess so."

Except I don't think I do understand. I think that feeling she's talking about is something I've wanted, but not something I've ever had. It's easy to confuse a craving for wanting with the wanting itself.

But Lilia, with all her paintings in front of her, seems to know the feeling well.

"So when you saw the building lit up, what did you think?" she asks me, sounding hopeful.

"I mean, I thought it was pretty weird. I kept wondering about the people in there, and the people in the neighboring buildings. But I felt like no one was seeing the light except me." I didn't mean to tell her that last part, but there it is.

"Yeah," Lilia says. "I know what you mean."

"So how big is this series going to be?"

"Oh, just you wait." She stands up straight, hands on hips, like she's been waiting for me to ask her this question. "If things go as planned, it'll be huge. It'll come spilling out the windows. I'll have to double my rent for all the space I'm taking up, and I won't even care."

It kind of kills me that she feels so strongly about a building.

"Wow," I say.

"I mean," Lilia says, "it's okay if it didn't inspire you. We all have our different subjects."

Even my sandals are mottled with the remains of *FP #1*.

"Tell me if you want to paint together sometime," Lilia says.

And she turns to go, leaving me to look at the red and gray skies, and everything I have to clean up.

Victoria texts me that her Juilliard audition has been confirmed—it's three weeks away. *Cool, amazing, great, awesome,* I text back, at rhythmic intervals. She will make it: there will probably be an interview, during which she will talk about her worship of the queen of modern dance, Martha Graham, and she will scatter charming details about her many well-worn copies of *Blood Memory*, Martha's autobiography, and how she and her parents sought out Martha's childhood home on one of their leisurely yet educational summer vacations.

But none of that will even be necessary—the Juilliard people will know they want her for their school by the way she strides through the door and postures herself into a chair. They will see the streaks of music and joy and feeling left by her footsteps. They will say lovely, thoughtless things that will fall out of their mouths and crawl to the door. Her feet will turn out in the perfect way, and the Juilliard people will shove their smiles into the angle they make.

Ah, damn it. Juilliard. They're not even good enough for her.

"She responded today," Mom says. We're on the phone after dinner. "Just once, for a half second. And no one saw it but me! I don't even think the nurses believe me."

I sit by the window of my bedroom, braiding the fringe at the bottom of my curtains, the way I did when I used to talk to Bill on the phone. "What did she do?"

"I touched her hand, and it moved. I couldn't tell if she was trying to grab my hand or push it away. The nurses think I've been here too long and I'm making things up."

"Did they tell you that?"

"No, no. I saw it their faces. They've started smiling at me more. Longer."

"Maybe they're getting used to you."

The dogs are yapping, and Mom clunks around Abuela's kitchen, and it's so hard to imagine that apartment without Abuela in it. Who's watering the flowers, who's sitting on the big pink sofa? "I don't think so, I don't think so." She takes in a deep, deep breath, as though she is sucking air all the way from Florida to San Juan. "Mercedes, when was the last time you talked to her?"

"I guess about five days before the stroke."

"Did you tell her—did you—" She's crying now. Shit. I hate hearing her cry. It's long and loud and full of vowels, and sounds like she's releasing something held inside for years. "Did you tell her that we love her and we are always thinking about her? Because I feel like I didn't say it enough. I feel like it was one of those things I said at Christmas and on Papi's birthday and no other time. Did you tell her?"

"Yes," I say. Has she stopped crying yet?

"I didn't tell you this. But I remember a couple weeks ago when you said you were sending her some of your pictures."

"Not pictures," I say. "A painting." It was a little square of canvas that I had painted with sort of a representation of the colorful buildings in Old San Juan. It was sloppy in places, the paint too thick. But I liked it, because it reminded me of Abuela, and I was pretty sure Abuela would like it, because it would remind her of me.

"I'm sorry, mi vida." She sniffles. "I didn't send it. I took the envelope out of the mailbox. I couldn't let her see it, if it was going to be anything like that food poisoning thing you have in your bedroom."

That thing. That useless thing that isn't in the house anymore, that isn't anywhere. That I created, and that now has completely ceased to exist.

I am the god of my artwork. Unless, of course, my mother intercepts the US Fucking Mail.

"Well, where *is* it now?" I ask.

"At my office," she sniffs. "Locked in my desk drawer."

"Shit, Mom," I whisper. "Just . . . shit."

Angela finishes her evening practice with a note of finality that reminds me of the triumphant end of the Firing Squad album (track nine, "Always Something Left to Love," with the winding refrain that makes you think it's going to fade out—I hate songs that fade out—but then brings itself home), and then goes to her bedroom to do homework. I slip into the living room and sit on her makeshift piano bench, and I run my hands over the wood. Someone had loved this piano and polished its wood and kept it clean before it wound up on our lawn. I lean into it, rest my head on it, stare down its keys without touching them. Maybe it'll yelp out a note, or guide me to play a song that'll give me all the answers: about Victoria, about Abuela, about how to create something that's more meaningful than a mood piece.

Thrum-bum-bum. The sound is messy and tired. It's the sound of a girl who doesn't know how to play music banging on an old piano. The sound of my continued trying and failing. I run my hands down the keys, and I swear they un-tune themselves as I go. My eyes fill with tears. I can't play, I can't paint, I can't ever be Victoria's girl-friend. I can't, I can't, I can't.

The piano opens at the top, revealing a bunch of little pins and hammers that connect to the keys and their strings. Even the beauty of its pattern makes my chest ache. *This* is a work of art. This, too, can be destroyed.

I pull at one of the pins, bending it, and then another and another. Everything inside me tightens as I do this. I shouldn't have touched it, but to have its music out of our lives, even temporarily, is exactly what I need. If I could break the strings and crack the keys, I would. If I could tip the entire wretched thing over, I would do that too.

"Mercy!"

Angela's face is cracked. Pink. Something essential about her is torn apart.

"What?"

"What? You look at me with your hands in *my* piano and say,

'What?'" She rushes over and clutches both ends of the instrument. "Stop touching it! Are you trying to break it?"

I take my hands out and tip the lid until it slams.

"I can't believe you," Angela says. She sits at the piano and glares at me while her hands move up and down the keys. My face burns at the sound. The sound, the sound: it's perfect. Nothing has changed.

She's still playing as I put on my purple sandals and grab a sweater and the keys to Mom's car. She's still playing as I stare at her from the front doorway and she doesn't see me. She's still playing as I stumble out into the yard, and I can think of only one place that has given me beauty and sense and comfort and light. Only one place to go.

Firing Squad (track seven, "The Getting Is Good") pleads at me from the stereo, and I take the curve toward the gulf. If this is where Lilia gets her inspiration, then maybe there's going to be something here for me, too. I've always resisted using things like beaches and sunsets as backdrops for my art, but maybe ignoring them in favor of food poisoning is what's gotten me to this point.

The stretch of condo buildings comes into view. The normal ones first, with their dim orange lights burning in some of their windows and big sedans turning in and out of their parking lots. And then, yes—the building, mine and Lilia's, pops up from behind one of the taller ones. It's just as bright as it was the other night. My head hums like it did the morning that Angela played with Lilia for the first time, whirring with a pure sense of music, like I'm savoring the last beats of an amazing concert.

Or maybe not the last ones. Maybe this is the beginning instead.

A sign at the building's driveway reads *Red Mangrove Estate*. I signal right and pull the car (my mom's car) into the chipped parking lot. It's the only one here.

Because I left the house in such a rush tonight, I don't have any of my usual art stuff with me. I feel naked without my sketchbook and at least a couple of decent drawing pencils. The only thing in my tote bag is a verb conjugation worksheet from German class. I dig a pen out of the glove compartment and sketch the basic outlines of the building. There is something about this place that wants to be captured. (*Immortalized* is too grandiose, considering the fate of the two *Food Poisonings*.) In one way, it's a hulking mess of natural resources built when Florida was trying to cram as many rich senior citizens as possible along the shoreline. In another way, I want people to know how the moonlight hits it, and how the waves sound beside it. And the building seems like it wants other people to know, too.

Did it make you want something? Lilia had asked.

I tuck my phone into my tote bag and my bag under my arm, and I leave the car and take a few steps toward the building. The light's so bright I expect it to make a noise of its own, but the waves are still the loudest thing around. I'm closer to the beach than I've been in months, though there's a thicket of weeds around the Red Mangrove Estate and the parking lot that I'd have to drag myself through to get down to the water.

But that's not where I want to go.

I cross the parking lot. The windows' light glints on my skin for the first time. I want—no, I need—to see inside, but a set of tall glass doors stands as a fortress to the building's interior.

A terrible, mechanical squeak above me. One floor up, a window is opening.

"Hey, you made it." Lilia pushes her face against the narrow space where she has wedged the window open. "Come on up to the second floor. The elevator's broken. You'll need to take the stairs."

The doors aren't locked? I want to ask her, but she slams the window shut.

The once-automatic center doors stay tight, but the regular door on the right pulls open. The lobby is quiet, but not silent—somewhere there's a swish of air, as though the building is having its life breathed back into it. A lonely emergency light sears everything a dusty shade of yellow.

The doors to the elevator are open, but the actual moving box that would take me upstairs is stuck, suspended between the lobby and the second floor.

I used to have to go to my dad's office on school holidays when I was little. I would bring a case of markers and draw on scrap paper pulled from Dad's recycling bin. But as soon as he got up to go somewhere, I would escape. I would race to the stairwell and run up and down the stairs, stopping at each floor to poke my head out and see how the hallway on floor eight was different from the hallway on floor seven.

The stairs in this building are in almost the same place as the stairs in Dad's old office tower in Naples. It's hot in here and the walls seem to be sweating dust. If Dad were to find me here, now, he'd have the same reaction he did ten years ago: *Mercedes, why do you keep doing this?* I was never a good troublemaker—I was predictable, and I had no fear.

The door to the second floor swings open before I can grab the handle. Lilia, of course.

For someone who clearly didn't care for Vic's grand entrance the other night, she sure likes making them herself.

"Hey, Lilia."

She's still wearing the paint-splattered dress from earlier. Her hair is down and her face is smudged and dusty, as though she's had to crawl here. She smiles at me—Frida Kahlo again.

"Well, you're here. Do you want to get started?"

.

seven

"THIS IS YOUR studio?"

Lilia pushes a small brown chair toward the center of the room for me. "It's a temporary space."

"It's very quiet," I say. "My sister told me you had a commission." My sister, my sister. I feel like, before I do anything else, I need to dig through the photos on my phone and find a picture of a grinning Angela to remind me that Lilia has done brilliant things for her, that Angela lives with me in a house owned by Rex, who rents to Lilia, and that Lilia's space has a totally normal chair in it, waiting for me.

I sit.

"That's true," Lilia says. "What you're seeing here is part of it."

But what am I looking at? There's a canvas leaning against the wall, drying, but it's not much more than the fuzzy blue and green beginning of some sort of landscape painting. Maybe the real art is the room itself—it's an old living room, showing leftovers of the usual Florida pastels, but transformed into its own beast. It's as if she's taken Florida apart, squeezed out most of the pink and white and muted orange, and pieced this place together with the remains. The light pink carpet has been zigzagged with black lines, and the walls are murals, with the loose human forms on one wall giving way to abstract color and shape on another. Lilia is turned away from me now, so I dare to glance at the ceiling. Yes, it's been transformed, too: soft primary colors resting underneath a layer of household items. Empty plastic soap bottles, a couple of toothbrushes, a hair dye box.

"That's not finished yet," she says.

I've been staring. I keep staring.

"Don't worry, they're glued on well," Lilia says. "And they're clean. You won't get dripped on."

Maybe she's involved in some sort of condo building restoration project, like maybe the mayor of Sarasota realized they weren't having much success filling the beachfront buildings with rich seniors anymore, so they decided to try to fill this place with . . . rich people who like conceptual art? Who knows.

Lilia, figuring correctly that I plan to sit here and look around for a while, goes over to a laundry basket full of junk for the ceiling artwork and starts rifling through it.

"What kind of adhesive did you use?" Oh my God, of all the questions I have about this place, the one that pops out is about *glue*.

"Rubber cement at first, but I switched to superglue after a couple of the soda bottles fell." She holds up a Stove Top stuffing canister and a Goya black beans can. "Which do you think should go between the boxes of laundry detergent?"

"The Goya, I guess?"

She faces the can as if she expects it to smile back at her. "Okay. Why do you think so?"

"Umm, personal nostalgia, for one thing," I say, "but also I guess because there'd be some contrast between the height of the laundry soap boxes and the Goya can." Goya, though. Like the Spanish artist who started out painting royals and moved on to disturbing stuff like *Yard with Lunatics*. Maybe Lilia is pulling a trick on me. There are a couple of places in this room where a Goya-style lunatic could pop out. "But also, I don't know, the sizes of the stuffing can and the boxes work well together."

"Mercedes." My name said the Spanish way, with just the right shape of the vowels and the *r*. Hardly anyone says it that way. "So much of art is making choices, don't you think?"

"Sure."

"So which do you think?"

"The Goya can."

"Great. That'll give me a theme for the next section of ceiling." She tosses the Stove Top container back in the laundry basket.

I meet Lilia's eyes, interrupting her from surveying her work again. "So, when you asked me if I was ready to get started, is this what you meant?"

"Um. No." A small smile crosses Lilia's face. "You're at the beginning of something amazing, amiga. When you're here, you'll be able to create what you most want to create."

"I've tried that before, though."

"You haven't. Not like this." Her voice is firm. She turns back around to her recyclables and art tools. "Anyway, the last time I saw you, you were kind of doing the opposite of painting, you know?"

"I know, I know."

There isn't a single person in my life who would understand why I'm here right now, and I wouldn't even try to explain it, because, well, that's my choice. A conversation at the Dead Guy with Victoria about this place would lead to many horrified expressions and questions upon questions. Victoria would ask why I don't just take another painting class at Ringling. But I didn't tell her much about that painting class I took while she was off dancing in Alabama. I didn't tell her how my chest filled with rocks as I walked into class, and how I spent too much of my time in that classroom trying to get the air through the few tiny spaces. I didn't tell her how the older woman sitting to my right asked to "borrow" a paintbrush, and still has it on permanent loan. I probably *should* feel the chest rocks right now, but I don't. Lilia's studio is cool and quiet, and if it expects anything of me, I think I might be able to live up to whatever that is. If I really focus on sound and sort out the air, the conversation of the waves comes to me, their sentences long and overlapping.

"And you know what, Mercedes?" Lilia concentrates on applying glue to the Goya can. "No one outside this building ever has to see what you create here. No one even has to know you've been here."

I want to ask her, *Oh, and how does that work?* But everything about Lilia is so sincere in this moment. The truth of her words sinks into my skin. No one has to see or know. Maybe I could run down the halls hollering about my love for Victoria. Maybe I could stage a piece of performance art about the destruction of the *Food Poisoning* pieces.

These possibilities leak in and out. What I really want is what Lilia's doing, her carefree sense of creation.

I take in a breath. "So where do I paint?"

She looks over her shoulder at me. "Go down the hallway here. Try the second bedroom on the left. Oh, and there's plenty of paint and brushes and stuff in the kitchen."

I'm still sitting in the brown chair.

"Look, I felt scared, too, the first time I came here. But I promise you're going to discover something amazing. All you have to do is start. Think about what you've always wanted to paint, and you'll be able to do it."

"I'll try it." I stand up. "But I can't stay for too long."

In the kitchen, I grab a couple of colors of paint: red, blue, black, white. It's thick latex wall paint, but you've gotta use what you have. There are two new brushes and a cup of water and a palette. Sitting by the sink is a brand-new roller, which I tuck under my arm, because why not? Lilia nods at me from the living room, and I walk down the hallway.

The door to the back bedroom sticks at first, but then flings itself open. I flip the light switch and three dim bulbs hanging in a bent ceiling fan come on. How did so much brightness outside give way to so much dullness in here?

I guess I could do my part to make it brighter.

Think about what you've always wanted to paint.

Well, there's one thing to scratch off that list: symbols related to food poisoning. I flop down onto the carpet—thin and pink and rough. I hate trying to paint people's faces, and their feet. I have never wanted to paint dogs or horses, whether realistic or abstract.

My left hand twitches, and I grab my wrist out of instinct.

Just start.

The thought is thick and urgent, like when I wake up suddenly in the middle of the night, convinced I missed my alarm. It occurs to me that Lilia doesn't have any canvases or paper in her kitchen—I guess I'm supposed to join her in painting the walls.

I dump a small can of red paint into a pan and unwrap the new roller. Does the building make me want something? Yes, yes, it does, at last. I want something, and for now it's to cover these four walls in paint.

Red is the color of blood, of apples, of the T-shirt I bought on our last, worst all-Moreno family vacation to Key West. Red was Victoria's face that time I went to see her modern dance company's performance and I met her backstage and brought her flowers because Connor Hagins sure wasn't going to. Red was the cover of the first sketchbook I ever filled, when I would sit on the bench outside my middle school in Naples and draw the palm trees, and people's faces and their shoes. There are red hands and a red tide. Red is flame and fury. Red is a smack on the cheek. Red is thin and shallow and covers everything. Red loves you back.

By the time Lilia pokes her head into the room, I have painted an entire wall.

I don't want to tell her this, but it's the most I've ever painted. The most paint I have used in a day. The most space I have ever dared to cover. It's the equivalent of thirty big canvases, at least. I drop my roller in the pan and stand back as Lilia takes a walk around the room.

"So this is it," Lilia says. "This is what you most wanted to paint."

I shrug. For once, I'm not feeling apologetic about my work. "Yeah."

"Well." She runs her hand along the red wall. The paint is already dry. "It's bold."

"Thank you."

She leans against the wall, *my* wall, and her hair and skin are a striking contrast to the red, so much that I almost want to ask her to step aside so I can paint her portrait, right in the place where she was standing. But I think that might weird her out. I'm not even sure if we're friends, this odd girl and I. She let me into her studio, but I hardly know a thing about her. In the great school cafeteria of life, I feel like she's perpetually blocking the seat beside her, unwilling to let me in.

"Who's your favorite artist?" I ask her.

"Who's yours?" she shoots back.

"Rembrandt," I say.

"Liar." Lilia moves away from the wall.

"Fine," I say. "Kahlo."

"Nice," Lilia says.

"How long are you going to be here?"

She looks worried about my question, and after hearing Mom cry on the phone tonight, I don't want to have to deal with a crying Lilia again. But then, she softens. "A few more hours, I think. I just want to make some more progress on the ceiling. You can keep working too, if you want."

"I might."

Lilia heads to the doorway. "Oh, and if you see any of the others on the way out, be sure to tell them I let you in, okay?"

"Okay."

And from the hallway, she calls, "Your wall is perfect, Mercedes!"

I don't think I should be scared of the others. Maybe they're fellow high school seniors who need motivation and a place to work. Maybe they are fellow veterans of art destruction. Maybe they're just people who like nighttime and old buildings.

Still, I'd rather keep painting than risk meeting someone else right now. Brushes, rags, a refill of red paint. A cool, wet towel for my sweaty cheeks. Back to it.

Another white wall.

Perfect. Just like Lilia said.

The red goes on so easily, and when I'm finished with the roller I pick up a thin brush and start working on the corners and edges, making them straight and clean.

But there is something else this time, something beyond the neatness of my red walls. A pattern appears on the still-white spots of the wall. Something curvy and abstract, maybe. The lines are barely visible—it's as though they're being projected in dim light from somewhere just behind me. I grab one of the edging brushes, dip it in red paint, and follow the lines.

It is so easy.

The brush, a tough one without much give to the bristles, glides along the lines and leaves a precise, even trail of paint behind. I curve with the line, and where it ends I finish it off with a twisting flourish of the brush. I try it again. The brush makes a pleasant *swish*—the nicest a brush has sounded in a long time—and I create a perfect circle.

This is me doing this. I think. I hope. Even though the projection of the pattern seems to come from nowhere but the wall itself, the brushstrokes are completely my own.

I wonder if this is how Picasso felt when he was working on *Three Musicians*. Or Frida Kahlo when she was re-creating herself as a work of art. Or, okay, to bring myself back down to earth, how Gretchen

Grayson feels as she works on the lizards in the dining room.

There's something here. Something for me. A painting that wants to reveal itself.

I keep going, curving with the brush as an outline takes shape. The soft half-moon of a smile. The sturdy sweep of a neck and chin. The only thing abstract about this painting is what's going on in the background. The foreground of it is oh so real.

I hate drawing faces. I think I always have. The feeling of creating something that gets closer and closer to staring at me creeps me out. Should I go further with this painting? The push-pull of the question prickles the skin of my arms and cheeks.

Mercifully, the lines on the wall fade away. I flop onto the carpet, belly down, arms and legs out, my face way too close to this place that seems to have seen a thousand pairs of shoes and feet. Cleanliness be damned—there could be a clue here to whisper to me about this place, this Red Mangrove Estate, a piece of dust or hair that could show me the whole of this world. It's like when you meet a new person and you want to scrub away that first layer of awkwardness to get to the one thing that makes them make sense—*Oh, so* that's *you.*

But right now, this is me. Lying on the floor.

I guess it's true whether you're painting in a classroom or a back porch or a supposedly abandoned beachfront condo—after a couple of hours, you get tired. The paintbrush won't lift anymore. Lilia has left the front room, and I wash all my stuff and put it to the side of the sink, the same way I'd do at home or in Mrs. Pagonis's class. I've always called it "putting the brushes to sleep."

Stepping into the hallway, I want to tell someone what I did tonight: I found this place, I came inside, I started something, I finished something.

The shadows of sound seep in from other pockets of this building. Somewhere there's music and conversation and glasses clinking, like the noise of the sort of party that makes your head hum for hours after you've left. It's happening behind other doors, and I pause in the hallway to see if any of them open for me. Two seconds, three, four.

The brush of footsteps. Someone rounds the corner a few doors down the hallway and approaches me. A girl, maybe a few years older than me, with fair skin, short blond hair, and all black clothes. In this dim, crumbling hallway, she is striking. She's a flashlight. She stops a few feet from me.

"I was invited." I jab back at the door to Lilia's studio. "Right there. I was working right there."

And yet, this place is full of possibilities. Like the possibility that I could open the door to Lilia's studio and find a blank beige space. Or the place restored to typical Sarasota condo chic, complete with an elderly woman reclining in the orange light of a TV game show.

But the girl just nods in recognition at the door. "Cool. So you must be good."

I don't know how to answer that.

"Should I go out the way I came in?" I ask her.

She nods toward the stairway door, which hangs open under an unlit red exit sign. "That's the only way," she says. "But you shouldn't stay gone for too long, okay?" She smiles, but it's a first-day-of-school smile. Friendly but wary. It says she's not going to ask me any more questions right now. It says she's not going to walk with me down the stairs.

I let her go. She heads to the stairwell and shuts the door behind her. It sounds like she's going upstairs.

My purple sandals, which usually look so worn-out and dingy, positively gleam against the thin gray carpet in the hall. How many people have walked down this hallway, have leaned against this wall to find their keys in a handbag, have slammed one of these doors for the last time, have run away and then come back?

How many people are here right now, painting walls red or climbing stairs or playing songs that seemingly never end or begin?

The music again. It is guitars and horns, and it stops and turns back and picks up a few of the notes from before but then swirls off into something new. It's live. And even for all the sound, I feel alone here. It's time to go home.

eight

SHIT. ANGELA.

She's still pissed about the piano. I don't think she noticed or cared that I wasn't home until after midnight. She hardly said a word to me in the house this morning, and so far in the car, all she's asked is for me to play "that piano song" on the Firing Squad album. She left the front seat open for Victoria.

"Can we just put that on repeat?" she asks as we pull up in front of Vic's house.

I do, because why not? The palm trees wave in front of the Caballinis' house, and they're so relaxing that I wish I could sit in the yard for the rest of the day and absorb what I did last night. Vic comes out wearing a brick-red shirt and a black skirt, with her trench coat draped over one arm. Her walk lately has been her ballet duck-feet stride, a rhythmic reminder of Juilliard and how much she's been practicing for her audition.

"Hi, Victoria," Angela says, as soon as Vic shuts the Ford's door. "Can you please ask my sister to promise not to destroy my stuff anymore?"

So this is how it's going to go. Vic makes a terrified face at me and stays quiet.

"Ange, I said I was sorry. And anyway, the piano's still fine, isn't it?"

"Yup," Angela says. "But the point is that you wanted to mess with it. You *tried* to."

"I don't know why I did that." I brake to let a school bus in front of us. It's a gorgeous morning, and I am going to be slow and deliberate in it. "And I feel different today. Play to your heart's content tonight."

"I don't trust you," Angela says.

"Okay, seriously," Vic says. "If you two don't stop, I'm going to replace your precious Firing Squad with my Broadway playlist for the next month."

Angela is silent for a minute. We pass this cool house at the end of Victoria's street that looks like a castle. If it lit up like the sun one evening, what would Vic do? I can't imagine her feeling pulled there. She'd probably shut the blinds in her bedroom and go back to reading whatever book she'd pulled from the big stack of paperbacks on her nightstand.

Maybe that's the way to go. I could tell Rex to watch out for his renter. I could leave the secret painting unfinished and forget it ever existed.

"Mom called from the hospital last night," Angela says over the last quiet chorus of "Always Something Left to Love." "Nothing's changed with Abuela. I made up something about where you were and I probably wasn't very convincing."

"Hey." We're at the stoplight at Orange Avenue. I turn around and try to meet Angela's eyes, but she's staring out the window at an elderly guy riding a bike down the sidewalk. We used to call guys like that Sarasota's Official Mascots. Actually, we called someone that a few weeks ago, when we were passing Jungle Gardens on the way to the art supply store. It feels like a hundred years and a couple of versions of ourselves ago. "I said I was sorry. I'll be home tonight. I promise."

Mrs. Pagonis has a sore throat, so she's written the plan for today's art class on the whiteboard: thirty minutes of independent projects, and ten minutes of constructive criticism with the other members of our color-coded tables. Next to the whiteboard, the photo of the late *Food Poisoning #1* has fallen off the wall. I don't bother to pick it up.

Gretchen, having set her lizard painting to the side for now, opens her sketchbook to start something new. The scratch of pencil on fresh paper. Thumbnails, outlines, ideas, possibilities. Lines with no color. I get chills, and I don't know if they're bad or good. I settle on watching Rider for a minute as he continues to shade his paisley pattern. He'll notice me soon—ten seconds tops before he looks up and smiles and sends a practiced eyebrow raise my way.

Mrs. Pagonis paces the room while clearing her throat, and Gretchen shoots thick gray lines across the paper, and the only thing I can think to do is throw open my toolbox and take out my watercolor set. With the paints and brushes and everything ready, I face the first blank page in my sketchbook and make a stroke of red. And another. The brush wobbles in my grip and paint streaks onto the table.

Gretchen's eyes go wide with the realization that I could be bringing down the otherwise sterling reputation of the Orange Table. I keep going, pushing my way down the sheet of paper, covering it like the whiteness of the paper is my biggest secret.

"I just . . . I want to have something for the county show," I tell Gretchen, which seems to satisfy her, even though the county show has flown to some faraway corner of my mind.

Once the red page is done, I tear another sheet out of my sketchbook and dive into the blue paint. Blue like my mother's bathrobe that she was wearing the morning she left for San Juan, that's still draped over the armchair in her bedroom. Blue like the mac-and-cheese box. Blue like the houses in Old San Juan. Like track three of the Firing Squad album. Like the daisy-print dress Victoria had on for her birthday last year—worn once, and never seen again. Like that pair of shoes I had with the stars on them, the ones I begged my mother for and then left outside in a hurricane. Can anyone look at blue and not wonder, for a moment, if they're going to fall into it?

But as hard as I try to experience the colors, painting here is nothing like painting at the Estate. The red page especially looks so . . . flat. There's no urgency behind it, no danger, except for the possibility of making Mrs. Pagonis regret those recommendation letters she wrote for my college applications a few months ago.

Mrs. Pagonis taps on the board to signal everyone to switch to the constructive criticism portion of the class period. Oh, yay.

Rider pushes his pattern into the center of the table first, and Gretchen takes the lead on the critique, pointing out Rider's use of detail and some places where his lines could be cleaner. I confess I've never thought much about Rider's work, but I wonder if there's a central theme to it all that I've missed. I wonder what he'd say if I tilted my head and said to him, "Who *is* Rider, really?"

I snicker at this, then straighten up and stare into his picture.

"It's honest," I tell him, by which I mean, it is what it is. It is tiny angles and microscopic dots of color. It's repetition. I kind of want to turn it into a shirt or a tablecloth. This isn't a bad thing, but I still don't think I'm going to say it.

And then Gretchen's lizard picture hits the table with a clatter. "Okay," she says. "Okay, have at it."

"I have a question," I say, meeting Gretchen's eyes instead of the lizards'.

"Sure," Gretchen says.

"How did it feel to paint this?"

"Horrible." Gretchen glances over to be sure Mrs. Pagonis is occupied at another table. The Yellow Table, where everyone creates appropriately cheery pieces. "Every moment of it was terrifying. I've never had a paintbrush feel so *heavy*, you know?"

I don't really know. But I nod.

"Anyway." She puts on a smile. "Like it or not, this is going to be my submission for the show."

"Well, I like it!" Rider says. I try to shoot Gretchen a look that says, *Hey, can we get this dude transferred to the Yellow Table?* But she's busy taking the lizard picture to a shelf in the back of the room.

When the bell rings, I fumble with my paints and the wet, messy slices of red and blue. Mrs. Pagonis comes over and taps me on the shoulder.

"Nothing for critique today?" she whispers.

"Not today." It's hard to talk normally when the other person's whispering.

"You've been off task a lot lately."

"I'm putting a lot of ideas together." I point to the blue-painted paper, the paper part of which seems like it's going to collapse under the weight of all the paint I slathered on it. Is it even worth setting this page, and the red page, on the back counter to dry?

"Ideas are fine, Mercedes." Mrs. Pagonis walks away to cough, and on her way back she grabs the fallen *FP #1* picture and tapes it back into place. "But I need to have something to grade you on. I'd love to see you do something like this piece again."

"We'll see." I drop the red and blue pages in the trash can on the way out the door.

*   *   *

The Dead Guy's memorial bench is not quite long enough for Vic—her arms and legs dangle off. But she makes it look comfortable. She even manages to keep her legs together so that no one walking by is able to see up her skirt. Her eyes are closed. It's always weird when you close your eyes at school—it sticks you in an uncertain place, like when you wake up in the middle of the night and the power has gone out. I try not to get to that place very often.

Victoria's tired, though. I know this. Last night was her late practice. The Juilliard people are coming to Miami in less than two weeks, and she's got her end-of-the-year show to practice for.

"Gershwin again," Vic says. "Just like last year's show. Wait! No, sorry. That was two years ago. You know I never got *Rhapsody in Blue* out of my head? I still hear it when I'm trying to fall asleep."

That was the first show she invited me to, and I remember how nervous I was for her when she stepped out to do her solo. It was the climax of *Rhapsody in Blue*, the moment where the orchestra sounds like it's diving down into itself, and you're not sure if it's coming back up. But then, ah, it does, and you can't believe you were ever uncertain. Victoria danced beautifully, gliding alongside the melody, leaping into it and landing in place. And so it was strange when I went to the R&B-themed spring show a year later and felt the same heart-stop when she danced. Process of elimination—it was not the music this time, it was not her dancing, it was something about *her*, something else entirely.

"Vic, I need help," I tell her quietly, figuring I'll only expand if she asks.

"With what?"

"You know, shit. Life."

"Oh, dearie. I don't know what I can tell you right now that doesn't involve dance." She turns her head toward me, puts a hand on her brow, and opens her eyes.

"No, that's perfect. Tell me again how you started to dance. Tell me anything you remember."

"Mmm, okay." She's quiet, and she has her eyes closed again. Across the courtyard, Connor Hagins and his buddies still occupy the tables we sat at last year, and strains of their nonconversations threaten to drop into our spot if someone doesn't start talking soon. "Well," Vic says, slowly, "there was a little girl in an apartment in Brooklyn, and there were her parents, who traveled a lot, and there was this girl's nanny, Celine. So one day, the girl was supposed to be watching *Sesame Street* while the nanny did whatever the nanny did, but the girl started going through the big cabinet by the TV, and she found her mother's collection of Broadway cast albums. And she put one on the CD player and started to move around."

I finish my fries and place my empty lunch tray by the Dead Guy's plaque. (O Tim Gelpy, here is your offering of ketchup residue for the day.) And I scoot backward across the ground one, two, three times so that I am in the shadow of the bench. One more and I'd be leaning against it. I want to, but she'd notice, even though she has her eyes closed again.

"And how could you not move around, you know? It had all the steps shouted out right in the beginning of the first song. It was *A*

Chorus Line, have I told you that before? I guess that's kind of key to our story, because I—I mean, *she*, our heroine—had no idea that good old Celine the nanny was going to hear some of the words in the music she was dancing to and get really pissed off. So she stopped the music and locked me in my bedroom."

"What?"

"Yeah, I bet I never told you that part before. She was planning to lock me in there just until my parents came home, but then she remembered that, oh, my parents were flying back from the West Coast and wouldn't be home until late."

"How long were you stuck?"

"I don't know. Long enough to have to empty my box of Legos and pee in it."

"Damn, that's awful."

"And I didn't tell my parents what Celine did. She asked me not to tell. So she was my nanny until we moved to Seattle."

The leg of Tim Gelpy's memorial bench is cool to the touch. I can see why Victoria likes it. I lean against it, with one shoulder.

"But you started taking lessons in New York. The place above the dry cleaners, and the teacher with the pink hair and the cat she brought to class, and all that."

"Yeah," she says. "Yeah. All of that totally happened. My mom came to me a few days after the locked-room ordeal, and she was like, 'Celine said you might like some dance lessons,' and I agreed."

The fifth-period bell.

I dart away from the bench, and Vic sits up and for a second her legs come apart, but she smooths out her skirt and gets back to herself.

"So, wait," I say, picking up my lunch tray.

"Hmm?"

"You started dancing because your nanny traumatized you?"

"That's not what I said," Vic says. "I dance because I love it."

We're back in the building, and I'm walking too slowly. Vic stops to let me catch up, and the crowd slides back and forth around us. It's the weird post-lunchtime dimness after being out in the sun—dim vision, dulled senses. Vic still looks gorgeous, of course, but her face is hazy.

"So I'm working on a new piece," I tell her.

"That's great, dearie! What is it?" We're walking in step again.

"It's totally different from anything else I've done. It's kind of abstract, but also not?" She wouldn't believe me even if I told her about the Red Mangrove Estate and what Lilia has done there. So why should I even try to tell her? While I'm creating it, my project can be my own perfect secret.

"Here's to the girl on the go!" Victoria grins. "Tell me when it's ready. I want to see it."

I wish Vic's story was different. I want it to be a story of pure love for her art—of inspiration and creation, a sense of having had her vision. She leaves for French, and I head in the opposite direction for trigonometry, and with every step of my purple sandals, I'm trying to make something happen. For her, for me, for us. Moving forward . . . well, I'm always moving forward when I walk, but this time seems more solid than usual. I'm going back to Lilia's. I'm going to finish the red walls and the secret painting. What would it be like to bring Victoria there someday, to let her try to see what I'm seeing? The beauty, the simplicity. Just love. Just art.

The clock by my mother's bed says 10:02.

Angela is the champion sleeper in our family. She doesn't remember a single one of our flights to or from San Juan because she always zonks out before takeoff. She slept through hurricanes while my parents and I stared down the trees closest to our house in Naples, willing them not to fall.

But I feel like my taking a single step in the house tonight will wake her up. And, you know, if life was fair and logical, that's what *should* happen. Angela should catch me trying to leave, should remember that she's still mad at me, should force me to sleep on the floor next to her bed to make sure I don't try to leave again.

It's so easy to go out the window.

In the imaginary conversation I'm having with my sister, I'm explaining the unexplainable. I'm telling her about the Estate and its weird energy. Its patient doors and its musty stairways and its secret paintings. I'm telling her about how I've got to go there, right now—that everything I've ever wanted to do with my art seems possible in that place. And somehow, I'm able to say this in a way that makes sense to Angela, and she smiles and remembers Abuela's mofongo recipe after all, and tells me it'll be ready when I get home.

I wonder how Lilia leaves the other half of the house. I can't imagine her saying to Rex, "Hey, I'm going to my studio. I'll be back at six in the morning." I bet she just shuts the door and is gone.

But she doesn't have anyone expecting her to be in a certain place.

Does Victoria feel this way when she's going to the dance studio or to one of her company practices? Does she feel this pull toward the art, a pull so hard that I think I might wake up with sore muscles tomorrow?

I leave the light on in Mom's room. "I'm sorry," I say, to the whole Moreno half of the house.

Outside, it's colder than it's been in weeks, and a chilly mist of rain moves in and sticks to me as I'm climbing into my car. I don't know why, but I feel like taking my cranky old Pontiac tonight. Poor thing needs to get out of the driveway and see the sights. It grumbles at me as I'm maneuvering around Rex's Jeep, but on the main roads, it doesn't make a sound. It's like it knows where I need to be, and that I need to get there as soon as I can.

At a stoplight, I turn the wipers off and the windshield blurs over with rain. A sheen of tiny drops, all of them trapped in the glow of the stoplight and reflecting red onto my hands and face and neck. It's beautiful. *I'm* beautiful. There's no one around to see it, but maybe that's okay. I flick the wipers on again to wash it away, and then the car pushes on toward the Estate.

nine

"I'M BACK."

I say it to the room, to the walls. I thought I'd feel relieved to be here, but it's more of a shout than a sigh. *Yes!* I'm here. Time to work.

The paint and supplies have already been set up for me. My circle and lines from the secret painting are there, but the projection guiding me is gone.

Okay, fine. Back to the red walls.

I wonder what led Lilia here, if this room I'm standing in right now is a place she's lived in, or if it's truly nothing more than an adopted studio to her.

I wonder if she'll ever tell me.

I've swept across another white wall with red paint. All I need to do is edge around the door to the empty closet, and it'll be done.

The door to the bedroom is open, and Lilia walks by. She pauses, peers in, and says nothing to me. I figure if I were doing something wrong, she'd tell me, or take away the paint. Maybe the room is starting to look how she pictured it would. *Yes*—the word strums in her head. *Yes*. And there's a warmth in my chest and my knees as Lilia returns to the living room.

There's only one more thing to do: I need to take on the secret painting again. The lines on the opposite wall are back, having faded in like sunlight. I abandon the closet and go straight to them, to catch them before they disappear. They seem clearer this time, though, and less likely to dance away. I grab a thin brush and a palette of colors and go.

I'm quick and smooth—like scribbling with a brand-new rollerball pen. Like Angela's hands across the piano. Like Victoria in the Gershwin show, making effortless leaps across the stage and falling into a pirouette. There's a move in modern dance called the downward spiral—Vic is always trying to perfect hers. Maybe this is my downward spiral, careening yet controlled. When art is like this, when the work is so hard and so easy at the same time, I feel like I'm breaking all the rules of the universe. It's thrilling. It's terrifying. I may as well be falling through the floor, down to the beach and the gulf, straight down to the water, all the while managing to bring this painting to life.

It is taking shape. Curves and thin lines. Wrinkles. Eyes that are open and wide and friendly. It's a portrait of the person I most want to see and most want to avoid seeing right now. Abuela Dolores.

Abuela, who loves her dogs and mofongo and flowers and funny nicknames. Abuela, who has always accepted my art even when she hasn't loved it, and loved it when she hasn't understood it (which is great, considering all the times I haven't understood it either), and now I guess it's fitting that she's part of it herself, here on my wall.

And I want to tell someone, or show someone, but can I? Should I? Is this painting even mine?

Elsewhere in the Estate, the music starts up again. Quietly, like a footstep on carpet. Like it's coming toward me but has a while before it reaches me.

I sit on the floor next to the painting and work on the corner and the bottom, which seems to be some sort of background pattern. The guidelines are barely here now, but maybe they'll stay long enough to let me finish this corner. It's coming together. The pattern down here, whatever it is, is more intricate than the rest.

Actually, it's not a pattern—it's a word. *This.*

I keep going. More red paint and clean brushstrokes. More spiraling.

The next word: *really.*

And one more: *happened.*

And a dot at the end. Final.

I drop the brush and stumble to my feet. *This really happened.* Okay, but *what* did? This is where I need the English-class analysis skills of Angela and Victoria. Maybe I'll let the painting hang out and be on its own for a while. At the doorway, I peer out into the rest of the apartment.

The music is clearer and louder now, like bells, or a brand-new piano. Every note, no matter what instrument makes it, is full and bright, bursting through the walls of the Estate like a searchlight.

"Lilia?" I say into the hall.

No reply.

"Hey, I'm going to take a short walk, okay?"

She has left. In the living room, she's finished a whole new ceiling section of Goya cans, and cleaned up her supplies. She told me before how we wouldn't be alone here, how this is a community of artists, so maybe she floats from one place to another, checking on other people's red or purple or orange rooms. I just know that my urge to find the music tonight is stronger than my urge last night to leave without seeking it out.

Out in the hall, it sounds different. It's still bright and brilliant, but it's clearly coming from somewhere farther away. Another floor.

I take the stairs one floor up. Still farther away.

Two more floors, and I peer into the hallway. I'm on the fifth floor. The hallway is identical to Lilia's floor. The music seems to be coming from an even higher place now.

Sixth floor. Seventh floor.

Finally, at the eighth floor, the music stops.

I step out into the hallway.

There. A note. The strains of a new song. They start as whispers with glances of a tone, but they fold on top of one another and now the music pours over me. It floods from the end of the hall. As I walk closer, other instruments announce themselves: bass, keyboard, and saxophone. The door to number 810 is ajar. I push it open only enough for me to slip through.

They're all here. In the living room, in the kitchen, in the hall. These must be the other working artists Lilia talked about. The rooms glow a dim orange, and the artists cluster in groups, shoulders close together. I have walked into parties before: Bill's pool parties where he would grab my hand and jump with me, fully clothed, into the deep end; Tall Jon's parties, full of members of two-month-old bands; a popular-kid party I went to with Connor and Victoria; a cast party for one of Victoria's shows, just after the lead dancer had announced that she was leaving; weed parties and cheap-beer parties, all of which smelled more like guy sweat and microwaved food than anything else. But I have never walked into an artist party.

I don't even know what it smells like here. Not smoke, not paint, not food. Maybe just like people.

A few steps forward. There's a group of three women talking. They look at me—they are older, like in that big swath of time between Tall Jon's age and Abuela's age. Like when you're supposed to be doing things and making things.

"Do you know what band this is?" I say. "They're really good."

They all look like they're trying to signal one or the other to speak to me. "Are you Lilia's new friend?" the tallest one asks.

"I guess so." Maybe I look nervous. I uncross my arms, let them hang by my sides. It's easier to do parties when you have a Tall Jon–donated cigarette in one hand. "My name's Mercedes."

"We're glad you could come up tonight," another one says. She is strikingly pretty, a mix of colors: brown eyes, medium-tone skin, a striped scarf in her dyed red hair. "This isn't a band, not in the usual sense of the word. They're here most nights, though, just experimenting with different songs and sounds. You might hear some of them again, one day." She winks at the other ladies.

"Cool. Thanks." I move farther into the crowd. People say *hello* and *excuse me* and sometimes nothing. But I am supposed to be here, I'm pretty sure. They haven't turned me away. And—yes—there's Lilia, heading toward me down the hall, and people step aside to make sure that she, now wearing a floaty light green dress and sandals, can get by.

Her eyes lock on me. "Did you finish your painting?"

"Yes," I say, "with the wall I came to finish. I mean, I didn't originally plan on coming back tonight. I know I didn't tell you that earlier. I really needed to stay home with my sister. But I just couldn't stay away. I just had to—"

"Your sister will be fine," Lilia says.

But. Angela. I can see her, as if an image of her was being hazily projected onto the living room wall. She's asleep—covers kicked off, Tweety Bird pants making another appearance, ceiling fan swishing her bangs around. I can stop looking at her, can't I? There's nothing to see, nothing that's going to change in this picture until her 6:33 alarm because she hates even numbers.

But. She's mad at me.

When she was in kindergarten, a bunch of the boys on the school bus called her Miss Piggy, apropos of nothing, and I, a cool if not ice-cold third grader at the time, didn't say a word about it.

When she was starting middle school, our parents bought her a new desk and chair, and I said I liked them more than my own desk and chair, and before I knew it, hers were in my room.

Last summer, when I told Mom that I'd broken up with Bill and that I thought I might go out with a girl next, and when Mom looked at me sideways and walked out of the room, Angela sat with me for a long time, the two of us staring straight ahead at *Antiques Roadshow* as I burned at my outburst with its ridiculous overrehearsed casualness. And Angela ate chicken soup with crackers and didn't seem to mind living in my world.

Also, let's not forget all my smoking.

Shit.

"Lilia." I shift to looking at her—well, at a noncommittal place on the top of her head—and the image of Angela vanishes. "Can I bring her here? Is there a place she can practice?"

"Your living room works for now, doesn't it?" It's like she's daring me to say no, to complain about how the piano and its teacher's randomness bother me.

"But Angela's about a million times better than I am. I mean, good Lord. She'll probably be playing Beethoven's unfinished symphony or whatever by the end of the week."

Lilia pushes back her hair. For the first time, she looks

exhausted. "No. That can't happen right now. I'll let you know if you can bring her in the future. But now, absolutely not."

The music swirls around us. It's only a guitar and drums right now, and has that classic feeling about it, like something I'd hear if Abuela took me to her favorite place for lunch. I should stay here a little longer. I should. I open my mouth to say something to Lilia—a protest, a question—but nothing comes out.

"Mercedes," Lilia says, "enjoy the music." She turns away and walks back down the hall.

I finished tonight's red wall. And Angela will be fine. And I am wearing my purple sandals.

Moving forward.

"Hey!" The voice comes from behind me, and I turn and it's her—the girl I met in the hall last night. She's behind the kitchen counter, with glasses and bottles in front of her. It's an oddly comforting sight. Ah, so this whole shindig does have something in common with a Bill Stafford or Connor Hagins party.

"I thought I'd see you again. Can I make you something?" the girl asks. Tonight she's wearing her same black clothes, but with a blue-and-white-striped necktie, and no makeup besides a shock of red lipstick.

"What do you have?"

"Anything you want." She opens a cabinet door to show me the selection.

"Um." What did Tall Jon make me that one time that I really liked? I told him I wanted a glass of whiskey, and he laughed and told me I'd hate it, but that he could mix it up in something and I might not spit it out. And I didn't. And that was the night I made out with Callie.

"There was this thing I had once, with whiskey and lime. Do you know what I'm talking about?"

"I'll see what I can do." She winks at me. "Give me a minute. I'm Edie, by the way. Tell me about you, while you're here."

I'm Lilia's new friend, and I paint walls for her, and that's currently my main contribution to the world of art. I've destroyed everything else. My sweet abuela is too asleep to care about me right now, and my mother is far too awake and knows too much about me and still doesn't care. And I know this amazing girl named Victoria, and I've always thought I shouldn't tell her I think she's amazing, but now I'm not so sure. My little sister is a musical genius, and I don't understand how Lilia is bringing that out of her. I'm at peace here, by the way. Maybe because no one knows about it. Because whatever expectations Lilia has for me, I guess I'm meeting them by painting walls. Because I don't have to show those walls to anyone else.

"Eh, that's okay," Edie says. "Plenty of people come through here whose names I never even know."

"I'm Mercedes Moreno."

"Well, Mercedes Moreno, I'm curious about what you're working on down there on the second floor."

"Me too." I don't mean to smile, but there it is. "I don't know what it is yet."

"Hmm." She mixes my drink with a metal stick. "I think you'll like this. Try a sip."

It's sour, and it's got a bite. I guess my face gives all that away.

"Hand it over. I'll add some orange zest. That should do it." She flings her tie over her shoulder and starts grating an orange. "So who are you thinking about tonight?"

"What?"

"You have that look." She pushes the sweetened drink toward me. "Wistful, sort of. Like you've got people on your mind. Maybe just a person."

"People, I guess. People in my family. But also this girl."

The drink is perfect.

"A girlfriend?"

What would it be like to say yes?

"No."

"Tell me about her."

"Um, she's from New York." A gulp. "Her family's Italian. She's a dancer. She's one of those people who's good at everything." Another gulp.

"Tell me what the nicest thing you ever said to her was."

The first time Victoria and I went out for coffee was also the first time we played "How Many People?" It was a Starbucks in downtown Sarasota, toward the middle of fall semester, sophomore year, and we both laughed ourselves into a state of happy diziness. I think we knew at that point that we were going to be good friends, that soon we would stop counting who owed who money for coffee, that we were going to learn (most of) each other's secrets.

I kept thinking that I needed to tell her one very true thing: "I'm glad I met you."

I couldn't get it to come out.

And then Vic said it, like it was the easiest thing in the world. She twisted the cap back on her water bottle and said, "Mercedes, I'm *so* glad I met you this year!"

"I am, too," I told her.

If the heart of "How Many People?" is infinite possibility—that, yes, any bizarre theory you suggest in the game either has happened, or will happen, or is happening right now—then maybe that was the heart of our friendship, too. I would have a million more things I would want to say to her, and a million more chances to say them.

And the possibilities are here, as well. Each room, each step, each floor, each person. I feel them all.

Edie slides another drink toward me. "I think you need this."

The party dwindles. The three women I talked to earlier wave at me as they leave. Everything softens and slows, and the only conversations happening are the low-voiced ones that are too close to their end to be able to join. A few more people come by for drinks, and so Edie helps them. She glances at me every time she serves a drink, and I keep thinking she's going to ask me more questions. She doesn't, though now I'd probably be more likely to answer.

Then Edie places a cup of hot coffee at the spot next to me on the counter.

"You good for now?" she asks.

"I think so," I tell her.

It's Lilia who saunters up and grabs the coffee.

"Oh my God," I say, "so you *do* caffeinate yourself!"

Lilia looks sideways at me and smiles.

I know I'm drooped over the counter. I know the whiskey has gone to my head. But I can't leave here just yet.

"There's a secret painting." The music is quiet enough that I can whisper over it. "In the red room. There's like a freaking *secret* painting on the white wall. Did you know that, Lilia?"

She's quiet for longer than she should be. "You might not want to go back to that room."

"But I *love* that room." I say this too loudly, but so what? It's nice to realize that. It's nice to finally love something I've created. "It gave me exactly what you said it would. Why shouldn't I go back?"

"You'll find out," Lilia says. "I know you can do good work here, but you have to trust me when I tell you these things."

"Oh, you sound like my mom." That's my loud laugh over the music, isn't it? Shit. "Sorry. Sorry, Lilia. Where are your mom and dad?"

She gives me a strange look, and I cringe. Maybe that's a raw question for her, for some reason. Edie pokes her head in and places a glass of water in front of me. "We're her family. This whole wonderful motley crew we've got going on here. Wouldn't you say, Lilia?"

Lilia seems to be taking in the scene the same way I was a few minutes ago. The sliver of gulf you can see from the living room window. The other party guests sighing out their last words. The old, scratched-up glasses we're using as partyware. My water glass has Ronald McDonald on it.

"My parents don't live around here," Lilia tells us. "The last time I saw them was back when I lived in Miami."

Edie shrugs and goes to wipe down the counters. It's probably a hint to leave, but I've got one more thing to tell Lilia.

"Beethoven," I say. "What's the famous one—the *Moonlight* Sonata."

"It's a nice piece of music."

"Angela's gonna play it. I know she will."

"She's not at that level yet."

"But she will be." I can see in Lilia's face that I'm right. "She will be, and maybe then, there'll be, like you said, a place for her here."

The music has become kind of disjointed: a line of notes from the saxophone here, a few drumbeats there. I push down the hallway, holding my water glass up, trying not to spill it, trying also not to make eye contact with the few people still here. Don't ask me about my work, don't ask me what I'm doing here, don't ask me who's on my mind. I stumble into an empty bedroom—the second one on the left, just like in Lilia's studio—and its walls and carpet are comfortably beige, and I settle onto the carpet, in the corner of the room, where I can have a view of the uncovered window. It's strange how close together the buildings look when I'm driving by, but from inside, it's as though the condo tower across from this one is a mile away. Its windows are dark—the old women have gone to sleep.

I finish my water.

Somewhere in San Juan, there's a hospital room. With monitors beeping their monotonous ballad of green and life. With too much light streaming in from the doorway. With nurses breathing out too hard and whispering in Spanish. With Abuela unmoving in the bed.

But tonight, I think, it is different.

I think my mother was right.

I think Abuela's fingernails are still painted purple and I think one of her fingers moved earlier and I think another is moving now. And I think her knuckles are wrinkling and I think she still needs her sleep for a while but I think, I think, she will wake up.

It's insistent.

She will wake up, she will wake up, she will wake, she will.

ten

WHEN I'M OUTSIDE, in the parking lot, I'm absolutely alone yet again. The waves crash on, not bothering to include me in their conversation anymore, and as far as I can see down the beach, the lights in the other buildings are out. Behind me, the Red Mangrove Estate is dark, too, each floor of windows a slice of the night sky. No one else goes in or out. The leftover music from the party can't be heard. Plus, it's like I never had the drinks at all. The flavor of the orange mixed with sour mixed with booze is gone. And the dizziness I felt in the beige bedroom is gone. There's no real urge to sleep—I could probably go to school feeling like this.

Well, maybe physically. Not mentally. Who knows what weird shit I would create at the Orange Table right about now.

My body's relaxed, but my mind is all over the place. It's not a good combination.

I need to talk to someone.

And there's only one person I know who's usually awake at this time of night.

"Moreno, good God."

Okay, so this one time, Tall Jon was actually asleep sometime before two a.m. I've never seen his apartment completely dark. It looks strange, but no stranger than the place I've just been.

"Can I come in?"

"I mean, I guess so. You need a place to stay or something? Did Angela claim the Moreno castle as her own?"

"I won't stay long. I need to talk to you. And do you have a cigarette?"

We smoke on the balcony. I keep waiting for total silence, but it's broken by the clatter of college kids coming home and talking about how fucking late it is. Yeah, guys, we know.

Tall Jon stubs out his second cigarette. "Did something happen with you and the Vicster?"

I laugh. "I—wow, no one has ever called her that. I'm going to think of that next time I see her." A deep breath. "But, no. I have to tell you about my new art studio."

I'm ready to tell him about everything, from the burned-dust smell of the lobby to the feel of the roller in my hands to the sweet taste of the drink. I'm ready to tell him about how scary it was to walk into that party at first, but how I felt like a queen when Edie served me a drink and when people knew I was Lilia's friend. And I'm ready to tell him about Lilia herself, the way she comes and goes, the way she creates so effortlessly.

Wait a minute.

The Estate is my secret. If I let out anything about it, will that dim its light for me? Will it even let me back in?

"You know Firing Squad?" I say to Tall Jon.

"Yeah, I know Firing Squad. Did you really come here to talk about music? I'm not sure I have all my synapses working on that topic right now."

"You know how Firing Squad just lays it all out there, like they kinda sound like they're crying out all their wants and fears right there in the music?"

"I guess so."

"Well, I think I can do that now. With my art. Something clicked and now I feel—" I don't know. Powerful? Changed? New? All those words are suddenly huge to me again, like it would wake everyone up if I tossed even one of them out into the quiet night. "I feel like me, I guess."

"That's cool," he says. "What'd you say this place was?"

"Um. It's more like a state of mind."

Tall Jon studies my face. He pushes his pack of cigarettes toward me, but I wave it away.

"You look like you're gonna cry," he tells me.

"I'm fine."

"Because, from my perspective, you've reached some kind of new metaphysical plain, where the inspiration flows freely and the nights are long. Does that make sense? Shit, I'm tired." He gets up and opens the balcony door. "I think you're going to come out ahead in this one, Moreno."

"Maybe so."

There's a weird commotion in the living room. Not a piano. Not the thud of my strange new neighbor becoming a presence in my life. Something that seems more alien than both of those things right now.

It's the TV.

Angela has the morning news turned up to a horrifying volume. She sits in front of it, while drinking a huge glass of my orange juice and eating cereal. The stock market is up (UP!), and apparently I'll never guess which celebrity just donated a hundred thousand dollars to a dog park.

I sit beside her on the couch. She doesn't look at me.

"I want to list all the lies I had to tell Mom about you last night," she says, her words weaving underneath the pumping music of a Cadillac commercial. "I'll just write them down sometime today, because I don't really feel like talking to you."

The remote is in its usual place between the couch cushions. I grab it and click mute. "Fine. Make a list. Tape it to my door or text it to me or whatever. What did Mom say about Abuela last night?"

"Why are you asking? It doesn't even seem like you care."

"Because," I whisper, "I felt something so strongly about her last night. I was in this . . . place, and I was thinking about her, and it was clear to me that she's getting stronger. Getting better."

"Mom didn't say anything about Abuela. She went on a fifteen-minute monologue about having to walk the dogs, and then she asked me a bunch of questions, which of course resulted in a bunch of lies." Angela finishes her orange juice. "Why would you even say that you think she's doing better? How would you know?"

"I can't explain it yet."

A thud outside. A taxi has pulled up in front of our mailbox, and Lilia is home. She's got the rumpled look that anyone who works a night job probably has, but the effects of the Estate cling to her, too. There's a brightness to her hair and face, like she's speaking a secret in a language that so few of us can understand.

She sees me.

Our eyes lock.

She's my neighbor. Rex likes her. We all live within the same walls. She used to live in Miami. (I've been to Miami!) She takes taxis and probably watches the news sometimes and maybe cares a little about which celebrity donated to the dog park. She drinks coffee, for fuck's sake. And I told her about the secret painting.

I push away from the window, stubbing my toe on the piano as I do.

"Gonna get ready for school," I say, hobbling out of the living room. "I'm sorry if we're late today."

I grab my army jacket from where I hung it over my desk chair a couple of weeks ago—the day before the piano arrived, actually. We sit together, the jacket and me, on the floor next to my bed. My knees pulled to my chest, I settle the jacket over them like a blanket and put my face in it. I bought it right after I broke up with Bill, and it was perfect at the time, like every time I put it on I was wrapping myself up in myself.

But it's not comforting now. For one thing, it smells like stale popcorn and needs to be washed. For another, wrapping up in myself seems uncomfortable and paradoxical today, and maybe every day from now on.

Angela knocks on my bedroom door. We need to get to school. I throw off the jacket.

Sometime this morning, Angela stuck a note inside my backpack. During first period, it flutters out onto the Orange Table:

Lies I Told about Mercedes:
She's home right now.
She's just working on a painting.
Yes, it's that one she left on the porch.
Yes, she's taking good care of me.

And at the bottom:

Mom wants us to get Abuela a special pillow for
her hospital bed after school today. No lie. This pillow
better be special.

"Listen to this, Ange. His voice cracks here and it drives me nuts. Like, the first few times I heard it, I thought he was doing it on purpose. But now I don't think so. I think he just can't hit the note." It's Firing Squad track four, "Head on a Train," maybe the only good thing about this drive from school to an appropriate pillow-buying location. "It's cool. I mean, I still like the song. But it's weird to hear someone's mistake like that, over and over."

In the passenger seat, Angela shuts her book. She's reading *A Separate Peace* for freshman honors English. It's one of those hardcover books the school loans out. Someone who probably graduated ages ago drew pointy ears and fangs on the characters on the cover, and so now Angela is stuck carrying around Gene and Finny's devilish counterparts.

"I never liked that book," I say. "Needs more girls."

"It's set at an all-boys' school," Angela says, not looking at me.

"Hey," I say. "You said something earlier that was really hurtful. You told me it doesn't seem like I care about Abuela. But that's ridiculous. You know that Abuela's one of my favorite people in the entire world. You know that."

Angela picks at the spine of the book.

I luck into a parallel parking space with no one in front of or behind me. It's been a shaky day, and I wouldn't trust myself to use my Advanced Parking Skills right now. "What you meant," I say carefully, "is that it doesn't seem like I care about *you*. Is that right?"

She ignores me. She's right to do it. We get out of the car and it's the type of afternoon that reminds me why old people move down here from Connecticut and why mothers come up here from Puerto Rico. We're at St. Armands Circle with all the snowbirds and tourists. The water is a block away. The Estate is around the corner. I could turn and run and go there. But would the doors open for me right now? Would the secret painting be ready for me? Something says it's not time to go at all. It's time to buy Abuela a very special pillow.

St. Armands is where we go when our tíos and their families visit, where everyone gets ice cream and Tía Elena always buys a gauzy bathing suit cover-up. This is the home of "nice" souvenirs, many of them with Florida-themed puns on them. Angela walks along in steady silence, but she's so happy to be here. She stops to pet a dog, and then to listen to a guitarist playing at one of the outdoor restaurants.

"Oh my God, every time I've ever walked by here, that guy's playing 'Brown-Eyed Girl,'" I say, because it's true.

"Shut up, please." Angela sways to the music. When the song ends, she pulls a dollar from her pocket, steps toward the guitarist on his stool, scribbles a song request on a piece of paper, and drops it in the guitarist's straw hat.

"What about the pillow?" I ask.

"I want to wait and see if he plays my song," Angela says.

"He plays every song the same way," I say. "He's not very good."

"Who are you to say what's good?" Angela says this loudly enough that the guitarist, who's now playing "Stairway to Heaven," which I only know because of Tall Jon, and which I don't think was Angela's song request, looks over at us.

Angela looks horrified to be singled out like that, so I don't expect her to go on.

But she does.

"Seriously, Mercy, you act like there's no *way* I could know what's good or not." Her voice is lower, but some of the people who noticed her before are still paying attention. She's drama. She's confession. "Maybe you're avoiding me at home because you're jealous. You never expected me to be good at something, especially something artistic. And now, you know what? I am. I don't know how I did it, but it's real. It has to be."

"I know," I say out of the side of my mouth. "I know you're good. And I probably was jealous."

I stop myself before I can say more, about why I'm not jealous anymore. About how I have my own place where I can go to be good at something. I catch the attention of a man and woman eating fries and having drinks out of coconut-shaped cups. It looks like the greatest and easiest thing in the world.

The guitarist stops "Stairway to Heaven" before the big climax. I think he sees that Angela is still red-faced and fuming at me. He starts in on a new song.

It's Angela's. It must be. Of course she would pick this one.

It's "Quizás, Quizás, Quizás," made famous in the US by Doris Day, and in my life by Celia Cruz, and also by Abuela. She loves it.

Abuela with her purple fingernails in her hospital bed with its sad lack of decorative pillows. Abuela who needs to wake up. Abuela, who had a stroke in her kitchen and who fell and hit the floor, and whose dogs yapped for long enough that the neighbors busted in and found her and called an ambulance. I hope that wasn't luck and luck alone—I hope there was a strain of her fighting her luck, or fighting *for* it. And I hope if it was her luck, that her supply of it hasn't run out.

Every note of the song hits like a firework in my chest. I turn and run to the center of the circle, where the statues of Greek gods preside over flowers and crosswalks and trash cans and benches, and where I sit and stare at the Red Mangrove Estate while Angela listens to the song. Bits of it trail over here, and I exhale in the music's direction.

She will wake up.

Angela crosses the street and sits next to me on the bench. I don't meet her eyes, concentrating instead on the statue of Aphrodite on my left. It seems like it must be a rough life for a statue here, but besides a wad of chewing gum stuck to her, Aphrodite looks pretty good.

"I was worried about you last night," she says. "I was trying to get to sleep, and of course I made up this whole scenario in my head where you weren't going to come home at all. I decided that you were tired of Florida and everything here and you were driving to Ohio to live with Dad."

"Oh, Lord."

"I almost called him. I really was convinced that's what you were doing. I was going to be like, Dad, when Mercy gets there, can you send her back home, please?"

"I wouldn't have made it. I would have gotten as far as the Georgia state line and wondered what the hell I was thinking."

Angela tugs at her hair. "He doesn't know we're here by ourselves, does he?"

"Nope." Across the street, the song—Abuela's song—has ended. Some polite applause. "Mom said she was going to tell him, but she never did. If she told him, he totally would have called."

"'Hellooo, girls, what's the story in old Floridy?'" For a fourteen-year-old girl, Angela actually does an excellent impression of a forty-six-year-old guy, born in Ohio to European parents, who thinks he's secretly descended from a Spanish prince.

"That's perfect." Now that we're safe from the song, I start wandering back toward the shops. "And I'm not planning to say a word to him about all this, even if he does call. Can we agree on that?"

"Sure, I guess." Angela walks a step behind me. "You know I wanted to live with him at first?"

I stop in front of the Ben & Jerry's, in its sharp and sugary-scented cloud. "What? You never told me that."

"It's true." She looks in the windows at a big family eating ice cream cones. She looks a little too long, to the point where one of the kids glares at her and sticks out his tongue. "You remember how much Mom and Dad used to talk about starting over? Well, I felt like, if they could choose to start over, then I could too. And I thought living with Dad would be my chance to do that."

"But they didn't let you."

"Nope." She starts walking again, and this time I'm the one who's a few steps behind. "Okay, your turn."

"My turn for what?"

"To tell *me* something."

"Ah." I keep thinking about Angela starting over, and what that would look like for her. And for me. "Okay. I remember a drawing I did a couple years ago. It was the last one Mom ever put on the fridge. It was of sea turtles—you know, how they hatch and then race to the water. That was the first time I ever drew something that was, like, symbolic of me and you."

"A turtle drawing is your secret," Angela says. "Well, great." She blows her bangs out of her eyes. "Let's go get a pillow."

Here is the pillow. It is thick and purple. It has *SEA LIFE'S BEAUTY* in big, swoopy script in the middle, and *Sarasota, Florida* in small letters at the bottom.

Angela settles herself at the piano as soon as we get home. I consider staying in my bedroom for the rest of the evening, but something doesn't feel right about that.

"Hey." I flop into the recliner, grip its armrests. "Do you know any Beethoven?"

"What? Do *you* know any Beethoven? I think that's the real

question here," Angela says without looking at me.

"I just thought . . . it might be something you can play."

"Lilia's always saying weird things like that." Angela taps out a melody on the far right side of the keyboard. It sounds like the birds that wake me up in the morning in the summer.

"I'm confident in you, Ange. That's what I'm trying to say. Let me try to find a recording for you."

Angela plays pieces of songs while I do a search for Beethoven on my phone. Her playing reminds me of the way the music changed at the Estate last night, from long songs to broken experiments, and how, just like Angela's music, it always sounded good. Mrs. Pagonis told me last year that *Food Poisoning #1* seemed "so inspired," and at the time I mentally rolled my eyes. Well, of *course* it had to be inspired by something, or it wouldn't exist. But there's another level of inspiration, I think.

Angela's back tenses as she plays.

Anyway. Beethoven. I'd forgotten that he was deaf when he composed a number of his pieces, and even when he performed his Ninth Symphony. I pull up a video of a woman playing the *Moonlight* Sonata and show it to Angela.

She nods along. She grabs the phone and puts the tiny speaker up to her ear and she sweats beneath her too-long bangs and she lays a hand on the piano and taps out a few notes. "Okay," she whispers. "Okay, let me try."

It seems like a private moment between her and the piano, as weird as that is. I duck into the kitchen to get her—and me—some water. In the other room, Angela fumbles with the melody. Stops and starts. Maybe this was a bad idea. I should leave this stuff to the actual piano teacher. I load some silverware into the dishwasher, some of them right side up and some upside down, because that's one of the ways to call for the Dishwasher Lemur. What would the Mercedes and Angela who invented the Dishwasher Lemur think of us now? Probably that we were screwing up this amazing opportunity to be parent free for a couple of weeks, wasting it on arguments and the pursuit of classical music. We should be inviting all our friends (I mean, the collective seven friends we actually like) over for dancing and movies and junk food.

But.

In the living room, the song comes together. Really, that's what it sounds like—all the notes meeting one another and having the fantastic party that the alternate-reality Angela and I are meant to be having.

She flies through the song, up and down the keyboard. I have no vocabulary for what she's doing, so all I can do is watch her. How she's more athletic playing the piano than she ever was at tennis camp. How she's breathing hard and ragged, but not in a way that worries me. How I really need to take scissors to her bangs, or make sure we have the money this week for a haircut. How she's taken to this piano the same way she learned to ride a bike: one day she was barely keeping her feet on the pedals as I held on to her, and the next she was off like a shot down the sidewalk.

Our water glasses sweat in my hands.

Angela finishes the song with a heavy, low note. And then she's still. I sneak around her—her eyes are closed, her cheeks are pink—and put one of the water glasses on the top of the piano.

"No!" she shouts.

"Whoa! Okay, then." I take the glass back.

"It might damage the wood," she says. "That can't happen. I need this piano."

"Sorry," I say. "That was amazing, though. You picked up the song in, like, five minutes."

"Yeah." She looks down at her hands.

"And, seriously, please have some water."

She does.

A single knock on the door. Rex says, "You girls okay in there? I heard someone yelling."

I glance at Angela. *Are we okay?* She shrugs. And I invite ourselves over for dinner.

Everything seems more possible in Rex's half of the house. Lilia isn't here. Rex and Angela are in the kitchen, putting the finishing touches on a casserole. Here in the living room (which is positively expansive without a piano in it), the TV is on, switched to one of those channels that plays the same three or four twenty-year-old movies on a loop. I think this is what my parents watched, in separate rooms, when they were going through the divorce. Except this one time that I caught them sitting together on the couch, their hands almost touching, watching *Jurassic Park*. It was two days before the movers came. I don't think they were sad about not being married anymore—I think they were sad that they were probably never going to watch TV together again.

"Is Lilia around a lot?" I wander into the kitchen and ask this, fake-casual in a way that Rex probably won't pick up on. "I feel like I only see her when she's doing Angela's piano lessons."

"Oh, you know, she's in and out," Rex says. He sprinkles cheese on the top of the casserole. "We have different schedules. She's a night owl, I'm an early bird. It's a good arrangement."

"Have you ever talked to her about her work?" I ask. Nothing's different about the walls (and ceilings) I can see from here—no murals or Goya cans added to Rex's place.

"Not really. I asked about it once, but she said it was in transition."

"Like, she's changing her style or something?"

"You got me. You're the other artist here," Rex says. "I think she's just private about it. Which is fine. I understand being a lone wolf." He scratches his beard, and Angela snickers. "I thought the two of you would find that common artist bond, Mercedes."

"Yeah. I'm trying."

While Rex and Angela serve the plates, I duck out to the bathroom. I take the one in the hallway between the smaller bedrooms, and use the opportunity of the loudly flushing toilet to open the door to Lilia's bedroom.

The whole Estate series greets me. It's more extensive than Monet and his precious haystacks and bridges. It's the Estate over and over, against color after color of sky, in daytime and nighttime, some versions more slanted and abstract than others. The paintings lean against the wall, or are propped up on the dark brown antique hulks of furniture that sit awkwardly in the Florida-colored room. For as much as Lilia said the paintings were her way to escape, they seem more like a trap to me than anything else. They take over the room—the only clue that a human occasionally lives here is the small suitcase on the floor.

It's red, and made of worn-out leather. A pink dress spills from one side. Lilia is living out of a suitcase.

I take a few tiptoed steps forward, as though any larger movement would set off some sort of alarm. The suitcase is zipped halfway, but I hold it tight and open it tooth by tooth. I'm a nosy person, and I've always justified it by telling myself that an artist needs to know other people's secrets, and needs to be able to twist them enough to use them as material. But this— going into Lilia's life feels so wrong, but so necessary.

Three floral dresses on top. Well, yeah. If anything, I expected more.

Sandals made of sturdy leather. A beautiful headband. Plain button-down shirts and some pants and even a pair of jeans.

A few books. She likes philosophy. Kierkegaard and Nietzsche— I remember trying to sound out their names on my dad's bookshelf a long time ago.

Under the books is a folded piece of paper. Thick paper, like out of a Canson sketchbook. I peek inside it, as though Lilia herself could come roaring out. But what greets me is a colored-pencil sketch of a small white house. It's a peaceful scene, the house surrounded by palm trees, the sky bright blue, and a couple of goats in the yard. It's a pretty good sketch, not quite finished, but it makes me want to be there, to know the place.

Oh. Wait.

I *do* know this place.

I've seen it in a few photos and I've been there once, a couple of summers ago, when Mom was so proud to show it to us. It's the house in Guaynabo, outside San Juan, where she lived until she left Puerto Rico for college in Florida. The place where she grew up with Abuela and Abuelo and her two brothers. Lilia drew this—she must have. It's clearly made by the same hand as the Estate paintings.

My hand shakes as I snap a picture of it with my phone. Then I lay everything back where it was and join Rex and Angela at the coffee table for dinner.

Rex's place is so jumbled after being in Lilia's room. Too many boxes, too many ingredients in the casserole in front of me. Rex asks what Angela and I are doing this weekend, and my sister fields the question by pointing a fork in my direction. "I have no idea what we're doing," I say, disappointing both of them.

Angela eyes me. I must not look right. I've barely touched my casserole or my orange juice. And my heart is beating so hard and fast that I think Angela might be able to hear it. Rex goes to refill his water, and I open my mouth as soon as he's around the corner.

"She has a studio," I manage to say. "Lilia." I feel the tension draining. "I've been working there with her."

Angela tries to respond, but Rex returns, and I jump in to ask, "Hey, I was just wondering, how did you find Lilia?"

"She found me!" he says. "I had barely put the 'For Rent' sign in the yard before she was knocking on the door. It was lucky for both of us. I think . . . I mean, I don't know, but I feel like she came here out of desperation. She needed a place right then. I didn't ask why, but I was happy to help."

Angela and I raise our eyebrows at each other in harmony.

I need to get back.

The house phone rings at nine.

"Mijita." I think calling me by a diminutive is my mom's way of kinda-sorta apologizing for the way we ended our last phone call.

"Hey," I say.

"She hasn't moved since the last time I told you she moved." Mom's voice sounds tired and wrung out. "I think I was imagining things."

"No. You saw what you saw. I'm sure of it." I lean against the fridge and concentrate on the mostly bare wall across the room, trying to will an image of Abuela to appear in the space above Mom's spoon rack. Nothing happens.

"That's nice to say," Mom says with a sigh. "And it's nice to talk to you, at last. I'm worried about how much time you're spending on that painting of yours."

Painting. I peel back the layers of the last few days to find what she means—ah, yes, a painting that no longer exists.

"It's for the county show, Mom." I try to push some enthusiasm into this. "I'm so close to finishing it."

"So close. I remember that from last year. I remember how I would find you out on the porch with that painting at midnight, and then you'd be back at it before school, at six in the morning. I let you stick to it because you kept saying you were almost finished, almost finished. Think about time, mijita. Think about how you're spending it. You've got about two months left of high school, and are you going to be spending that time finding the right place for, I don't know, a purple dot in your painting? Is that what you want?"

There's a cloud of noise from her end of the call. Beeps and dings and a murky announcement in Spanish. She's at the hospital.

"Maybe it is what I want," I say. "Also, the painting is red."

"Let me talk to your sister," Mom says.

There is only one place right now that I can feel as comfortable as Victoria feels in modern dance shoes, and as Angela feels with her hands on the piano keys. There's so much I want to do there: stare up into the Goya ceiling cans and see if they help me understand Lilia at all, hunt down the next party and say something to Edie about Victoria, and, of course, finish the red room. My heart flutters, my fingers ache at the knuckles, and a chill strokes my spine. I should be able to leave any minute now, but every flicker of sound in the house holds me back. The tree outside the window, once referred to by Rex as a bay laurel, moves as if shaken, probably by some hungry lizards. The air conditioner clicks on. And there's a knock at the bedroom door.

It could be Victoria, who rode a bike over here late at night because she wanted to sleep next to me. It could be Lilia, coming to tell me that if I can finish the red tonight, she'll explain why she drew that house, and why I felt so compelled to paint a room red. It could even be Mom, returning to lecture me some more about time and then kick me back to my own bedroom.

It's Angela, of course.

"Mercy." She hurls herself onto the bed, her knee jutting into my side in the process.

"Oh, come on."

"No, *you* come on. I want to know about Lilia's studio."

"I need to sleep."

"That's your own fault for being out too late. If I can figure out that you're sneaking out, you know I can figure out where the heck you're going."

"I don't think you will."

"That sounds like a challenge." She doesn't get under the covers. Instead, she props herself up on two pillows, as though it's noon instead of midnight. "Anyway, you owe me. For all the nights you've been away since Mom left. This isn't the best way to leave our sisterly relationship before you go to college."

"Why does everybody think I'm going to college? Jeez."

"I figured you'd heard from SCAD by now," she says.

"Not a word," I tell her. "And I would have said something if I'd heard from them."

"Uh-huh." Angela glances at me, maybe to make sure I'm telling the truth. In the half-light falling into the room from the moon and the street, her face is a lot like Dad's. The same down-browed look. The black hair on fair skin. The stillness of her thoughts. "So where's this studio? It's not in Rex's house, is it?"

"No. It's in this old condo building out on the Key," I say, and it's like letting out a breath.

"Okay, weird. So you and Lilia are working together?"

"Sort of. I think . . . I think we're at the beginning of a bigger project." This has to be right. I want it to be right. "It feels different, painting there, like I know exactly what I'm doing all the time. I feel like I could be successful—like, successful at making what I want to make. I feel like if I wanted to do a sad painting, I could do it there. I'd start it, finish it, put it on display, and bring everybody there to tears."

"Who's everybody?"

"The other artists."

"What about me?"

"What about you?"

"Could I do the same? With the piano. With the Beethoven piece."

"I don't know. Do you feel a pull to go there?"

"Maybe?" Angela hoists herself off the bed and paces around the room, her hands brushing some of Mom's things as she does. The pile of yarn from her knitting hobby, which never produced anything but three sad pot holders. Her collection of potted bamboo stalks on the dresser. My and Angela's school photos, but only the worst, most awkward middle school ones.

Angela leans against the window. "I think so."

"We can try," I tell her. "Maybe you'll get there and you'll realize that it's where you're supposed to be."

The last time I heard Angela yell, before this afternoon, was the day our dad announced that he was moving out. He had left before, but this time felt real, like all the anger from the other times he said he was leaving had been dug up and shoveled into this one phrase. He had conviction. But so did Angela. Right now, we're in the car with music on (Firing Squad, track four, "Head on a Train") and when I replay, in my head, Angela's shout from three years ago, it comes in louder than the stereo. "Stop walking away!" she yelled. And for a minute, Dad did. I stared at his boat shoes until they stopped on the driveway. It didn't last, but Angela knew how to set up a metaphorical wall covered with metaphorical graffiti. *Stop right there,* it might say. Or maybe just, *Fuck you, Dad.*

Angela says, "Lilia's been saying really nice things when I practice lately. Every time I work with her, she says I'm getting better, I'm finding my voice through the instrument, that sort of thing. What if she knows I'm coming tonight? I feel like she really could sense it, don't you?"

She gets so talkative when she's tired. I turn down the music so that I can better hear the rest of her monologue, but instead she leans against the window and is quiet again. Maybe this is how it's supposed to be—the unstoppable pair of Moreno sisters, creating stuff together. I don't know . . . we've never been that great of a team. But I like that she's here with me.

I crack the windows, and the air comes in cool and thin, like an *s* being pushed between teeth. It's going to be spring soon. It won't feel like this for much longer.

Angela tiptoes through the lobby, and she pauses at the door to the steps. "Maybe I should stay down here."

"Look, if Lilia's in the studio, then we'll go away and wait until she invites you. But if she's not, then we can peek in. It's only up one floor."

She walks up behind me, two-footing each stair. The stairwell smells like salt water and old paint, probably toxic if you had to stay here too long. She holds the door as we head into the hallway. No one, as usual. It feels strange to have the presence of Angela tailing me. Angela wearing a Harry Potter T-shirt and dark blue jeans. Angela with her black hair tied up in a messy bun. Angela who feels ready but who has not been invited.

"There's music," she says.

"Yeah. It's upstairs, usually."

"Oh, let's go there." She moves back toward the door. "This floor creeps me out."

We take the stairs up three more floors, because that's where the party was last time. And, yes, the music is here again, starting and stopping and leaning into itself. Piano, drums, guitar, and bass. I keep thinking that for as long as I was at the party last night, I must have seen the band, but no, I never did. They were off down a hall, in a room that felt like it wasn't meant to include me. The music kicks into gear, and Angela and I walk toward it. But as we do, it seems like the music is moving toward us, as well. It's louder and louder, and I swear that more instruments are joining the band every second, and the music has direction now, and it's like a cloud of noise in the hallway.

"Angela!"

She turns around.

"This is hurting my head!" I yell.

She says something I can't hear.

"I'm going to walk back the other way!" I call out, pointing at the door to the stairs.

I'm walking, and now jogging, and now running. I hope she's behind me. She's not. And there are vibrations under my feet, and it's not just my shoes coming loose because I'm a terrible runner, or the floors shaking because I'm a terrible runner, but really, the floors shaking because . . . the floors are shaking.

"Angela!"

The music stops. The noise in the hall is of the metal doors shuddering in their door frames.

Angela walks fast from the end of the hallway, and I start toward her again. My head rings with the echoes of the music, and the floor rumbles as though it is a piece of sheet metal being shaken from one end, and we have got to get back to that stairwell.

We meet in the middle. This time, she opens the door to the stairs, and we begin rushing down. One of my purple sandals falls off and tumbles ahead of me down a flight of stairs. I kick the other one off too, and it's much easier going. I'd leave them here if I didn't need them—they're the ones still stained with the mess of the *Food Poisoning* duo.

"Has this ever happened before?" Angela is much quicker on the stairs than I am.

"No!" My breaths are raspy, and they keep getting stuck in my throat. "Honest to God. There was a party last time. A girl mixed me a drink."

Angela reaches the lobby and waits for me. I run out, but maybe I don't even need to now. The shaking has stopped. The lobby is still and quiet except for the hiss of air in the vents.

"I think we're good," I tell her.

"Maybe you are," Angela says. "I don't think I should come back."

eleven

"I HAVE REGRETS," Mom says. "Things I was going to tell Abuela when I got older. *Older!* Can you believe how ridiculous I was? I've been in denial. And now she might never know."

"Tell her anyway," I say. "Whisper them in her ear." I take the last bite I can stand out of my toast. It has reached that state of trying to turn into its former self—from warm and crunchy to cold and chewy.

"Is there anything you want me to tell her for you?"

"No. I think I've said it all."

"Hmm." Mom sounds unconvinced, but she doesn't press. "I didn't mention any of this to Angela, by the way. She sounded strange. Is she okay?"

"We're just tired. We got to bed late."

"You shouldn't do that. You've got school."

"It's Saturday, Mom."

"Oh." The dogs yap. I bet she doesn't walk them on the beach like Abuela did. Three dogs and Ceci Moreno, all bored and restless and shedding hair, in that one little apartment. It probably doesn't smell so good right now. "I've been thinking about coming home."

"No." I bolt off the dining room chair. "I know you don't think she's going to wake up. But I do, and someone should be there."

"I called Tío Mario this morning."

"He'll probably poke his head into her hospital room once, be like, 'Oh, she's fine,' and then go back to whatever the hell he does."

"Mercedes. He's a policeman. And he loves her, too."

"If you don't want to stay there, then I'll come down."

"Mija, please."

"I will. Angela and me both. You can come home—we'll just trade places."

"That's ridiculous."

"It's not. She needs someone there. Imagine what would happen if she woke up tomorrow and there was no one there to help her get back home."

"I'm sure I'll stay through this weekend."

"You didn't even know it was the weekend."

"I'll talk to you tomorrow, mijita."

Angela stares at me from the doorway. I suppose it's a good thing that one of us is frightened to talk to Mom like that and the other isn't. She looks mad at me, but what was I supposed to do, say *mm-hmm* a lot and shoot pointless smiles at the phone? Say, *Sure, Mom, come on back, and we'll meet you with flowers at the airport*? Damn it, no. Between Angela and me, there's one perfect person: this fabulous Renaissance girl who paints and plays piano and speaks with kind confidence to everyone. She arrives fashionably late to parties and then leaves tantalizingly early, as though she's got somewhere more important to be, but she's really going home to finish her precalc homework. Perhaps she manages to carry on two best-friendships without anyone getting jealous. She speaks elegant Spanish, grammatically correct from subjunctive to swear words. She's vice president of the National Honor Society. She only skips school for socially useful events like beach bonfires. She knows the mathematics of risks to be taken: a Coke and rum, plus or minus an herbal cigarette.

Angela waits for me to bring her phone back. I press it into her hand and rub her mess of hair as I leave the room. "I'm going to have some orange juice," I tell her.

A knock on the door. It's the same one Angela uses to signal Lilia.

"I'll get it!" Angela calls.

It's almost noon, but neither of us have bothered to get out of our pajamas, and even though Lilia's assured in her floral-based fashion, I still don't want her to see me looking like I just rolled out of bed. Like I was tired from running down stairs and like I told Angela to come sleep in Mom's bed next to me and like I woke up at two thirty thinking about how we shouldn't have gone there and like I sat in the kitchen for a while and couldn't force my damn imagination to abandon a version of Victoria's Juilliard audition where they say yes to her and whisk her away right then and there. Like that.

In my bedroom, I do homework that doesn't require a sketch pad. Thirty pages of *Slaughterhouse-Five* for English (so it goes), and an in-depth look at the endocrine system for human anatomy. I sketch it in the margins of my notebook with a plain old mechanical pencil, and it comes out looking like one part female anatomy, one part Florida highway map, and one part drunken hippo. Blast. Angela's current song resounds through the house, stops, and then rushes down the hallway again. It is not a song I know, and she's playing the same part over and over, and it's like the song is trying to trap me in. The song and the piano. Not Angela.

Silence.

"I wanted to get closer to the music was all," Angela says.

More silence.

"I wasn't trying to cause any trouble."

Her voice is barely there. Lilia's voice. She's whispering, but it cuts. I can't let Angela take this verbal beating. I move toward the living room.

"I told your sister that you would need to be invited before you could come to the studio." Lilia standing is barely taller than Angela sitting in her usual piano chair, but she holds her head as though she towers over Angela.

"We didn't go into your studio." I sound loud and brash compared to the two of them. I sound more like the piano than anything else in the room. "Okay? I didn't even touch the doorknob. We were in the hallway on the fifth floor and the second floor. But we didn't go inside a single room."

Lilia, in her light blue dress again, stares me down. "That doesn't matter. You were there, weren't you?"

"Well, I took Angela there myself, so blame me if you have to blame someone. I'm the one with the car."

"She could have stayed in the car."

"That's not the point. She played the Beethoven piece *perfectly*, Lilia. I thought she was good enough to come inside."

Angela looks like she wants nothing more than to hide under her bed and never see Lilia again. She also seems like she could stand not to see me for a couple of days. Lilia considers the both of us, seeming lost, as though she is stuck listening to repetitions of a song she's never heard.

"You could have caused so much damage with what you did," she tells me. "I trusted you with that space."

"I know, I know."

"You don't!"

Her voice slices the room. It is gravelly at that level. High and low at the same time. I hate it. I want Rex to come running in to see what's going on. I want to throw a pillow at her to make her shut up and go away. I want to crawl under the piano until she leaves.

"Okay, I'm sorry. Do you want us both to stay away?"

My chest aches as I say this.

It is not what I want.

I want to go back.

But I want her to want me back.

"No," she says, taking a few steps backward and leaning, almost collapsing, against the door to the rarely used coat closet. "But there's a moment when it's right to arrive there. And that means there's a whole lot of moments when it's not right to be there. You don't want to ruin your work, do you, Mercedes?"

Lilia pushes her long hair out of her face. I think of the house drawing, and how she *knows* us. She knows things about the Puerto Rican side of our family that I'm not sure I'm okay with her knowing. It's as though she's sifted through our history the same way I rummaged through her suitcase.

"Of course not," I tell her.

"There's a plan." She says this quietly, looking out the living room window instead of at me or Angela. "For the studio. For all of us to be able to work there. It's more, I don't know, mechanical than I would like. But it's there. Can you come back and finish your work, Mercedes?"

"Yeah. I'll finish it."

"Okay." She looks over at me. Her face is drained of color. "Oh, and since I never told you the other night, my favorite artist is Calder."

She has no other words for Angela, nothing but a glance back at her as she heads for the door. I almost want to run and try to beat her to Rex's, so I can steal her safe place the way she's stolen ours.

The one good thing about all this is that my work and my space are still safe at the Estate. It's not just that the work needs to be finished—it's that she needs *me* to finish it. The idea takes hold in me and whirls around.

Angela slumps against the piano. "I'm sorry."

"Don't worry about it. It's my fault," I tell her. "Seriously, don't think about any of this for a while."

"Who's Calder?" Angela asks.

"This guy who made mobiles," I say. "It makes sense, I guess, that Lilia likes him. She does enjoy suspending crap from the ceiling."

My sister takes refuge in her bedroom, and I slip in after her and sit on the carpet beneath the framed portrait of Supreme Court Justice Sonia Sotomayor. Angela sits on her bed with a book called *How to Say Goodbye in Robot*, but the pages aren't turning. I message Victoria and then Tall Jon, asking what they're doing tonight, wishing I were feeling direct enough to ask the real question: Do you want to do something with *me*?

"Abuela always liked the Dishwasher Lemur," Angela says, with the book still in front of her face.

"I know. She never asked where he came from or anything. She was just like, 'Yeah, a Dishwasher Lemur. Of *course* a Dishwasher Lemur.'"

"Well, it couldn't be a dishwasher meerkat."

"No! God, no."

"Let's draw him," Angela says, hopping up from the bed. "It'll be something to send to Abuela."

I bring in my supply toolbox and my sketch pad and some nice microfiber paper and some cardboard. Angela looks excited by all the choices I've given her, like she's just entered the notebook aisle at Target the week before the beginning of the school year. She's probably debating whether to ask my permission about using this or that, but I don't even want to start that discussion. Yes—take the oil paints and the watercolors and the drawing pencils. Take them all. I grab a sheet of the fancy paper and a couple of markers. Purple, blue, yellow, and orange. Oh, this lemur will be festive. Oh yes, he will.

My phone bleeps. Tall Jon says I should come over and there'll be some other friends and it will be "a thing."

"How's this?" Angela holds up the sketch pad. She has an outline of a lemur-ish creature and our dishwasher. The lemur stands next to the dishwasher, back up against the cabinets, trapped by his overwhelming desire to get to the clean dishes. It's pretty great.

"It's cool. Keep it up," I say.

Mine is a little more abstract. Everything is square-based: the lemur himself, the dishwasher, the dishes the lemur has stolen, et cetera. It's kind of like Picasso's cubist period if he had studied Warhol and then had a little sister who was afraid of opening the dishwasher.

The phone again. Victoria. She's leaving dance class, and after she showers and eats, she will be "up for anything."

I text back and tell her about the thing that Tall Jon is having.

She is actually up for that.

"Angela, how do you feel about parties and things?"

"I'm drawing a lemur picture right now and am therefore

ignoring any and all of your bizarre ideas."

"It's not a bizarre idea. It's a party. I thought we should both go."

"Look." Angela drops her colored pencil, and it lands on the lemur's face. "I know you don't think I know what a party is, beyond, like, some rich girl's country-club quince or a third-grade sleepover. But I get it, okay? You want to go and hang out with people and smoke. I get that."

"Hey. Okay. I get that you get that. And that's not even what I'm going to be doing. It's just an excuse to hang out with Tall Jon, and Victoria, and maybe even you."

Angela looks away for a minute, perhaps seeing if Justice Sotomayor is going to indicate whether I'm serious.

"I mean it," I tell her (or maybe them). "I just don't want to be here tonight."

"Yeah, me either," Angela says, "but I think I'm going to call Hannah and see what she's doing."

We are off. I leave a message on Rex's phone telling him not to worry, we're staying with our best friends. I will drop off my sister at Hannah's house and wait, like our mom always does, until she has gone inside and shut the door. Angela has a backpack and I have my trusty purple tote bag, and we say farewell to the piano and our half of the house as though we are going away for a long time.

twelve

EVERYONE'S HERE. PEOPLE from the University of South Florida and Ringling, people who've been in bands for five minutes, people who Tall Jon probably met in the parking lot outside his apartment complex, because people see Tall Jon and want to know him. And there are a few others I recognize from Sarasota Central High here, but they are mostly this year's smoking-corner residents. And then there's me. And Victoria.

Victoria can't hear the word *party* without thinking of some fancy *event* that likely includes a sit-down dinner and a live jazz trio. Or at least something that doesn't take place on grungy carpet. I would never turn down the opportunity to see her in a satiny, short gray-blue dress, though (but anything she wears that's *satiny* is prob-ably actually satin). Her heels are tall and silver and impressive, but they're silent as she walks across the living room to say hello to Tall Jon and . . . Bill. Shit.

I step outside on the balcony to smoke, but about twelve people have already had the same idea, and there's not enough room for us all. The threshold between the balcony and the living room is a good enough place to wait for the inevitable reunion.

Tall Jon wanders up. "Hey, Moreno. Sorry. It's just that I didn't know he was coming when I invited you, and then he said he was coming and then I didn't want to disinvite you or him. You know?"

"Yeah."

"I bought you some extra smokes to make up for the discom-fort."

"I'm sure I'll need most of them."

"Vic looks good."

"Doesn't she?"

I sort of hate it when he winks at me. He's so bloody sincere about it.

"I'll make you ladies some cocktails."

"She doesn't drink."

"Oh, right."

A couple of people push between us to leave the balcony, and we slide into their spots. Tall Jon produces two cigarettes and lights one off the other. Smoking doesn't seem as appealing as it did a minute ago, but I take the cigarette and hold it by my side.

"You should talk to Bill, though. You know he's in a new band, right?"

"Nope."

"Well, he is. And they're busting up the place. They're playing in, like, Tallahassee and Jacksonville later this month. They might even have a gig up in Atlanta. I saw the show last week. It's something."

"It really fucking is," says one of the girls behind Tall Jon.

"It ends with this hugely loud metal-cabaret cover of Leonard Cohen's 'Take This Waltz,'" Tall Jon says, to the balcony citizens in general. "It is the most unexpected, and yet also grandest damn thing you've ever seen. It will burst your eardrums while making you wish you had dressed up like you were going to the opera."

"That's so true," says the girl, who is fumbling with her lighter so much that she is coming close to setting her hair on fire.

"Here." I snatch Tall Jon's lighter from his hand, ignite the girl's smoke, toss the lighter back to Tall Jon with a ballet-like swoop, and leave the balcony.

I take to the sad little half bathroom off the living room to flush my cigarette. Tall Jon still hasn't bothered to hang toilet paper or a towel in here. The lights are four bare bulbs stuck horizontally in some fixture above the mirror. It all gives me a brutal look, like one of those high-contrast photo filters, my eyes so dark as to be opaque.

"Mercedes, are you in there?"

It's Vic.

"Yeah. Just a second."

"I wanted to make sure you were okay."

I poke my head out of the bathroom. Vic's face is right there, like she was leaned up against the door a second ago. Like we missed each other by an inch.

"Bill was wondering where you were." Vic takes a step backward and fiddles with one of her silver barrettes. "He wanted to say hey."

Bill is in the kitchen, having a beer and hovering over a plate of mismatched snacks. Fries and cheese slices and potato chips. His T-shirt is partially obscured by a gray jacket, but it's not worth looking at because I'm sure it's a cheeky reference to some movie or old cartoon that he would have to explain to me. His jeans I recognize— the rip on the right-side pocket.

"Well, well, Mercedes." Bill cracks a smile through about a week-old beard. "I thought you were a myth these days. Every time I'm here, Jon's like, oh, I'm seeing Mercedes Moreno tomorrow, or, Moreno was here yesterday and we ate hot dogs and sang the blues together, or something." He puts a hand on my head. "You're larger than life."

"Thanks, I guess." I take one of the fries. It's cold and shiny. "I heard about your band. What are you guys called now?"

"We're Self Saint Rage," Bill says.

"What's that mean?"

"It means whatever you want it to mean." Bill smirks. "But our bassist got the idea when he drove by a self-storage place."

"Oh. Clever."

"Are you still doing art about salmonella?"

"Sort of."

He takes a swig of his beer. "I've learned an important lesson this year. About, you know, the philosophy of creation." He waits for me to ask him what this is. "I've learned that if you have hope, you can make anything happen."

"What?"

"I know, you think I sound weird, but I'm being one hundred percent sincere here. It's important to visualize exactly what you want."

"I do that, you know. It's one of the few things I'm good at."

"Well, then, if you don't have what you want, then you're not visualizing hard enough."

"That's ridiculous, and I have an example for you. My grandmother, you know, my abuela Dolores, is unconscious in a hospital in San Juan. She had a stroke."

"I'm sorry, Mercedes."

"Well, it's been a few weeks. I'm getting used to it. But seriously, how in the hell am I supposed to visualize her out of her current state? That has nothing to do with how hard I think about her, and everything to do with her own body and how she responds to treatment."

"But you're thinking about her, right?"

"Oh my God." I take a few more fries. These are even colder, and they worm around my mouth as Bill stares me down, as though he is visualizing me visualizing Abuela. "Imagine a time machine, Bill.

Visualize that thing really, really hard. Okay? See if you can make it happen. And if you can, let me know so I can take it back to last year and never go out with you."

The party is migrating. Expanding to the apartment below, and out to the parking lot. Contracting here in Tall Jon's place, in the rooms I've felt so comfortable in. Tall Jon moved out of his dad's house the second he turned eighteen: signed a lease, amassed a collection of free furniture, covered the walls with band posters and old maps and framed album covers and photos of his mom. This one he's placed in the hallway, next to the light switch to the unflattering and perpetually paper-free bathroom, has always haunted me. Tall Jon's mother is beautiful. Was. She's standing next to Tall Jon on the beach, and Tall Jon is middle school age but already taller than his mom. And both of them are staring straight at the camera, and their eyes are smiling, and I never understand when I see her how she doesn't exist in this world anymore. I know she wasn't saintly or anything; even if she'd lived, I think Tall Jon still might have moved out on his eighteenth birthday.

"Ah, here's your latest hiding place," Vic says from behind me.

I sit on the carpet beneath the photo, and Victoria fumbles herself into a sitting position across from me, slipping out of her silver heels as she does. She kicks them aside, braving the old carpet on her bare legs and feet.

"What's up?" she says. "Why did we switch social roles at this party?"

"I can't deal with these people. They're all good at things. Even stupid Bill." I glance at her face to see if she knows what I'm talking about. "How in the hell did he do it?"

"Probably just practice, you know?"

"You and him, I swear. Both of you serve up these easy answers for these things that to me are huge and impossible."

"I don't mean to make it sound easy. It's just that it's not that mystical for me. By the time I got old enough to think too much about why and how I dance, I had already been doing it for years."

"Because your nanny locked you in a room."

"See, I never should have told you about that."

Vic crosses her ankles and doesn't seem to realize she is putting her poor, wrecked feet on display. I guess she has been dancing in pointe shoes for about six years now? But her feet are like that of, well, if not an old lady, then at least a Mom-aged one. But they are small and tough and have created lovely things and have been around the world.

Maybe the problem is that I can't imagine Bill or Gretchen Grayson or sometimes even Victoria doing the work. I experience every second of my own work, and then I ponder on those seconds and chew them up and relive them too many times—why *did* I decide to create a painting called *Food Poisoning #1*? (Oh, right, because I was grumbling about Bill's musings.) Once I started it, how did I know I wanted to stick with it? Why did I choose purple and yellow and newspaper? Why did I add a tiny pink flamingo in the top right corner? Why did I decide it was done? A hundred little choices, each of them so critical.

I suppose Vic has made those choices, too.

"Anyway!" Vic sounds too bright for having danced most of the day away. "You know what I was just remembering? That time Bill said he had a surprise day trip for all of us, and it turned out to be—"

"Disney World! Except that the pass that was supposed to get us in turned out to be, what, someone's expired family pass?"

"Something like that," Vic says. "Let us concentrate briefly on the symbolism of being locked out of Disney World, staring at the gates."

"Bill was so pissed. I thought he was going to try to find a Mickey to kick in the balls or something."

"Oh, come on, dearie. That was all for show."

"You think?"

"Absolutely. He knew all along that pass wouldn't work. But once he got it in his head that taking you on an impromptu trip to Orlando would be the greatest thing in the world, he couldn't shake that idea."

"I guess I can buy that. But how did you fit into this plan?"

"I'm an excellent travel companion." Vic slouches, and she looks at me seriously. "How much did you like him, really?"

"I liked him." I did, even though he occupies a fuzzy place in my brain now. When I think of him, the images come at me fast and jumbled, like a movie trailer. He sees me at the Smoking Corner and smiles and rolls his eyes. Cut. I watch him badly play bad music with his bad band (and Victoria is there in the background, out of focus but empathetic). Cut. A close-up of his face: blue eyes and that indented scar on his upper lip. Cut. Obligatory sexy shot of him unbuttoning my jeans. Quick cutaway!

"He was . . . exactly the kind of person I thought I'd hook up with, or go out with, or whatever," I tell Vic.

"Yup," Vic says.

"Oh, you knew, did you?" I grin at her and try to kick her bare foot aside. "Did you know I was going to dump him? Did you have visions of the breakup?"

"Hmm, sort of. I mean, Tall Jon and I could see it coming a mile away. A hundred miles away. We just didn't anticipate the reason."

"I'm full of surprises."

"Indeed." She eyes me, as though she expects me to make some sort of grand, truthful pronouncement about how *that moment* was a victory for my whole identity. "Ugh, I cringe when I think about it. I didn't know what I was going to tell him, and I almost texted him instead of talking to him. Telling him about girls was an afterthought. Like, I was almost walking away when I said it."

It was a half-truth, anyway. I didn't break up with him because of *all* girls but because of Victoria. Still, it was new information for Bill. He didn't know what to do with it, so he left it lying there, flopping around. Or maybe I didn't sense that he picked it up and threw it back at me, *Oh, and I like girls* attaching itself to me in the form of wings on the backs of my feet, sometimes propelling me forward and other times catching under the weight of air and stopping me in my tracks.

Like right now. And any other moment I'm with Vic.

"Were you with him when you realized that?" Vic asks.

"No. It wasn't a realization all at once." It was something that was always there, but was quiet in letting me know. "And I didn't realize it because of Bill, though I remember this one day, I was leaving his house, and for some reason, I whispered to myself that I was bisexual, and it felt right." Like putting on a shirt that fits. Like saying my full name.

Someone slams out of the apartment, and there's the hollow clamor of empty beer cans falling to the floor. It's possible the Drama phase of the party is happening now. I'm glad we're out of its immediate orbit.

"Well, fine," Vic says. "All I know is what I see or hear. I should never think I knew what was going on in Bill's head. Or in yours, for that matter."

I smile. "It is a bizarre and frightening place."

Her foot touches mine again. On purpose. I think.

I leave my wall and scoot over to the other side of the hallway. Next to her. As if this is less dangerous.

The apartment door opens again. "Jon, where'd you go?"

"That's Bill," I whisper, my lips about two inches from Victoria's ear. I can see her very attractive ear veins.

"Hide!" Vic jumps up and opens the bathroom door, leaving her shoes in the hallway. I rush in after her and shut us inside, in the dark, our backs against the wall. I snort-laugh.

"No!" Vic whispers. "There is a delicate *art* to staying hidden.

We need to be quiet and still."

"Like the shoes you left outside the door?"

"Totally part of the strategy."

I don't know why we're in the dark bathroom, but I do know this is the Victoria I like best. Victoria when she's come out from under her superhuman sense of self-control. When she's about as far away from a performance as you can get. She vibrates differently—her voice, the way she moves, the way her hair is down and sort of frizzy and brushing against my shoulder in the dark.

This really happened.

It flashes quickly, in the mirror. It's the only light in the room.

"Did you see that?" I ask.

"I didn't see anything," Vic says.

And they're back, those same three words, lit a wavering orange, hovering in the mirror in front of me.

Vic says nothing.

I take two steps away from Victoria's hair and reach toward the mirror. *This really happened.* The words flicker, but their color stays bright.

"How long do you think we could be in here before someone notices?" Vic says with a snicker.

I turn on the light. The words disappear, but my head floods with warmth. It's like the way it feels to get into my car on the first hot day of the year—comfortable in the center, but the edges burn.

I lean over the sink and splash cold water on my face.

"You okay, dearie?" Victoria asks.

Oh, right—this bathroom remains a stubbornly towel-free place. I swipe at my face with the back of my hand, smearing my eye makeup in the process. "I think it's time to go."

"Back to your house?" Vic opens the door and reaches down for her shoes.

"No, not yet." The apartment looks so normal—the framed Ramones album covers on the wall, the beer cans, the old pull-out couch, the picture of Tall Jon's mom.

Who found me here? Was it Lilia, or was it the secret painting itself?

My hand grapples around for Victoria, but finds a wall instead.

"Vic, I'm going to show you my new project."

It's late. Almost one in the morning. This is the latest I've arrived at Lilia's studio. Or tried to.

The Red Mangrove Estate looms above us, its windows dark. It's an overcast night and if the clouds get any lower, I think the top floor might end up swimming in them.

"Just a second." I pause at the glass doors, Vic ten silver-shoe steps behind me, almost definitely assuming that I've become a vandal. "Something weird happened when I came here with Angela last night. So we need to go inside really slowly and make sure that the building is, you know, secure."

"What do you mean?"

"Like, the foundation and shit." My voice is a bit wavery on the *shit*.

"I'm sorry, should I have worn my spelunking gear?"

The door on the right opens as usual. The heavy air of the lobby, the hiss in the vents. No movement.

"Follow me."

She does, and I wait until she closes the ten-step gap before I move toward the stairs. She stays only a step or two behind me as we head to the second floor. I am ready to grab her hand or her shoulder if anything happens.

There's no music tonight. No noise at all that we aren't making: Vic's shallow breaths and my steady ones, our footsteps on the stairs. Vic wiping her sweaty hands on that poor satin dress.

"Okay." We're here. I open the door to the second floor. No Lilia. The floor seems to welcome my feet. Vic stays next to me down the hall to the studio. Lilia has either been there to greet me, or has left the door cracked, up to this point. But with a closed door, should I knock?

"Does someone live here?" Vic asks.

"It's Lilia's studio," I tell her.

Vic laughs—sort of a cascading, nervous giggle that falls to the floor. The floor which, by the way, is perfectly still.

"You're *working* with her?" Vic whispers. "I can't believe it. I hope she's not here."

"She says you're supposed to be invited before you can come in." It's silent up and down the hallway. It's how Vic would expect an abandoned building to look. "But, I mean, we're already here."

I tap on the door. Nothing. I try the doorknob, and the door swings open to reveal a dark house. Studio, whatever. To avoid scaring Vic off right away, I'm not going to bother turning on the lights, because the ceiling sculpture isn't the most welcoming introduction to this place.

She follows me down the hall, and I flick on the overhead light in my room. It's a single bulb in a plain round fixture, but it has served me well so far. It's better than painting under the bright fluorescent lights of Mrs. Pagonis's classroom.

Vic stumbles into the room. "Whoa! This is it?"

"This is it. The two red walls, and the picture over there," I say.

She gives herself a walking tour of the room, running her hand along the red walls and coming to a stop in front of the formerly secret painting. Abuela stares down Victoria, and both of them look perfectly serene about this arrangement.

Thanks to the presence of Victoria, I forget about the possibility of highly localized earthquakes. I flop onto the floor and hold my hands there. Not a single vibration. Would I suffer through another instance of the Estate shaking if it meant I get to see what Vic thinks of my work here? I think I would. And I think I might risk another if she were to say that she liked it.

"Wow!" Vic sits on the floor, too. She almost slides one shoe off, but seems to rethink this and keeps it on. She stares hard at the walls, her eyes scanning from one field of red to another, her gaze hanging in the corner, like she's waiting to see something burst forth from the place where the walls meet. And then she returns to studying the Abuela portrait. "It's amazing, dearie. Like, when I look at it, I feel like I've met her. And you said you couldn't do faces."

"Thanks." A nice acknowledgment from Victoria is not a thing that shakes the floors. Noted. Very much noted. "The red walls were the first thing I did. The Abuela portrait is something else entirely. But everything about painting this room has felt right, so I'm going to finish the red walls to see what happens next."

"Well, okay." Vic looks as overwhelmed as I have ever seen her.

I kick off my shoes, so she doesn't feel like she needs to wear hers. "What do you feel like doing?"

"Are you tired?"

"Not even a little bit."

"Then I'm going to tell you to finish your red walls already! I want to see what the end result of all this is."

There's still no sign of Lilia or a shaky floor as I go into the kitchen cabinets where she keeps all the paint and other supplies. I poke my head out the door, expecting to hear music or the strains of a party, but the hallway is silent. I wonder what would have happened if I'd brought Angela tonight, and if she'll ever get to see this place again. I kind of want to show her how inspired a person can become here, but it's possible that she doesn't need it. After all, the piano and Lilia came straight to her. I'm the one who has to go sneaking out of windows and dashing across the city in the middle of the night to do my work.

But that's okay. Because despite all the trouble, the rewards are pretty great. The red walls. The free drinks. And tonight, there's Victoria.

Back in my studio, she is sprawled out on the floor, so welcomingly out of place, like when your math teacher drops the name of one of your favorite bands in class. She is staring out the window; the view from here is nice because at night it is always the same. It is the dark rooms across the way, and it is the sky, and the gulf. You don't have to worry that you're missing anything, that something has changed without you noticing.

I start painting the third wall red, announcing myself with a wide slash of paint across the center of the wall, and then moving outward to the corners, becoming more strained and careful as I go along. Victoria doesn't interrupt—her view shifts from the window to me, but she doesn't say a word.

A sound from outside. No, from above.

The music. It's back.

"You hear that?" I put down my roller and brush.

Vic nods. Her eyes ask me to tell her something, anything about what's going on.

"They have parties upstairs. It's kind of a practice space for musicians."

Last night, with Angela, the music was chaotic, focused on the level of noise it made and seemingly nothing else. Tonight, it is quieter, and more settled into itself. It bounces along, assured, like Vic when she dances. Like me with the red paint. I sit on the floor (a few feet from her—now that we're not in an enclosed hallway, I can't figure out what is the best way to be with her). I stare at the wall across from me, the first one I painted. I stare at it long enough that it starts to have texture and movement. Almost. Maybe. And it is calling out for something more from me.

"Be back in a minute," I say to Vic, who is still taking in the music.

I grab more paint from the kitchen. Tubes of blue and black and dark green. Thinner brushes. A palette and some rags and a cup of water. I wish Mrs. Pagonis and Gretchen and Rider could see me now.

Or maybe not. Because this is my place.

In the room, I start with a black outline, keep my hand steady, decide on form and orientation and size and such. I shape a head and a back and arms and legs. I begin brushing in fur in strange shades of blue and green, because there have been enough paintings of brown and gray lemurs already, I'm pretty sure. They look just like the lemurs in the head-picture that I didn't even know I had—so much like them that I expect one of them to pick up a paintbrush himself and start drawing his own dishwasher.

"What is that?" Vic asks.

"Something inspired by Angela."

"Hmm. It's pretty cool." She has come up behind me and is looking over my shoulder, watching me craft the lemur's fur. Thick and thin strokes of blue and green, each made with a strategic flick of the wrist. It's sort of like when I would start off any picture I drew as a kid with a thick brown line for the ground, and then meander a zigzag of green grass across it. Actually, it is only a little like that, because my fingers are getting cold and shaky, and my knees are prickling, and

I'm not sure how many times Victoria has heard me swallow hard.

"Ooh, do you hear that?"

"What?" I let my brush hang at the top of the lemur's right paw.

"The music! It's a bossa nova. Don't you love it?"

She sashays backward—some sort of step-touch-step-touch movement that she makes look easy. Of course she knows the steps to this. Of course. If we were to find ourselves at a Self Saint Rage show (against our will, for sure), she would find the perfect way to dance to their cabaret metal. The music upstairs seems to get louder, and its melody changes a little, but Victoria stays right in time. It's as if the music is fitting itself around her steps. Maybe it is.

"Come on," she says.

I lay the brush and palette on the floor. "I don't have a clue what you're doing."

"I'll lead," she says. "Watch and follow."

She takes my hand. *She* grabs my hand and does not seem sure of what to do with it, whether to lace her fingers with mine, or to nudge my fingers at the knuckles to lock with hers, or to envelop my hand in hers. We do the knuckle lock. Her hand is cold and small and I don't even know when the last time was that I touched it. I think it was accidental, like I was handing her a pen or a spoon and she reached at the same time I reached. Or, no—it was when we both reached toward the stereo of my Pontiac at the same time, me to change the song, her to turn it up. I brushed her hand and she looked at me, and I let her have the control. Sure sure, I was totally going to turn up that song, too.

Step forward, step together, step back, step together. That's what we're doing. It's not that hard.

"You've got it!" Vic says.

I think I do.

I slip my fingers between hers without losing the rhythm. Step forward, step together. Maybe I am leading now.

The song flows into a different one with the same beat, and Victoria tilts her head upward, as though the musicians are sending a message down to her. "Yep, I thought I recognized it. I remember my parents listening to this song. It's called 'No More Blues.'"

"I like it." I tighten my grip on her hand, which is getting warmer.

"Does this always happen here?" she says, looking at our hands, and then at my face.

"No. You make everything here better."

And it is true, isn't it? It is the truest thing I have said all night. The music is brilliant and I have almost finished the red, and I have new ideas for my work, and I can dance a little bit, and the floors are still and solid and are holding us, and Victoria is my best friend and I love her. Her hair is falling out of its silver clips, and I think it is the first time I have ever seen her dance with a curtain of dark brown alternately hiding and revealing her face. Her eyes are shining, and her mouth is not caught in its usual stage-ready smile, but instead lazy and heart-shaped, so much like it has looked in the morning of all those times I have slept in her bed or she in mine, being and breathing but not touching. And this—this. Her tired satin dress and the step forward and together and back and her falling hair—is this my best chance, my only chance?

Step forward, step together.

Our lips meet.

She is leaning into me, and with the hand that is not holding hers, I touch her side, gently, the way you touch something you weren't allowed to for a long time. And her lips move against mine. She is kissing me back. *She is kissing me back.*

I think I could live here.

thirteen

AT SOME UNIDENTIFIED hour of the early morning, there is nothing to do but go home. I was hoping Victoria would sleep in the car on the drive back, but instead she is looking at me sideways from the passenger seat, and not in a way that makes her meaning apparent. She might be thinking, *I can't believe I kissed a girl who paints lemurs.* Or she could be thinking, *I can't believe I kissed Mercedes.* Or, *I can't believe I only kissed Mercedes once. We should have lain down and made out for hours, and instead I quietly let her go back to painting—God!* Or maybe just, *I am so tired and weird things are happening and I'm considering telling Mercedes to take me back to my house so that I can sit in my room and listen to Broadway songs until sunrise while trying to sort out everything in my head.*

There are a thousand ways this could go. More. I don't think we know all the possibilities anymore. They are flying at me from all directions—each streetlight I pass, each pair of taillights, they send new possibilities careening my way, some of them almost too much to let in as I drive from the key to the mainland. I let them in, I breathe them out. They'll fall on her and cover her and maybe she'll start to know them, too.

Firing Squad plays on the stereo. I open the windows, and the car is filled with cool, salty air. We head on toward the Moreno-McBride residence.

She stands in the dark living room holding the little overnight bag she always brings over, the one that has dedicated pockets for every-thing and seems to keep her clothes unwrinkled, and she smiles with half her mouth. Sleepy, crooked, unsure. Oh God, I have completely confused her, to the point that she doesn't even know where we are going to sleep. I lead her to my mother's room, mostly because that's still where my toothbrush is, and when I come out of the bathroom she has already made the satin dress disappear, and she is wearing yet another American Ballet Theatre T-shirt and a pair of gray shorts. My head is fuzzy and my eyes burn and my fingers should be paint-stained but they're clear. We left the door to the studio unlocked and we never did go upstairs to find the music and also I kissed Victoria Caballini.

Light off. Covers. Dark hair and a disproportionate sketch of a ballerina in my face. I want to catch her in that floaty place between wake and sleep.

"Vic."

"Hmm."

"I didn't plan that, okay?"

"Okay."

As though our trip to the Estate tonight transported us to an alternate universe, I sort of want to call up Connor Hagins and ask him what did he do, how did he get this amazing girl. I feel like I know the answer, know the story, but I've stuffed it in the back of the mental folder labeled *Caballini, Victoria: romantic life of.* And besides, to *get* a girl seems like she was tricked or trapped somewhere along the way. That's not what I want. I don't want Victoria to wake up wondering why she kissed me. I want it to be her truth that this place next to me is the warmest place there is.

I am closer to her. I touch my nose to her hair. She doesn't move.

I could see if she wants to kiss me again. I could tell her I think she's perfect, and ask her is this how it begins, is she going to be my girlfriend now? No—that's too much. I just want to be in this time with her, to live as long as I can in the same night I danced with her. Okay, I think she's asleep now, but maybe I can make up for her unconsciousness by keeping hold of this moment as long as I can. Holding on, holding on.

I'm awake and she's still here.

The sunlight crashing through the windows tells me it's mid-morning already, that, somewhere across town, Angela has been up for hours and is imagining me hungover at Tall Jon's apartment, that my mother is going to visiting hours at a hospital in San Juan, that Abuela Dolores is asleep in her persistent way.

Vic turns over and startles herself awake. She stares around at the room, at the light. And then at me. I try to smile. I know that she's not one to confuse reality with dreams—she knows where we were last night. Surely the music is running through her head the same way it is through mine.

"Morning," she says, and rolls onto her back.

"Morning," I say. I check my phone—ten thirty a.m., and two generic *where are you*'s from Angela. "Can you hang around a little longer?"

"Sure." She gives me a sleepy smile. "Before I left last night, I told Mom I was going to keep you company today."

"We have to pick up Angela soon. I get the feeling she chose her friend's house over the party only as the lesser of two evils." I lean on my side. The sun catches me at that angle, hits my eyes and strips my sight for a minute. I'm here, but I'm nowhere. I'm with Vic, but without the prodding hum of the studio, I don't know how to do anything but long for her. "Hey, Vic."

"Yeah?" She looks at me like she's expecting something, but she's not sure what. It's probably like when she's at a Broadway show and waiting for that one last big revelation before the intermission.

I am above her, sort of. I can see what it'd be like to lie on top of her and kiss her. I can see it, I can see it. But it's the fading image of a dream—if you catch it at the right time, you might live in it for a minute more. And if you don't catch it, it's just gone.

"We have to talk about it," I say.

"What?"

"Last night. In the studio."

Vic narrows her eyes. "The dance studio?"

"Come *on*. No. I mean the Red Mangrove Estate. The place where I'm working with Lilia. I mean the red and white room and everything that happened there."

"But we couldn't get in, dearie," Vic says in her matter-of-fact way. Her pointe-shoe voice. "I would have loved to have seen it, but it's kind of hard when the doors won't open, you know?"

The sunlight is too much. I get out of bed and pull the curtains closed, but they're so sheer that they don't make much of a difference. I push them aside again, because I have to accept this day. The doors—they *opened*. The door to the right of the formerly automatic doors, the one that let us into the lobby, the one that trickily seems like it should be pushed rather than pulled. And then the doors in the stairwell, and of course the door to Lilia's studio. I didn't consider the physics of opening or not opening them, not with Victoria there. To say I didn't open them—that *we* didn't—is like saying I never lived in Florida, or I don't have blood, or I don't love her.

"I don't understand," I tell her. "We were there. We were. I painted some lemurs on the wall. We heard a bossa nova, and you were dancing, and then—"

Vic has no idea.

She gets out of bed and she's still wearing the gray shorts and the T-shirt with the contorted ballerina, and her hair has that same humidity-tinged messiness to it as at the party last night, but she has no idea.

"What happened after the doors didn't open?" I tug on one of the curtains as Vic heads into the bathroom to wash her face. I almost want to tell her not to, to leave each fleck of dust from the past twelve hours on her as long as she can.

"We came here," she says as the water runs. And she recounts the whole sleepy drive with Firing Squad, and coming into the house in the dark and putting on her pajamas and crashing into bed.

She dries her face, and I go and stand next to her, and she's kind of startled to see me when she drops the towel. Here we are again: Mercedes and Victoria, Mercy and Vic, *dearie* and all the pet names I've wondered if I would call her if she ever became my girlfriend. I consider her lips, and how, despite the insistence of *this really happened*, Victoria's lips in Victoria's reality did not touch my lips at all.

"I'm worried about you," she says. "You weren't drunk last night, were you?"

"Don't ask me stuff like that."

"Hey, sorry." Vic squeezes my shoulder. "Last night was fun. I just feel like we're starting to run out of weekends like this, you know? My audition's coming up, and then there's all the BS before graduation. I think we're both getting our foundations thrown off, you know?"

I don't know, not really. If anything, I have a fully new foundation, with ten floors of apartments on top of it. *That* foundation is as strong as ever, in the way it pulls me toward it, and the way it is pushing itself into my life. Clearly, the space within the walls of the building knows what happened. Lilia must know. And yet, the person who was *right there*, who touched those walls and those stairs and those floors, who spent several hours cloaked in the salty, musty air of the Estate, does not know.

"Yeah," I say. "There's a lot in my head to sort out."

When Victoria has left the bathroom, I throw her face towel at the mirror. *Thwap.* The towel collapses onto my mom's soap dish. I grab the soap and it snaps in two without a fight. I fling the soap dish at the tile floor, and the metallic clang it makes is finally satisfying. But now I need the towel again, for my own eyes and face.

I read something recently about stroke recovery, about how the rehabilitation process from a moderate-to-severe stroke (that's what Abuela had) can involve the victim becoming highly suggestible. They will believe anything you tell them. They'll believe two contradictory statements, one said right after the other. I know I am a ridiculous person, but I want to bestow this power on Victoria for five seconds, ten, twenty. Long enough for me to tell her what happened again, and for her to believe it, and for her to know, just for a moment longer.

Angela emerges from Hannah's house looking dazed, and she heaves her backpack into the car as if it weighs two hundred pounds. As soon as she's in the backseat, she leans against the window and closes her eyes.

"Didn't sleep well?" Vic asks from the front seat, observing

Angela with the same wary stare that she's been directing at me all morning.

"I hate sleeping away from home," comes the fuzzy reply.

"Did you have breakfast?" I ask.

"I don't remember."

"Screw this not remembering. Girls, we are going out for breakfast," I announce. "Moreno family treat. And it's gonna be amazing."

I turn on Angela's favorite Firing Squad song, the one with the pianos, and Vic sings along as I drive all of us through the city on this unreal day. "And as the hours go by, there's always something left to love."

Coffee all around, even for the historically noncaffeinated Victoria. She dumps milk into hers and takes a sip and then looks at me cross-eyed over the top of the mug. Angela snickers, dumps three packets of sugar into her coffee, takes a huge gulp, and then holds the mug on top of her head.

"I'm not taking part in this piece of performance art." My hands shake as I fix my coffee with normal amounts of sugar and milk. Anything I say or do could reveal how wrecked I am. "After my attempts at food-related art, I think I'm gonna sit back and enjoy my coffee for being coffee."

"Aw, come on, Mercy," Angela says. "You're not going to get away with looking like the normal one here."

"Ahem." I put down my spoon, move my shoulders from side to

side, and pick up from where Firing Squad left off in the car:

"The time is trickling low
The sun is bleeding slow
But since you're here with me
There's always something left to love."

At first, I'm singing only to Vic and Angela, but then they join in and there's too much energy to be contained by our table alone. It has to go somewhere else, to catch in the restaurant's ceiling fans and be whisked out to everyone else brunching here this late morning, to cling to the windows as condensation, to seep out to the parking lot. Maybe the people driving by will feel it, even for a moment, and know that we are a part of something, a certain vibration, a home for all the parts of us that do not fit anywhere else. The lonely and bright and discolored and weary and sad. The satisfied and the terrified and the longing.

Every little sound unsettles me tonight, from my and Angela's jeans clunking around in the dryer, to a pickup truck barreling down our street, to Angela tapping a mechanical pencil against her math book. Lilia has never come bursting into our half of the house before, but I'm building up a scenario in my head where she could, where she rips through the screened porch and tells me how I've fucked things up at the studio and how she knows I went through her suitcase and how she's going to take something important from me.

The dryer buzzes. The jeans clunk one last time.

Angela and I sit on opposite ends of the couch, feet up, laps full of things we are supposed to be doing. The pull to go to the Estate isn't around at all—I think the walls and the paint and I need to rest after last night. I keep glancing at my phone and wondering if I should send Victoria the smallest of messages: *It really happened.*

"I tried to go last night," Angela says from behind her geometry book.

"Shit, Angela." I throw my paperback copy of *Slaughterhouse-Five* in her direction. It bounces off the math book and lands on my sister's feet. "Why would you think that's a good idea?"

"I didn't think it was a good idea?"

"Okay, forgive me, that was poorly worded. Why did you think that was something you could do?"

"I felt like I had to be there," she says. "And I felt like, if you weren't there, if I could just find Lilia there, then it'd be okay. You know?"

"No, I really don't. Lilia said you weren't invited, and clearly I messed something up by taking you there the other night. And beyond that, I *was* there last night, so you could have royally screwed up some shit. But I'm guessing you didn't make it?"

"No." Angela closes the book and sets it aside without looking in my direction. "I was able to get out of Hannah's house and down her street, but then I realized I had no idea which way to turn from there."

"And you didn't want to end up walking alone down Tamiami

and across the bridge at three in the morning? Yeah, a sound decision, I'd say."

"I can't explain it," she says. "It's like the building was calling me, and I feel like I let it down by not being able to make it there."

"Well, I was there, and the floors never shook."

"Did you go to the party?"

"Yep, but it was boring, so we left early."

Angela knows who the "we" is. She wants to know what happened when I brought Vic, but she's not asking, and I'm glad.

It's midnight and Angela slips into our mother's room and, without a word, slumps onto the bed and nudges me. I guess she wants to be sure that I'm not leaving tonight. I give her some room and an extra pillow, because she can only fall asleep with her head propped up. Mom has said she's been like that since she was a baby.

"What if Abuela dies?" she asks.

"I don't know," I tell her, even though, technically, I *do*. I mean, we have the plan: we will tell our dad and he will help us make the arrangements to meet our mom in San Juan, and there will be a funeral and we will have to be kind and familial to our uncles, who have pretty much never extended the same behavior to us. Abuela has never been shy about talking about her last wishes, to the point that we all know exactly which songs she wants played at her funeral, and how I'm supposed to read something from Romans ("And hope maketh not ashamed; because the love of God is shed abroad in our hearts by the Holy Ghost which is given unto us"), and Angela is supposed to read an Emily Dickinson poem, both in English and en español.

So, yeah. We know this.

But also, we don't. I don't know when we will start crying. Will it be the moment we hear the news, or will it be later, like standing in the security line at the airport, my shoes off and my backpack churning down the conveyor belt and tears running down my face? Who will cry the most? Will my uncles cry at all? I will want to take care of her little dogs, but I don't know how you're supposed to transport dogs from an island to a peninsula. I don't know how I will feel at the funeral, and the burial. I hate crying in front of my family, especially Angela, because I don't ever want her to think that I am not okay, but I will do it, this once, for Abuela.

I don't know how I will feel a week, or twenty days, or three hundred days later. And I for sure do not know how to comfort my mother, or if I should even try.

This is why I'd rather paint at night.

fourteen

I COULD TELL her about the kiss.

It'll be at her house, the two of us sitting by the pool, the sun streaming in and dancing off the water. *Dance.* Shit. The Juilliard audition has to be kept in mind—should I, as she put it, throw off her foundation before the audition, or after it?

I tap my paintbrush against its palette in a bossa nova rhythm. When Tall Jon gets into his amateur music critic mode, sometimes he refers to a beat as a tattoo. I like that. But Gretchen and Rider clearly do not find anything inspiring about what I'm doing. Well, fine. Back to my absentminded work on this week's assignment, which is to create a piece about an early memory.

"Green carpet," Rider says to me, pointing at his sketch pad. I guess I've been staring. "The absolute first thing I can remember."

My earliest memory is of my mom telling me not to climb the ladder to the slide at the big playground in Naples, and of me doing it anyway, and getting to the top, but then being too afraid to attempt the slide.

I remember her yelling my name over and over. *Mercedes, Mercedes, Mercedes! Mercedes, no!*

It's so easy to say what you need to say—to yell it, even—when it's that crucial.

It should be easy to tell Victoria.

By the pool. Or at my house, whispering it to her in the kitchen while Angela pounds on the piano. Maybe even during lunch this afternoon by the Dead Guy. In any of these places, the words will be the same: *I kissed you, Victoria. And you kissed me back. And it was perfect.*

But it was perfect because the Estate made it perfect.

Can we ever get back there?

It's possible that telling her could screw everything up, that the memory was taken from her for a good reason. I spent so long planning to never say a word, and now the Estate has worked it out for that to be reality again. Maybe I shouldn't disturb that.

Rider finishes another dizzying corner of his green carpet sketch. I drop my paintbrush and work on a rough pencil sketch of the slide's ladder. I want the focus of the picture to be the insistence of my mother's words. The viewers should have a sense of being shouted at to run away from the picture, but—I hope—a couple of them will make the choice to stick around and climb the ladder.

How do I accomplish this?

The ladder looks disproportional and weird. I start an outline of my mom on the left side of the paper, but no, it's not the physical presence of Mom that stuck with me, it's the sound of her.

Maybe there is a cloud of sound coming from that side of the picture, a distracting smoke bomb of Mom's favorite shade of blue.

Maybe Mom's voice comes through in a barrage of *M* shapes.

Maybe this idea won't work at all. The viewer could sense that something's wrong by the mixed-up proportions of everything else in the painting, and the skewedness of it could be the distraction.

All of these things.

None of these things.

Rider makes his way through the green carpet, and Gretchen draws a close-up of a dog's face, and here I am with half of a messed-up ladder. I wish they could have seen me painting those lemurs the other night, or discovering the secret painting. I wish they could know. Where is the moment where it becomes easy and beautiful and mystical? Where are those moments I remember when I was only a few years older than the Mercedes who climbed the ladder, the afternoons of wearing down colored pencils and crayons, of showing off the thick stain of marker on the side of my left hand, of preparing a new box of watercolors and watching the first drops seep into each little oval of paint. And it's not even that I didn't appreciate those things when I was a kid—I totally did. There's something so true and solid about being a seven-year-old in paint up to your elbows and thinking, *This is the best thing ever!* Especially when you see your parents going off to work and then coming home and arguing. That's enough to help you confirm it: *Yes, this really is the best thing ever.*

I want to be there again.

But the possibilities—for Victoria, for me, for this useless ladder picture—are crowding me out.

There's always something satisfying about ripping a piece of paper off a spiral binding.

I fold the paper, rip it in two, keep ripping, keep multiplying, letting the pieces fan out in front of me on the table. I should tell her, I shouldn't tell her, I could, I couldn't, I can't.

Rider and Gretchen are staring at me.

"I can't do this," I tell them.

She's at the Dead Guy.

Even though it's threatening to rain and no one else is outside today, she's there. Because that's what we agreed on this morning. She moves to the edge of Tim Gelpy's marble bench to let me sit next to her, all the while balancing a bag of baby carrots on one knee and a tiny cup of ranch dressing on the other. She is totally getting into Juilliard. I start in on my fried chicken sandwich.

"Are you okay?" she says after a while.

We turn toward each other at the same time. She has the front of her hair pulled back with barrettes, and she's wearing a navy dress with the gold bracelets I gave her for her birthday. It's her, but it's not her. It's a version of her that doesn't know all the wonderful things about a bossa nova. It's a version of her that never watched me paint in a moment when I felt I could do no wrong. There's this crack—no, at this point, it's a damned canyon—between my reality and hers, and I don't know how long I can keep talking across it before we both fall in.

"Vic, good God," I say. "Is anything okay? Abuela's still in the hospital, and she might never come out of there alive. I'm going to hear back from my damned colleges soon. I'm tired of cooking and doing laundry and getting the side-eye from Angela. I miss my mom. I miss feeling like I was a decent artist. I miss everything."

If nothing else, I'm good at making a carefully worded outburst.

Not that I have Vic particularly fooled. She waits a minute, probably to see if I'm going to mention the studio I insisted that she visited.

"Take a deep breath." Vic dips a carrot stick in a dangerous amount of ranch dressing. "Let's talk about infinite possibilities. Name a place."

"Right here." I smack my hand against the corner of the bench.

"Have we seriously never done a Dead Guy–themed edition of 'How Many People?'"

"I don't think so."

"Wow! This should be good, then." Victoria considers for a minute. "Obvious one. How many people before us have called Tim Gelpy the Dead Guy?"

"How many people before us have called Tim Gelpy the Dead Guy and have defaced his bench out of a fear of their own mortality?"

"You're weird, dearie. Okay, how many Dead Guy–naming, mortality-fearing, bench-defacing people have eventually cried over their guilt for screwing with the Dead Guy's memorial bench?"

"All of them," I say. "Definitely all of them."

Angela and Vic find each other at the front of the school and run to the car together under Vic's polka-dotted umbrella. They both look so themselves today, like no one would ever mistake them for being anything other than an aspiring Juilliard dropout and a piano player with Sonia Sotomayor bedroom decor.

I got here to the Ford as soon as I could after last period, to cower in the driver's seat and be sure that I'm feeling it again. Yes. It's back. It started in English class and stayed through trigonometry. The insides of my fingers were itching. The veins in my legs were throbbing. This was stronger than it had ever been, and it was clear where I needed to go, as soon as I could.

There's no way I can drop them off and then come back. There's no way.

"I need to run an errand," I tell them as we turn out of the school. "Can you both stand to hang out with me in the car for an extra thirty minutes?"

Sure, they both say, and I wonder what they're imagining. It's quiet after that, and I'm relieved when Vic plugs her phone into the Ford's stereo and coaxes it until her playlist comes on.

"This is my new one," she says. "I call it 'Broadway Beginnings.'"

"Oh yeah?" I click my fingernails against the steering wheel.

We're out to the main road. Ten more minutes to the Estate.

"Yep. It's the best opening numbers of various shows—not, I should say, the opening numbers of the *best* shows. There's a difference. *Some* of them are my favorites, but some of them are just, like, eh. But the beginnings of them, you kind of want to live in forever. This is from *Thoroughly Modern Millie*, of course."

"Of course," I say.

I'm jerking the car in a way I haven't since Mom gave me driving lessons at the back of the Publix parking lot. I am punctuating each stop. My legs ache, and the clouds push more rain down at us, gray water upon gray water, all of it piling up at the intersections until it's hard to separate sky from land. Vic has her eyes closed and is humming along to the music. But every time I glance at Angela in the rearview mirror, she's straight-backed and unblinking.

Finally, we cross the bridge and have the gulf on our right side, though it's blue-gray and indecisive about its direction in the wind and rain. The car behind me honks when I turn without signaling into the Estate's parking lot. Look, dude, I'm a confused driver just turning around or checking my GPS. Why would anyone be stopping at this deserted place on purpose?

Vic looks at me but stays quiet. Oh, good Lord, she definitely thinks something's wrong with me, the way I'm trying this place again and hoping to get a different result.

"I'll be right back," I tell her and Angela. "Just stay here."

Vic glances down at her phone—the picture of us on the beach, and the time. 3:32. Angela nods at me.

I run through the parking lot, resist my urge to punch the front door as it opens smoothly for me, and tear up the stairs to the second floor. The lights are off in the hallway, and it looks about as lonely as Sarasota Central High on a Friday afternoon, or like the Naples house after the movers had already come and it was just Mom and me left to scrub the floors. Lonely in the way that makes me feel foolish for being here.

Lilia isn't in the studio, but her terrifying purple bathrobe hangs on a ladder, and she's made progress on the ceiling of household products. A cluster of plastic butter tubs. A circle of Dawn dish soap bottles. It seemed pretty brilliant the first time I was here, but now I think it'd be a pain to have to clean out all that crap. A pile of cans sits on the kitchen floor, and one kick scatters them all. Lilia clearly does not have a Victoria, or a Victor, for that matter. Lilia has this building, this project.

Down the hallway. Everything looks so different here during the daytime—bleached and shallow, showing all the ways that the Estate has been baking in the sun too long. Out the windows, the gray ocean and sky look bright compared to what's in here.

Except the red room.

I let out my breath and drop onto the floor.

Everything's gone. The lemurs, the secret painting, and even the walls that were so red they practically strutted. Everything has been returned to white. I run my hand over the wall by the closet, as though it will give me answers. Nothing. The paint is smooth and dry. It may as well be the first coat ever painted on this wall.

"I didn't think you'd be here so early."

I turn around, my hands still on the wall. Lilia is here, with the bathrobe back on, with a look on her face that says everything's okay. I'm relieved. But wait—why? She's still taken the secret painting, and my moment with Victoria. All she hasn't taken is my ability to be here.

"What happened? Why did you do this?" I scramble to my feet so I can face her.

"I'm trying to help keep your secrets for you."

"Well, please don't," I tell her. "I can decide which ones are worth keeping."

"Mercedes." Every time she says my name, it sounds so earnest. "Remember how I told you that no one ever has to know what you create here? That's such a gift to be given. Everyone here understands how rare that is. What would it take to help you understand?"

"I don't know." But as I say this, I do know. To be able to confess these things to the four walls of the Estate, to be able to face Abuela even while she's ill, to be able to paint far better here than I do in studio art or on the back porch—these things are incredible. Maybe it is worth going deeper into the Estate's potential. Maybe I'm only scratching the surface of what I can do here.

"Why don't you try painting again?" Lilia says.

"Fine." The white walls are wearing me out, which was maybe Lilia's desired effect. I try to sneer at her a little as I leave the room, annoyed at her for creating successful art out of the destruction of my paintings. It bugs me that for all the evidence of expression she has in the Estate, and for the whole series that's still hanging out at Rex's place, I know so little about her. From here in the kitchen where I'm grabbing the paint and brushes, I consider the ceiling art again. While it's visually cool, it doesn't hit me emotionally in any way. Is that my fault for not finding a way to connect to the piece, or is that Lilia's fault for not putting enough of herself into her work?

The one piece of hers that tugs at me is the picture of Mom's old house. Maybe I could ask her about it. Sure, fine—this is the house of all secrets being free and easy and beautiful. I trudge back to the white room with a cup of brushes and a nice palette of paint, and Lilia is sitting against the wall, waiting for me.

"Whatever you want," she says, her face bright. "I'm interested to see what you do."

Never mind. I'm quiet. I can't break this spell. Whatever courage I have, I need to save it for the painting.

I dive in, taking the white wall across from where Lilia's sitting. I remember the way it felt to trace the projections in the secret painting. How I didn't have to think about the amount of paint to put on the brush, because it was right each time. How I didn't have to consider the weight of each brushstroke, or the angle of my wrist. All those pricks of worry that appear every time I put a brush to canvas in the non-Estate world—all of them were gone.

It's like that again. And maybe it's better. Because I'm painting Victoria.

She's dancing in this picture, and the best thing about it is that it's a performance I've never seen. It's something I'm creating for her in this moment. I like to imagine that it's choreographed to Firing Squad's "Always Something Left to Love," and that I'm front and center in the audience. And she notices me, and breaks her concentration for half a second to meet my gaze and smile.

"Do you see this?" I suddenly say to Lilia, jabbing the opposite end of my brush next to painted-Victoria's outstretched arms. "Do you see this? I love this girl. I love her."

Lilia looks like she could cry. Good.

"I love her, and I brought her to this ridiculous room, and I think for a second she knew that I loved her. But then all of that was gone."

"It's not gone," Lilia says, getting to her feet and shoving her hands in her bathrobe pockets. "*You* know exactly how it happened. You still have that beautiful memory, and you can relive it. You can even paint it on the wall, if you want."

But painted-Victoria, even for being the best work I've ever done, isn't nearly as luminous as Victoria when she was dancing with me here, when the room was red.

"I don't want to paint it," I tell Lilia. "I want it to be real."

"Then tell her," Lilia says. "Tell her again. See what happens. I'll let you finish your work by yourself, okay?"

And she marches out of the room, bathrobe ties flying. The front door slams shut.

I run out of paint at exactly the right time.

There's nothing more to add to this painting.

I hardly know what to do with myself. I haven't finished and been satisfied with enough pieces to have any sort of ritual for this moment. So I just do what I always do when I'm done painting on the back porch, or when I end Mrs. Pagonis's class in a normal state of mind—I go to the nearest sink to wash my hands and my painting supplies and put the brushes to sleep.

I've been working long enough that I've got layers of paint on my hands and wrists, some of it still sticky, some of it totally dry. I—how long *have* I been here? I race to the nearest window, the one in the living room that cowers beneath Lilia's ceiling art, and outside everything looks the same as it did before. The Ford is down in the parking lot. It's still raining. My sense of time is skewed—I feel like if Lilia came back right now and told me I've been painting five minutes, or five hours, I'd believe her either way.

I duck back into the bedroom to take a picture of the Victoria painting with my phone. My phone, which tells me it is now 5:41.

5:41. I blink, disbelieving.

That means Angela and Vic have been down there in the car, in the storm, for two hours.

Doors and halls and the stairs and more doors and the lobby. Stupid purple sandals, getting swallowed by the murky water gathered by the front entrance. The Ford is still the only car in the lot. I run to it, waving, tepid rain dripping down my chin and arms, and my shoes slapping the whole way.

"Oh my God, I'm so sorry." I fall into the driver's seat, let the sandals thud to the floor. My feet are freezing and the rough carpet doesn't dry or warm them one bit. "I didn't mean to stay there for so long. Vic, you can totally yell at me if I make you late to dance."

"There's still plenty of time," Vic says.

"Yeah, maybe if I speed the whole way there."

"Hey, I have an extra hoodie if you want to dry off with it," Angela says.

I turn around and meet her eyes, expecting the same girl who yelled at me at St. Armands Circle. But she's not mad at all—she really wants to give me the damn hoodie, so I take it and rub at my hair while my sister looks at me, concerned.

"What were you doing in there?" she asks.

I take a deep breath. "I'll show you." I grab my phone from my back pocket, where it only got slightly wet. 3:42, it tells me, the numbers clean and white over the photo of Vic and me at the party.

"Hey, what's the time on your phones?"

"Three forty-two," Vic and Angela say in unison.

They don't look tired or rumpled or like they were trying to call me and not getting through. They don't look like they wore themselves out on Vic's Broadway playlist and went wild and jumped around in the rain and then got back in the car to nap. Nope. They look like two girls who've been sitting in a car for about ten minutes.

I click over to the photos. The most recent one is of Tall Jon and me at his party on Saturday. I close out of them and go back. Nothing from today.

No pointe shoes or outstretched arms.

No evidence of the painting at all.

It's still up *there*. I mean, of course it is, because Lilia herself approved of it. But here in the rest of the world, it doesn't exist.

"Never mind," I say as my cold feet drain the warmth from the rest of me. "We need to go."

fifteen

AT LEAST WHEN I'm at home, I know the general rules of permanence of the things I create. I alternate between making enchiladas and sketching out a few more versions of the Dishwasher Lemur and his friends. A kind, trusting lemur with a mischievous side. An ornery lemur who is convinced he wants everyone to leave him alone, until the moment when everyone actually does. A lemur in the spirit of Abuela Dolores: elderly, a little stubborn, strong, and proud of the gray-white stripes in her otherwise black fur.

Hmm, do lemurs go gray?

Across the dining table, Vic is putting on a good show of making notes on some poems for AP English (by "The Idea of Order at Key West," she has written, *layers of disorder??? or order??? I don't knoooow*), but mostly she has not taken her eyes off me. I wish this was for some reason other than her thinking I'm ridiculous.

Angela is practicing on her own in the next room. Sort of. A chord here, a scale there, all of it sounding like she's dusting the piano rather than playing it.

"How about a song?" I call to her.

"Eh," comes the reply.

I go to her wearing oven mitts, reach over her shoulders, and plunk both hands down on the keys. *Thrum.* "Is that what you're so scared of? A little noise? Well, if your esteemed teacher comes over now because of that, you can tell her I was making all that racket."

Angela looks up at me, her cheeks and eyes red. Oh shit. I wipe at her cheek with the oven mitt from my right hand.

"You realize she hasn't been here to help me in a while?" she says.

"I know."

"I get that she was mad, but I thought we'd still have our lessons. What's so wrong with me?"

"Nothing, I dunno." I flop down on the couch. Beside me, the tissues Mom left behind stand guard on the end table. Oh, the things those tissues have seen. "I'm going to find out soon."

She isn't surprised that I'm going back. She just tosses the oven mitt back to me, as though I will need it for strength and courage, and she leans back against the piano. *Doop doop dop*, say the middle notes.

It keeps raining. I go out to the screened porch with my cigarettes and wait among the remains of the vanquished *Food Poisonings*, because I know if I stay long enough, she'll be here.

She is. And she even has the pink floral dress on.

"Hey, Lilia, do you want a smoke?"

Lilia stares at me like I am every obnoxious thing about next-door neighbors, which is exactly what I was going for, so at least I know that I can fool her occasionally. I shrug and take a drag on my cigarette and wait for her to lay into me.

She says nothing. She looks out at the flat gray-green pad of yard beyond the porch in a way that tells me she is remembering another place, that she is taking this little piece of earth and the memory of another and watching helplessly as it becomes a third place, a place that never existed.

This would be a great moment for Rex to barge in and offer us some casserole leftovers or at least harangue me for smoking.

"So I finished that painting," I tell her.

Lilia pops out of her memory. "I know."

"So?"

I'm not sure if she looks tired, defeated, pensive, or some combination of all three. "What do you want to know?" she asks.

The words are going to tumble out of me, and I start walking from one corner of the porch to another so that I don't bury myself in them before I can finish. "I want to know why you offered your help but then destroyed what I created. I want to know why I felt like I *had* to paint a room red. I want to know why Angela's not allowed in the Estate yet. And why Victoria doesn't remember being there.

And why I keep coming back. I want to know when the hell you're going to help with my work, or if you had ever planned on doing that, or if you're using me for free labor for some weird renovation project." I stop pacing at the screen that divides us. Her straight face is inches from mine. "And despite all that, I still really want to know what you thought of my painting from today. And of my lemurs from the other night, for that matter."

She smiles a little bit. "I don't know what a real lemur looks like. But your paintings were good. Unexpected colors, nice technique."

"I wasn't finished, you know. They probably would have gotten even better, if they hadn't been painted over."

The rain is indecisive: it gets harder and then slower again, as though Lilia and I are standing in the midst of a sped-up video version of this day. Maybe Victoria has already finished her poem notes and called her mom to come pick her up. Because Mrs. Caballini would do that, no questions asked. Or, well, some questions asked, but nothing where the answers would rattle her.

Lilia seems to be considering everything I have asked to know, and maybe more than I have asked.

"Okay," she says. "Come meet me tonight. In the studio. We'll work together on a project, and I want to explain something to you."

And Rex pokes his head out of the sliding glass door of the McBride-Solis half of the house. "Well, hey, Mercedes!" Refreshingly, he has traded his bathrobe for a Tampa Bay Bucs hoodie with a coffee stain on one sleeve. "I feel like you girls have been quiet lately.

Let me know if you need anything."

What I really want, in this one chilly, humid, impossible moment, is to talk to Abuela again.

"Oh, Victoriaaah!" I jingle my car keys from the living room and try to sound like a Broadway star.

Vic stumbles around the corner with her purse, backpack, and dance bag. "That was lovely, dearie. Was that the beginning of your opening number or your 'I want' song?"

"It's the triumphant song where the heroine escapes her humid-ass house by taking her friend to dance class." Major props, self, for keeping composed while saying this. "Where does that come in the show?"

"Hmm. Could be a nice transitional moment in the first act." Despite the stuff hanging off both her arms, Vic opens the front door for me. "See you later, Angela!"

For now, Angela has abandoned the piano to watch anime. Vic and I head out into the drizzle, this March day that is basically the Marchiest day I have ever seen, and for once I don't want to be alone with her.

"I'm worried about you," Vic says as soon as she shuts the car door.

This is why.

"You have to stop going to that creepy building. I don't care if it's helping you create the best painting of all time. I swear I'm going to see you on the news if you don't quit going there."

"Maybe it *is* helping me create the best painting of all time."

"Oh man." She drinks from her massive purple water bottle. "You're not telling me something, and it's bothering you, and it's bothering me."

We pass the 7-Eleven where Angela and I haven't missed a Free Slushie Day in three years, and the church that Mom drags us to on holidays. The wipers swish and squeak as the rain lightens. Vic weaves and unweaves her fingers, knowing that she's thrown down a line that can't be undrawn.

"I can't talk about it yet," I tell her.

Lilia didn't give me a time, but by eight p.m. I'm getting restless, drinking orange juice until my stomach hurts, staring at my phone, and letting Angela load the dinner plates into the dishwasher.

"Scratches," I say under my breath.

"Not again," Angela says, but she grins.

Scratches is the only word the Dishwasher Lemur can say. It's a question, it's a request, it's an exclamation of anger or surprise or joy or confusion. And when your vocabulary is so limited, and your communication so reliant on tone, you consider what you say so much more carefully.

"Scraaaatches," I say, a suspicious lemur, my voice appropriately gravelly.

"Scratches, scratches, scratches," Angela says, head shaking and voice low.

She fills the top rack with glasses and shuts the dishwasher. She has left the messiest pots and pans for me, but I am all kinds of tired and jumpy and hollowed out, and cleaning will have to wait until tomorrow.

On my way out the door, Angela gives me a small smile and a whispered "Good luck."

The clouds move out, shoved to sea by an expanse of black. There's a new warmth in the air, one that feels like it's settling in for the spring and summer. And for the first time ever, when I pull into the Red Mangrove Estate, there's a vehicle beside mine in the parking lot. It's an old green minivan with an Alabama license plate.

In the lobby, she's there. Lilia. She's rushing to open the door for me, but I make it in before she can. "Come on, come on," she says, which is the best greeting I think she's ever given me. We rush up the stairs and she leads me not to the second floor, or the third, or the fifth. I'm breathing hard and Lilia is half a flight of stairs ahead of me the whole time.

"You should stop smoking," she says.

"It's the shoes," I tell her. Purple sandals again.

She waits at the landing for the seventh floor, and she opens the door for me, and the music floods in. *Always something left.* It is the next best thing to hearing Abuela's voice beside me. It is every time Tall Jon gave me pizza and smokes and a hug. It is the steady ground under my feelings for Victoria, as if I could pluck a beat or a line of the song out of the air, lay it down for her and say, *Walk on this*, and she would understand.

It is Firing Squad.

sixteen

LILIA STANDS BACK and lets me open the door.

They are here—in the living room, all four of them, looking like they do in the videos I have watched and watched of them online. Brad, the lead singer and bassist, calling out the words as though he is pulling them up from the soles of his feet. Nelson, the drummer, making it look easy, wearing a smile as he beats away. Jake on guitar and Mae on keyboards, sneaking glances at each other. There's nothing that divides where they're playing from the rest of the living room. They're here, in front of me, playing their hearts out.

Lilia joins me inside, stands next to me. It's kind of like the time my dad gave me tickets to my first concert, and then I noticed there was one for him along with the tickets for me and Susana Romero.

I had thought it was going to be weird, rocking out with Susana in general admission, in full view of him, wondering what he was thinking as he watched me have this notable Growing Up experience. But then the band came on, and my dad started nodding his head, and then his whole upper half. He was having an experience all his own.

I nudge Lilia in the side. "Have you heard them before?"

"No," she says. "It's their first time here."

"Well. They're my favorite."

How ridiculous are the other people in the building tonight that there's only a small crowd gathered here? There must be a cruel variety of soundproofing on this floor that's not letting the songs carry to the floors above and below. I want to kick off my purple sandals and run up and down the stairs, knocking on doors and telling everyone to stop what they're doing and come listen to the band in 723. But then I'd be missing their set, and who knows how long it's going to go on? Maybe I've caught the second encore of their one-night-only engagement.

This is the eternal problem with concerts, I swear. I have to remind myself to be in the moment, but to do that, I have to slip out of the moment. *Enjoy it, enjoy it,* goes my usual refrain. *Don't start counting the songs. Don't start guessing which is going to be the last. Don't look at the time and realize they've played ten minutes longer than you thought they would. Just enjoy it.* But trying to enjoy it is as bad as losing time reminding myself to enjoy it, because it comes with the same force of expectation. I'm standing here waiting for the amazing piano work in the middle of "The Getting Is Good," but

I'm not sure how to deal with it when it comes. If I stand still and let it wash over me, is that enough? What's the next level of enjoying something, and how can I get there, and how will I know when I arrive?

Mae does the piano solo, and it hits me from all directions. I am a seashell in the gulf, alternately floating and sinking in sound. I am a hair in Picasso's paintbrush . . . no, Botticelli's. And I am whirled about, helping to birth Venus. I am losing myself and finding myself in note after note. Damn it, Angela would love this.

They play and play, and I am completely taken over, the beat of each song in my chest as though the music is keeping me alive. My knees and ankles ache from standing for so long, and Lilia stands next to me, seeming to enjoy the music on the proper level, but also staying aware enough of me that she'd know if I, say, texted Tall Jon and told him to get over here as fast as possible.

But hey, there's Edie the bartender. I figured she'd have good taste. I keep my eyes on her for a second, three seconds, and yes—she realizes someone's staring at her, and she turns, and she sees that it's me, and she waves. I'm here. I'm really here.

It's over.

Not in the way you'd usually know a concert was over, like with a long, improvised guitar line or a triumphant waving of hands at the crowd or a particularly electric but painful-looking dance move committed by the lead singer.

No.

"Head on a Train" finishes with the same bass notes as on the recording, and they don't linger. The notes fall into us, the fifteen of us (unless we lost another guy from the back of the room), and as soon as we've caught them, the band lets out a collective breath. They're done.

Usually when I cheer at a show, my voice folds in among the rest. Not this time. It's me above everyone. Lilia, applauding the way Mr. and Mrs. Caballini probably applaud at the symphony, looks at me and smiles. So does Edie. So do the members of Firing Squad. My heart leaps not only for this moment, but for the moment that I will shriek about this to Tall Jon, and all the moments afterward that I will think about this. This one area of my life, the Concert Satisfaction Area, is ever so brilliantly complete.

"Do you think they'll come back?"

I'm ahead of Lilia as we head to the second-floor studio. She's wearing a plain, light blue dress. Without her usual bouquet of fabric flowers, I have no idea if she means business or not.

"They should, shouldn't they?" Lilia says.

I wait for her and close the door behind us. The studio is looking like itself again, lit by a new floor lamp, free of dirty paintbrushes and piles of soap bottles. I lean against the wall dividing the living room from the kitchen, where a tower of soda cans points down at me from the ceiling.

"How'd they find their way here, Lilia? Did you invite them?"

Lilia yanks shut the black curtains over the door to the balcony.

"People find their way here when they need something from us."

"What," I say, heaving my hands in front of my chest, a classic Abuela gesture, "does that *mean?*"

Lilia starts walking down the hallway, heading toward my studio, clearly having planned for this moment (planned, even, for the desperation steaming out of my hands and face and voice). I follow her, and in the studio I stand with my back against the Victoria picture, facing the wall where my Abuela portrait once had been.

"The Estate guides us to fulfill its needs," Lilia says, "with art and music, structure and form, color and light. But it knows what you need, too."

I stare at the white space on the wall instead of at Lilia. "I still don't think I get it."

"Follow me," she says. "Let's get out of this apartment for a while."

She leads me past the ceiling art and into the hallway. As always, the red exit sign shines from one end of the hall, and I could turn and run and never come back. But the Abuela portrait, my Victoria picture, and even the lemurs—I created those here. That experience felt like nothing else. I can keep going for a little longer. I can keep going until I've created what I really need to create.

We pass scuffed doors leading to other rooms. "Are people working in there right now?" I ask Lilia.

"In a few of them, maybe," Lilia says. "But definitely not all. We've got people who stick around for a while, and people who come and go."

I keep walking. My purple sandals kick up dust as I reach the window at the end of the hall, as far from the exit as I can get. "Lilia!" My voice echoes. It feels good to disturb things here, if only for a second. "Do you know this place, like, bends or erases time? Is that part of what it needs? Because that was really a mindfuck the other day."

She sort of laughs as I walk back toward her. "Yeah. It'll do a lot of things to keep inside what needs to be kept inside." She runs her hand over a dingy green door. "Let's look in here for a minute. It might be a little . . . I don't know. Disturbing."

Lilia opens the door for me and flips on a light as we step inside. Instantly, I feel like I've gone back in time—the living room and kitchen are in the same places as in Lilia's (and my) studio, but they're still the classic pink, beige, and white, and the carpet looks so damned pink and fluffy that I almost want to lie down and take a nap on it. It's like no one has touched this place since before I was born.

"Down the hall," Lilia says. "Try the first room on the left."

I grasp the cold silver doorknob and turn it.

I swear it's ten degrees colder inside the bedroom than outside it. The walls are all a deep gray, and the carpet has been pulled up, though a few bits of pink remain. Stuck to the walls are the torn pieces of photos: school pictures, family pictures, and I think someone's wedding portrait. Black paper or fabric covers the ceiling, and coming from somewhere, maybe the closet, there's a recording, playing on a loop, of someone whispering.

My head feels like it weighs a thousand pounds, and I can barely stand. I take a step back and brace myself with a hand on Lilia's shoulder.

"I need to get out of here," I say.

"I know. Come on." Lilia takes my wrist and leads me out.

"God." I flop down onto the pink carpet of the living room. It really is as soft and wonderful as I thought it would be. "Who *did* that?"

"Her name was Anna," Lilia says. "She was here a long time ago, probably years before I came here."

"And she's gone now? What happened to her? Is she okay?"

Lilia sits in front of the door to the balcony. The vertical blinds, pink and plastic, clatter against one another. "I'm sure she's fine. She unburdened herself here. And we've kept her art safe all this time."

"Can I do that?" I say it to the carpet at first. "I want to have my own space to do, you know, what Anna did. But mine won't be as scary, I swear."

"You don't know that yet. Yours could be scarier, in its own way," Lilia says. "And it's hard work."

"I'm sure it is, but I think I can do it."

Lilia crosses the room and opens the front door. "Maybe. First, let's work on something together."

Back in the Land of Ceiling Recyclables, Lilia takes out a bunch of paint and a rectangular canvas. (A big one—twenty by twenty-four. I hardly ever dare to get those. There's so much space to mess up.) We sit on the living room floor, beside the canvas. On her hands are bits of glue, the kind that's satisfying to peel off.

"Do you speak Spanish?" Lilia says.

"Ugh, Lilia, these things you ask me." I smack my palm against one of her strange wall murals. "My Spanish is terrible. I used to take it in school, but I got tired of being the Puerto Rican girl who couldn't get an A, and so I switched to German in sophomore year. My mom is still pissed about it, and my German grades aren't any better."

"There you are," Lilia says. "A secret."

"Not really," I say, though maybe she's right.

"I express myself better in Spanish, I think," Lilia says. "I wanted to tell you something."

"Oh yeah?"

"Uh-huh." With one pink-socked foot, she nudges at a can on the floor, one that once held chicken broth. "I think I might be leaving here."

"Why?"

"I've had a sense of dread. You know? Every time I come here, I keep thinking it's going to be the last time. I'm waiting for the day the door doesn't open for me anymore." She clenches her jaw and hurls a paintbrush across the room. It lands with a sad, quiet clatter in the kitchen. "I've been trying to do whatever it takes to stay, but I don't know if it'll work. I don't know, I don't know." She looks over at me. "You saw my terrible paintings at Rex's house. I might be stuck making those forever."

"They weren't terrible," is all I can think to say.

"Hmm, maybe not," Lilia says. "Anyway, you're here now. Let's get to work."

"Sure." But I'm terrified. I don't know what time it even is, and since time doesn't seem to matter much here, I wonder if I could go back to the Firing Squad show and live in it for a few hours. But Lilia's face is pleading, and I'd rather do art than try to bend time. I pick up a drawing pencil.

"What do you see when you close your eyes?" Lilia asks.

Muted colors. Orange and yellow and red dancing behind a black curtain. Hazy lines of light, like the projection that appeared and directed me toward the secret painting. And then—an image. Abuela asleep in her hospital bed.

But the thought of painting her in that state makes my chest ache, as does the thought of even telling Lilia that this is the image in my head. I know so little about her—why do I have to start *unburdening* myself in front of her? Why do I have to prove to her that I can do it?

I open my eyes. Lilia is looking off toward the window. She wears no makeup, has long eyelashes and a new-looking zit on her chin. "Let me guess," I say. "If we finish this, I'll never be able to take it to school to enter it in our countywide art show."

"That's true." She hands me a sketchbook.

The idea of spending hours on a painting of Abuela in a coma is just—I don't think I can do it. I shut my eyes again, will another image to appear. The house: Mom's house, Abuela's house. The one Lilia drew. If there's anything burdening me that's not related to Abuela's coma or Vic or my art, it's that picture.

I steady the pencil, start drawing the outline.

"So this is going to be good, I bet," I tell Lilia.

"It is." She looks over my shoulder as I position the roof and then the windows.

"Better than anything I could create in art class, huh?"

"It'll be exactly what we need here."

"But it's still *me*, right? It's not, like, the spirit of you working through me or something creepy like that? I seriously need to know."

"It's the best version of you," she says.

My arms and hands and fingers chill at the thought.

If she doesn't know yet what I'm drawing, she will soon. She'll know it the second I put in the little semicircular window above the door, or when I start drawing the goat. And so I sit in this moment for a little longer, this shiny glass of perfect expression. The house has the physical presence and the feelings I wanted. The palm trees wave at the right angles, framing the house and ushering the viewer in. And God, do I ever want to go in. If I could step inside and see the living, breathing younger versions of my grandparents and my mom, even if only to watch them for a minute of their lives, I would do it.

I draw the goat. Lilia peers over my shoulder again.

"Mercedes, what are you doing?" she asks, her voice at once high and low, warm and cold.

I shiver. "I'm going to go downstairs and have a smoke."

I place the sketchbook next to the canvas and start backing out of the room, watching the canvas, watching her.

* * *

Outside Lilia's studio, I pull off my shoes and dangle them from my hands, and start running up the stairs. What I'm craving right now is far more complicated than a cigarette—it's motion, it's time, it's a new space in my head for what Lilia showed me. Up to the fourth floor, the fifth. The seventh was where the concert was. Now, the eighth. I just want to see what's here, but the door from the stairwell has other ideas. The handle doesn't budge.

I head downstairs. The fifth floor. The door opens with no problem, and I put my shoes back on.

There's a whisper of music coming from one of the doors on the right—that's the one I'm looking for. The place that had the party. The music sounds like something that'd be playing in the background of a coffee shop, maybe another one of Vic's bossa novas, but I'd have to get her to listen to it to be sure.

The door opens easily, and I'm relieved to see I'll have good company. Edie the bartender is the only one here. She's drying glasses by the sink.

"Are you open for business?" I sit on a stool and rest my head on my arms.

"For you, Mercedes Moreno? Sure. Make yourself comfortable." She smiles and leans across the counter. "What can I get for ya today?"

"Whatever's your favorite, I guess."

"*My* favorite?" Edie says. "What if my favorite involves anise, and it turns out that licorice is your most hated flavor? You've gotta

211

give me something to work with here."

"Ah, okay. How about something with orange juice?"

"There you go," she says. She's not wearing her necktie tonight—just a red tank top and black pants.

I figure I will sit up straight and attempt normal chatter until I burst. "So do they pay you well here?"

Edie regards me knowingly. "Not too badly, considering the hours."

"Yeah. I work at the deli in my mom's office building in the summers. It opens at seven. And I have to be there at six thirty, ready to toast bagels and such. You think I'd be tired of orange juice after all that, but I'm not."

"This is a version of a tequila sunrise," she says, pouring something into a cocktail shaker. Our conversation takes a necessary break as she rattles it around in the shaker and then dumps it into a glass.

"Thanks." I take a sip. It's like orange juice poured through a loudspeaker. It's amazing. "Am I allowed to ask you questions?"

"About the drink? Sure."

"No." I sink back down again. "I mean about everything else. About how the Estate knows what people need."

"Ah. Well, give me a starting point, and I'll see where I can fill in the gaps for you."

"I just—I don't even know. Tell me how you started coming here. Did you see the windows all lit up one night, too?"

"Oh! That's a cool story. You're going to think this is so blah, but

I answered a job ad. It was almost two years ago. I was getting ready to go to college with my girlfriend to study photography—we'd both gotten accepted, we were going to live together, all that fun stuff. But, what do you know, she broke up with me a week before we were supposed to leave. I kind of snapped. I couldn't bring myself to go to the same school as her, and I also couldn't go back home, which is a long story. You bored yet?"

"Not at all."

"Good." Edie turns away, drinks from a bottle of water, and then whirls back to me and smiles. "So yeah, we're at the low point of the story. No home, no school, no job. But I'd worked in a restaurant in high school, and I applied here, hoping they'd overlook my lack of bartending experience. 'Barkeeper needed for onsite establishment at residential property. Photography experience preferred.' That was how the ad read." Edie raises an eyebrow at me. "It wasn't really lying."

I nod, and the amplified orange juice fills me with warmth.

"I think I'll have one of those, too." She starts mixing and pouring again, every gesture sleek and easy, like Vic when she dances, like Angela and the piano. "Anyway, Lilia wasn't the one who hired me. It was this woman named Mary-Louise. She's gone now, but she was the one who showed me the ropes, gave me a place to sleep, gave me a space to work on my photos. Pretty sweet deal, I have to say—Mary-Louise gave me a great new DSLR, and an old manual camera, and access to a darkroom."

"And what did you have to do for her in return?"

"Hey now." Edie looks over her shoulder at me. "I like my job. Didn't you see me take a lot of pride in mixing that for you?" She shakes up her own drink and pours it out. "Besides this, I used to do some projects for Mary-Louise, but now I'm free to work on my own."

"What happened to Mary-Louise?"

"She got tired. That's how she explained it to me. She went to Colorado and she was going to start doing nature photography."

"Because it's pretty hard to take pictures of birds or whatever from inside an old building."

"Hey, we're not trapped here. I could go out right now and do a shoot down the beach. But it wouldn't be my best work, you know?" She tries her drink and smiles. "I heard you're a painter. So think about those times when you're painting and it's going well and you're so into the work that six hours could pass and people could be yelling at you and none of that would even register. Because of your work. Because your work is so important. Think about scrubbing the edges off that time. Imagine that you never need to have those days when you're putting off getting started on a painting. And then imagine that you never need to stop."

The drink seeps into me, shooting warmth up and down my arms and legs.

"So, it's like anything is possible here," I say.

"Fast learner. You got it, girl," Edie says.

I finish my drink while she sits on the tall chair behind the bar and sips her own. The buzz of brilliant work, of art without an end, is everywhere around us. There are photographs on the walls of this room that I didn't notice the last time I was here. Are they Edie's? Are they Mary-Louise's? Do they belong to the Estate in such a way that it doesn't matter who took them? They are strange, close-up photographs of the faces of statues. Some are smooth, some are cracked. One shows nothing more than a big gray stone nose.

"So, okay," I say, "when you came here, Mary-Louise helped you out and you started a project. After you finished that one, what happened?"

"Ah. I see where you are. I see it, exactly." Edie puts her drink down and leans across the bar—toward me, sort of, but far enough away that I know there's no possibility of us touching. "You'll get another project. I don't know what it'll be, but it'll be perfect for you. Okay? It'll be daring. You'll love it."

Oh, never mind. She is touching me. My fingertips and her fingertips.

"You'll come back, right?" Edie asks.

I'm pretty sure I will.

seventeen

I TRY TO push through the morning like Edie would, if Edie had a best friend whose before-school texts were noticeably absent, and if Edie had first-period studio art, and then German and human anatomy, all before lunch. I spend part of Mrs. Pagonis's class with my eyes closed, willing the world of the Estate to show itself to me. But there's a lot to shatter my concentration: morning announcements, the nature sounds CD with its occasional shrieking frogs, and the other members of the Orange Table asking me if I'm okay.

I'm fine, I'll be fine, I tell them.

Between classes, I check my phone and an email from the Savannah College of Art and Design's admissions department pops up:

Dear Mercedes Moreno:
Your admissions status has changed.

In German, sitting at my desk not as Fräulein Marino but Fräulein Edie the Bartender, I resist checking SCAD's website for my admissions status. Let it wait. Edie got as close as the symbolic front door of art school, then turned around and found a much more interesting door to pass through.

Edie doesn't have a best friend lurking around corners. Crossing the school from German to human anatomy, I don't see Vic, but I feel her. She's so very *here*, in this place where we met. I imagine every place on this hall that her favorite red flats have touched, and soon enough the floor is awash with red, a red that doesn't love me back.

Maybe the Estate was right.

Maybe I should have kept on living in the reality it gave me.

I have never seen Vic like this. Hair down, flip-flops, jeans (jeans! I forgot she owned any), and a T-shirt from a Broadway show she likes: *A Little Night Music*. She forgot her usual insulated bag of various raw foods at home, and so she appeared beside me in the lunch line, shooting a longing glance at the pulled pork and fries but emerging with a limp green salad drenched in orange dressing, and, in a move of great recklessness, an oatmeal raisin cookie.

Her Juilliard audition is on Saturday in Miami. She and her mom are driving down on Friday afternoon.

"Maybe I'll save this for seventh period," she says of the cookie as we take our usual places at the Dead Guy.

I don't know if it's me or Juilliard who has broken her.

"Gotta have some refreshments when heads start rolling," I say.

"Huh?"

"Seventh period. Your European history class. All those poor folks who got beheaded."

She has no idea what I am talking about. Because I am not talking about ballet or modern dance or audition etiquette.

I wish I had gotten a cookie. Maybe I will go back through the line and get one and leave her to her endlessly pirouetting thoughts. Also, it's bugging me that every time I see the words on her T-shirt, I think of "No More Blues," and then of the Firing Squad concert, which Vic knows nothing about. How do I even begin?

"It's going to be fine, Vic."

"Thanks." She stabs a lettuce leaf, lets the orange dressing drip from it. "I have to confess, I don't really know how to talk to you right now."

"What do you mean?"

"Whatever you've got going on with Lilia and your project." Vic's voice is dry, about as far away from *dearie* as possible. "Like, the more I think about it, the more I get weirded out. Are you hooking up with her? Is that what all this is?"

"What? No."

"Because you shouldn't be afraid to tell me if—"

"I'm not. Really." I brazenly eat a fry in front of her. "Just forget it.

Forget you ever met Lilia. Forget I ever took to you to the building."

"I'll try." She swishes her plastic fork around in the orange dressing.

It's a terrible waste. All that fucking energy and time I spent worrying about how to tell her, if I could really tell her, and now I'm trying to wipe it away. It's better this way, though—I can live in my moment with her in the Estate, and she can have her audition and her "it's showtime, folks" and New York City all to herself.

"Vic," I say, "you've been preparing your whole life for your audition. That's what I want to talk about. You have, I don't know, the spirit of Martha Graham behind you."

She smiles a little while folding a lettuce leaf in two. "Oh my God, if only."

"Too bad you don't believe in spirits."

"I am willing to make this one exception. Oh, Martha Graham, please bestow your gentle ghostly presence on me this weekend in Miami. I promise there will be lovely weather and good food, if you're into that sort of thing." She flops backward onto the grass. She is pretty freaking into this. "Martha, Martha, I need you. I've spent my whole life waiting for this moment. I've annoyed my poor friend Mercedes half to death talking on and on about you. Surely you can take a few hours to visit me in my time of crisis!"

The kids in the middle of the courtyard look over at Victoria's performance, and I wave at them, even though they don't know us anymore.

* * *

Nobody looks at Victoria today in the hallway. (Nobody probably knows what *A Little Night Music* is. Well, maybe some of the theater kids, but Vic doesn't hang out with them very often.) I wish I could grab her hand so that we could stride together down the center of the hallway to our fifth-period classes. Anyone who had delicate feelings about such things could move off to the side, but anyone else could fall in behind us and join our confident walk. We could sing the song from *The Sound of Music*. You know, "Edelweiss." No, just kidding. And anyway, to try to hold her hand now wouldn't reek of confidence, but confusion, which is the last thing she needs going into her audition on Saturday.

I'm not messing this up. I'm not. We are steady and cheerful. We are saying *hey* to people we know from classes. We go into the girls' room before fifth period, and Vic stares into the mirror, pulls her hair up and knots it around itself, and then turns away.

Dear Mercedes Moreno:

The Committee on Admissions has completed its review of applicants to the first-year class at the Savannah College of Art and Design. Following a careful consideration of your application, I regret to inform you that we cannot offer you admission to the college at this time.

The only dusting spray in the house is the lemon-scented stuff Mom has always cleaned with. I used to think it smelled terrible, but today it's okay. Nostalgic. I knew the lemon spray before I knew of SCAD. I knew the lemon spray before I knew Victoria. I can carve out a space in one of those memories that's little more than a frozen moment: Angela and me sitting on the couch eating tostones and watching cartoons while Mom dusted.

As the lemon spray hits the piano, I swear the smell gets better.

"Hey, Angela!"

I know she is in the next room doing homework. A page turns in a book.

"Ange, come sit here with me."

Another page.

I perch on the edge of the dining chair that has persisted in being Angela's piano bench. I position my hands at the keys, letting my fingertips touch them, in that way that makes anyone seem cool and graceful. *Moonlight* Sonata comes to me in my head, the beautiful way Angela made it emerge in this room, a fully formed thing with skin and hair and guts.

It doesn't work the same way for me. I run my hands over the keys, and the song in my head is still *Moonlight* Sonata, but the sound from the piano is something that would make Beethoven run away crying.

"Ugh, Mercy." Angela nudges my shoulder. Her way of saying, *Let me show you how it's done.*

She sits down and does it, and it is as beautiful as last time. And yet, that wasn't enough to bring her inside the Estate. This morning, I tried to tell her how Lilia and Edie explained the possibilities of the

Estate, but she gave me a glum look and walked away before I was done. I want her to know about it so badly. And selfishly, I want to see what she can do when she's there.

"What if it's not a song?"

Angela stops playing. "What?"

"What if the key to get you inside Lilia's studio isn't a particular song? What if it's more like a feeling?"

"Well, you're the expert," Angela says.

"I'm not," I say. "I mean, Lilia wants me to be, but I'm not. I feel like I'm such an impostor, thinking I can figure anything out about the damn place."

I hit the top of the piano with my palm. And again.

"Okay, okay." Angela grabs my hand and holds it down. "Tell me what you know. Tell me what you think I should do."

Out on our street, it's almost six p.m. and people are coming home from work. A pickup truck hauling ladders passes, then a minivan I've seen before, one that's covered on the back with Disney magnets and stickers. People are debating pizza or hot dogs in their kitchens. At some point today, Rex must have pulled our garbage cans back up to the house from the curb. The sun's going down and searing the gray clouds orange at their edges. I know this place so well, but sometimes I feel like an impostor here, too. Not Mercedes or Mercy or Dearie or Fräulein Marino, but rather someone who is caught between two worlds, the one in my head where I am my true, whole self, and the one out here, where I'm always waiting behind a canvas or sketchbook, where no matter how much I wave and jump around and call attention to myself, I still feel like I'll always be watching everyone else live.

I will probably feel like that anywhere.

Except, perhaps, the one place where I can be the best version of myself.

I keep thinking I could cry. My hand hurts, and there's a stuffy cloud of sad gathering behind my face. But maybe I'm mistaking the feeling. Because it hits me like a deep, low note of the piano, a *thrum* that fills my chest and head, that this is a feeling Lilia knows. This is the Estate's magic—either it has held on to me, or I've somehow grabbed on to it. It's like a helium balloon, bobbing above me, tethered to me by a thin string in my hand. I can keep holding.

"What do you want most?" I ask my sister. "Like, if you could have one perfect moment right now, what would it be?"

"Abuela would wake up," she says.

"Yes," I say, "but what else?"

"Isn't that enough?"

"I mean, yeah. But what about the other parts of your life? What's something you wanted long before Abuela got sick?"

"I don't know." She taps a few keys at the lower end of the piano. "Friends?"

"You have friends. You were hanging out at Hannah's place the other day."

She gives me a weak smile before staring down at the keys again. "Well, even someone who called you a bitch at the beginning of the year can't turn away the poor girl whose grandma is dying."

"Hannah's the bitch, then."

"Not really. I wasn't a good friend to her. I get, you know, closed off and weird sometimes." She sweeps at her bangs. "Anyway, you know what? I don't feel like telling you all this. You asked me, that's what I want. Friends, to do friend stuff with. Maybe one of them would like to play music."

"Shit, that's totally what I forgot to do."

"What?"

"Your hair."

Angela watches me run out of the room and come back with water and a comb and a towel and scissors. She sits with her back to the piano, and I stand facing her and comb her long, dry bangs into wet black stripes.

"Stay still," I say.

"You know what I want?" she says, her lips barely moving. "I want to have a friend like Victoria is to you. Someone who likes being in the same space as you."

"Mm-hmm." It is harder than I imagined to cut bangs. They're slippery, and they hold a lot of responsibility. On someone like Angela, with fair skin and thick black hair, they're the first thing you notice.

"But it's one of those things that feels greedy to want," Angela says. "I don't even know how to begin. What do I do, like, go up to someone in the cafeteria and declare my undying friend-loyalty?"

"That's not a terrible idea." Oops, the scissors move when I laugh. Snip. A half-inch chunk of one section of hair falls into my hand. I try to comb the shorter section under the longer hair, and mix up the strands so that the shorter ones are hidden within longer ones. "Keep thinking about it. And I'll do the same."

Because I will.

Because I think this could be her moment—and mine, too. This could be what gets her into the Estate.

After dinner, in my own bedroom, sitting under the *Three Musicians* picture, I keep writing and erasing texts to Victoria. *What's up?*, the usual standby, looks so self-conscious sitting there by itself on the screen. Delete. *I cut Angela's bangs*—one of those things I normally wouldn't think twice about telling her, but right now seems too invasive, for everybody involved. Like, why am I trying to nudge the everyday blahness of my evening into her life?

Better to go with something practical.

Do you need a ride tomorrow?

Her thoughts, her hesitations, appear as a series of three pulsing dots on my screen.

Vic: Nah my dad will take me

Me: I want to hang out with you before you leave for Miami.

Vic: I really don't have much time . . .

I'm thinking. She's thinking. I am about to dive back into practical suggestions of dates and times that we might be able to see each other, which we haven't done in years. We haven't needed to. I know her life, and she knows mine.

Vic: Maybe dinner tomorrow?? My mom is making cauliflower crust pizza

Me: Uhhh (deleted)

Me: Really? With your parents? (deleted)

Me: Wait, the crust is made of cauliflower? How does that even work? (deleted)

Me: [pizza emoji, trash can emoji, pigeon emoji] (deleted)

Me: Sure.

I turn off the lamp and lie on the bed with my hands behind my head. The house phone rings in the kitchen and I don't move to answer it, figuring that Angela will run for it in a minute. Yep, off she goes. Her talking-to-Mom voice appears, but I can't tell from what she's saying if there's any good or bad news. Abuela in the hospital in San Juan. Me in my bed here in the Moreno-McBride-Solis house of oddities. And Victoria in her room across town, probably getting ready to go to sleep in her big iron bed, underneath her Broadway posters and that one picture of a steely-eyed Martha Graham on her wall. I don't know why, but I like the mental image of the three of our beds lined up in a row, and all of us asleep, breathing through our dreams in succession.

"There's an email from Mom." Angela is about ten steps ahead of me in the getting-ready-for-school dance. Her cereal is the bow to the morning, while my messily peanut-buttered toast is the creaky warm-up. The tingle of magic from last night is gone, and I don't know how to will it back.

"Is she still annoyed at me?"

"If she is, she'll remember it in a couple days. She just wanted to let me know that Tío Mario is getting ready to take over."

"She's coming *home*?"

"That's her plan."

"And that doesn't piss you off? She's supposed to *be* there. God."

"I want her to come home, Mercy." A couple of weeks ago, she would have been teary, or close to it, while saying this. Now, she is dry-eyed and direct. "She can't stay on leave from work forever. And I miss her. I don't like any of this anymore."

Since we're not picking up Victoria today, there are still fifteen minutes before we need to leave for school. Angela realizes this too, and shuts herself in her bedroom to finish her cereal. I can't believe I didn't see that Lilia was the latest in a line of people to brush off Angela after Angela has given so much of herself. A line of people that includes Dad, Hannah, and me.

I take one more bite of the peanut butter toast and march over to the front door. Maybe Lilia is home, maybe she isn't. Maybe I'll tell Rex everything I know about his tenant. Maybe I'll inform Lilia that I'm not doing any more projects for her until she starts the piano lessons with Angela again. Maybe I'll sit on the floor of Rex's living room, among the pictures of dead redheaded folk, and I'll wait until Lilia gives me an answer or I come up with one myself.

On the floor of the foyer, something white gleams up at me. The sketchbook Lilia gave me the other night, the one in which I drew the perfect picture of Abuela's old house that could never have been drawn anywhere else.

I flip the cover open.

The house, the swaying palms, the little goat. They've all survived.

Somehow, Lilia kept the Estate's magic intact. Somehow, she got this picture out.

I clutch the sketchbook to my chest. It's clear Lilia knows what she's doing.

It's a beautiful morning, and I bet it's the same or better in San Juan and I'm thankful that Abuela is living through it even if she doesn't know she is. Angela throws her stuff in the backseat of the Ford, but I need an extra minute to be sure that my sketchbook has a comfortable place to sit. Every time I open it to look at the picture of the house, there's a strange, sweet pressure in my chest. I can't even talk about it—not yet. It's a newly cut feeling that still needs sanding down.

One thing is that I'm glad I didn't tell Angela about the impromptu Firing Squad concert. Talk about a way to make her never want to see the floral-dressed one again.

"Hey, you've been killing it at the piano lately, you know that?" I say to Angela over the music she keeps turning up on the Ford's stereo. "You should come back to Lilia's studio with me before Mom comes home. I feel like things are different now."

The speakers crackle. Angela switches the stereo off.

"I don't think anything's different," she says.

We pull into school and I grab a spot at the back of the lot. Some of the Smoking Corner citizens wave to me, and I smile back out of instinct, but I doubt any of them can see it. Angela falls into step with me on the walk to the front doors.

"Anyway," she says, "I'm sure we won't even *have* a piano in a few days. You think Mom's going to let us keep it in the living room?"

"I guess we'll see."

When she returns, our mother is going to feel like a visitor in her own house. It's our house now, isn't it? Rex pays the mortgage, and Mom's name is on the rental agreement, but it's really mine and Angela's and, in a way, Lilia's. It's our new habits, our new rules. It's how we've reversed Mom's cooking traditions and now we have enchilada sauce from the jar but homemade mac and cheese. It's how I always fall asleep alone in Mom's bed but sometimes find that Angela has crept in halfway through the night. It's when a couple of Vic's annoying shirts from Alabama popped up in our laundry. It's Angela not asking a thing about Vic, but seeming to know enough. It's all that, and the damned piano.

Mrs. Pagonis loves the house sketch. "You're really coming along, Mercedes," she says brightly, and I want to ask her if she'd like to go out to the parking lot and have a smoke and talk about this strange place I know, this studio where every beautiful and terrifying thing seems possible. But I won't.

"It's cool," Gretchen says after Mrs. Pagonis has moved on to the

Green Table. "Is that a real place?"

"It was my mom's house when she was a kid."

The story of the picture threatens to come out of me. But I push the drawing closer to Gretchen and let it tell her as much as it can.

I flip through my old sketchbook, the one that holds my art-class history, some of which looks a lot like Gretchen's. The shading assignments, the attempted still life, the practice on perspective. I'm tempted to tear the house picture out of the new sketchbook and place it in here, as if to say, yes, *this* is who I am now. But the picture seems too fragile for that, as though handling it in the wrong way could make its pencil lines retract from the paper, back into space.

Gretchen smiles and hands the picture back to me, laying the sketchbook lightly on the palms of my hands as though she knows how important it is. I will fill this sketchbook, maybe inside the Estate, maybe here in art class, maybe somewhere else entirely, but I will do it. I turn each page—blank and white, full of possibility. A zillion people have said that before me, but I think at last I understand.

Wait—there's a page in the center that has a telltale Sharpie marker stain on it. I flip another page to find what bled through. In one corner of the page, there is neat handwriting in bright blue.

If you still want to work here, come see me. I need you to do a self-portrait.

Ah. Edie was right. I have my new project.

eighteen

MRS. CABALLINI HAS never not been worried about me.

"Are you sure you want a second cup of coffee?" She squats beside me and looks straight into my eyes.

"Oh, yes," I tell her.

Meanwhile, Victoria, the refuser of dessert and coffee, is sitting in the chair across from me, drinking water as though it is the only thing holding her together. Her hands tremble and her face has almost no color. She has the Juilliard flu.

"Hey, Vic," I say, "let's go over your outfits for the trip one more time."

She takes several long seconds to realize what my motivation is here. At least she doesn't say something like, *Why would I need fashion confirmation from someone who always wears the same pair of purple shoes?* I take my coffee to go and we head to Vic's room.

She flings herself onto the bed, and I settle on the desk chair, which is willow-tree-draped with clothes of all kinds. I set the cup of coffee—which, okay, I didn't want or need—on top of a stack of books on the desk. Paperback novels, probably her comfort reading for the trip.

"You haven't packed, have you?" I say.

"I haven't even gotten the suitcase out of the closet."

"That's commitment."

"I know." She smiles. "I keep thinking about what I would be doing this weekend if I wasn't going to test the effects of extreme stress on my nerves in Miami."

"I don't know." I try to lock eyes with the picture of Martha Graham on the opposite wall, but it's impossible. Martha is staring at a point in the distance, and she's waiting for that point to move, but I don't think it ever will. "Maybe at practice?"

"No. That's what I mean. Even you can't imagine me out of that world—*this* world, I mean." She gestures around herself, at the stack of dance clothes topped with pointe shoes next to her on the bed. "I can't be anything but this."

"You can if you want. No one's stopping you. I mean, your parents might be sort of pissed, but they'd get over it." This is true. If Vic decided to take up physics in place of dance, her parents would spend about a week in mourning before buying her a graphing calculator. "But like you always say, you dance because you love it."

"I know," she says. "I'm sure this is just a temporary annoyance."

"Vic, go to the audition. If you decide you don't want to go to Juilliard, then you will have at least met some interesting people and taken a trip to Miami."

She nods—well, bobs her head up and down, as though tricking me into thinking she's nodding. God, I hope Vic doesn't pull something outlandish, like telling her mom she's going to the audition and then disappearing to spend a *Catcher in the Rye*–type weekend alone in Miami, having an odyssey of booze and self-discovery.

She studies the toes of a pair of pointe shoes. "I hope things aren't weird between us when I get back."

I grip the stack of clothes on her chair, their fabric soft on my hands, though the skeleton of the chair pokes out. "Yeah, I feel the same."

"It seems like you've got some magic or something, dearie."

Another second thought about the cup of coffee. I swallow a gulp. "It's not mine. I mean, I looked for it and found it, but it's still not mine."

Martha Graham keeps her eye on the prize, and I stare her down instead of looking at Victoria.

Martha, girl, you're so focused, but on what? Was your whole life about artistic expression, or was there something else you needed? When you wanted to tell someone how you felt about them, did you use words, or did you just downward-spiral your way across a stage and hope they understood?

It's not particularly graceful, but I cross the room, take her suitcase from the closet, and flop it open on her bed. I leave myself enough room to sit on the corner of the bed, with one of the four carved posts jutting at my back in uncomfortable places.

Vic shakes her head at me. "I almost want to ask if you'll take me back to your art studio, but I'm scared of what might happen."

"Me too," I tell her.

And we are close again, almost as close as we were that night at the Estate. Her right leg is up against the suitcase, and I grab the leather corner of it so that we're touching the same thing. She hates confusion. She hates the feeling of being on edge—she needs the steps and counts laid out for her. And yet, here I am, throwing deviations in the path of hers that leads neatly from here to Miami and then to New York. The look on her face is one I haven't seen before, and I've got a whole catalog of Rare Looks of Victoria Caballini from which to draw. The look from ten seconds after she broke up with Connor Hagins, as she strained to stay completely cool while he walked away. The look when she found out she was doing the *Rhapsody in Blue* solo in the first Gershwin show. Even the look when I brought her flowers to the theater. None of those. Or any of the dancing looks or any of the late-night looks or the early-morning looks.

"We shouldn't, though." Vic brushes her hair back and spits these words at the suitcase. "This audition is everything, and I just . . . I can't shake my confidence before it."

"Yeah, your audition for a school you're going to drop out of."

"Shh!" Vic points to the door. Then she pulls the suitcase to the middle of the bed and throws a pair of pointe shoes and an armful of tights and warm-up clothes into it. She's committed. For all our talk of possibilities, when it comes to Victoria, there is only one.

But after everything, after years of dance classes and companies and performances, the possibility quivers.

"You're scared," I say.

"Duh. We've covered this."

"No, I mean, you're scared of not getting in, but you're scared of succeeding, too. You're scared of dropping out of Juilliard, or not having the life you want by the time you're supposed to drop out of Juilliard. All of it scares you."

Victoria swipes at her forehead. Her hair is down and messy, and her dress is one I've never seen, purple with little birds all over it. Birds in nests, and birds suspended in fabric flight.

There's a possibility, small but visible, that I may never see this dress again. That she may leave for New York straight from Miami, and that she'll change her phone number and make her parents swear not to give me her address.

"But you're afraid, too, dearie," she says. "You're scared of what you want. Sometimes you take a step forward, but then you retreat again. Always."

Martha Graham has no use for me. I stare at the floor.

"If you need to tell me anything important, then just do it," Victoria whispers. "Because I think you're holding on to something."

She doesn't know how right she is. But she has been wrong about me so many times that I can't give in to her right now. Vic is not that good at commitments. Vic is good at moments—sometimes moments that last a few days, or a few years, but still, every time and place and person in her life so far is something or someone she's going to leave behind. I wanted to be more than a moment to her. I wanted the world to spin tightly around us, holding us close, keeping us together.

I don't think she's going to let me be that person.

"I mean, okay, maybe I'm wrong," Vic continues, grabbing the stack of books from the desk and layering them on top of the clothes. On one cover, a guy and a girl stare longingly at each other over a fence. On another, a silhouette walks through the rain in Paris. I want to sit next to her and read them (I'll take the Paris one). "But it bugs me to watch you get so close to what you want and then . . . you know, run away again."

"I don't know what you mean," I say quickly, hopping up from the bed and returning to the desk chair. "I'm, like, working on the biggest damn art project right now. I'm putting myself out there." But the center of me seems to collapse, my guts and heart trying to swap places. I steady myself with two hands on the side of Vic's desk.

Maybe Vic was right in calling the magic mine.

It is. I shouldn't ignore that anymore. I'm connected to the Estate just as much as Lilia is, and I need to get back there, to *my* studio, to figure out how I should do my self-portrait.

Vic goes back to packing, and I grab a handful of the clothes on the chair and bring them to her. She takes them without managing to brush my hand. She's coordinated that way.

Are you going to miss me?

Are we going to talk about this when you return?

Was this, indeed, inevitable?

These are the things I want to ask her.

But we're quiet until Angela pops in from the other room, finished with dessert and coffee with the Caballinis, hinting that she'd like to get home, hinting that it's getting awkward to be sitting there.

Vincent van Gogh wasn't a slouch about the self-portrait. Neither was Frida Kahlo. Rothko loathed them. Warhol consented to them. Marc Chagall parodied them. And the esteemed Lilia Solis claims she doesn't care for them, but that having one is "part of the project." And so, here we are.

"Nice view." I lean against the window and stare out into the Gulf of Mexico, which on a calm night like this seems black and tired and almost defeated. We're on the other side of the building now, and six floors higher than before, and from here the gulf announces itself.

"It really is." Lilia's voice is clipped and kind of sad. "Are you sure you want to do this?"

"Yes." I turn away from the window and continue not sitting on the dusty concrete floor. "But I need to know, are there some rules about what it should look like? Colors? Shapes? Size? Are you going to say something all mysterious-like, maybe along the lines of, 'Whatever you create, it must be true to yourself'?"

Lilia pushes her hair out of her face and actually sits on the floor. I think I wear her out sometimes. "It needs to fill the room."

As soon as she's said it, I realize I know that. Fill the room.

"If it helps, I know you can do it," Lilia says.

"Thanks."

The white walls here are uneven and smudged, brushed with nail holes and dust and the impact of hands and furniture. The door is even worse, with a jagged hole going all the way through. "It looks like someone got angry," was all Lilia said when we came in, and I was glad that my mind hadn't made that connection immediately.

"So I can use any of the materials in the kitchen?" I ask, though now Lilia is the one who seems to be daydreaming, staring at the maze of concrete bumps and swirls across the floor.

"And is there any hope of getting a rug or something, or can I bring one?"

Lilia says, "I'll find something for you." She picks herself up off the floor, gathers her dress around her, and takes stock of the walls the same way I've been doing. This is hardly an ideal canvas for someone who often sucks at painting on canvas.

I ask her, "Where are you working now?" Because I know she's not working here, and it's starting to sink in that I practically have my own house. Someone else's rules, but my walls to draw on.

"Down the hall. Eight oh five."

"Can I come see what you're working on?"

"Not yet."

"I saw the sketchbook. I mean, I know you intended for me to see it. But you got that picture out. You changed the rules somehow."

She gives me a slow nod, but says nothing.

"Did you know my mother is coming home?" I haven't told her this and neither has Angela, but it seems like Rex might have told her, or that it might be the sort of thing she picks up on without explanation. Like I'm standing in a certain my-mom's-making-travel-plans-right-now way.

"I hadn't heard," she says, and I think we both look surprised.

"So, ah, I might not have as much time to come here as I do now." I mean, there are methods for escaping the house when Mom's there, but I haven't tested them in a while. She could have figured them out. "I just wanted to warn you."

"When is she coming back?" Lilia asks.

"She thinks maybe Monday."

"Why don't you stay here for the weekend?"

"Here?" I thump the heel of my shoe against the concrete floor.

"In the other place," Lilia says. "Your white room. I can make some arrangements for you. Artists shouldn't have to sleep uncomfortably."

"What about my sister?"

"Are you saying you want to bring her?"

"Well, yeah."

"Do you think that's going to work?"

I look her straight in the face. Well, at her nose. "You know what? I think it will."

It's echoey in here. My voice, not hers. I suppose I should get used to it. This is where I'm going to be spending lots of time alone. I hope I'm able to hear the music from here, at least.

"Hey, is Firing Squad still here?"

Lilia brightens. "They're on about the same schedule as you are right now."

"Okay, cool." I take a walk to discover the walls, the same way Lilia did. "That's great news."

It's an odd thing to picture—Angela and me waking up in the weird white room with Victoria's picture on the wall, grabbing breakfast from the little kitchen, and then sitting and eating it beneath Lilia's artistic jumble of household objects. But Victoria is packing her bags to leave, and somewhere in San Juan, so is Mom. Why not the Moreno sisters, too?

The last time we went to visit Abuela Dolores, she surprised us before we had even set down our luggage. Her hair, once salt-and-pepper and then silvery all over, was back to being black. One hundred percent opaque black. "I missed this," she explained, puffing it up with her fingertips. "Black matches better with my clothes than silver."

Abuela was bouncy and bright for those whole two weeks. Waking too early, singing in the shower, teasing the dogs with a laser pointer, and going out in the early evening to play dominoes with her friends. Angela and I went for long walks to the beach—it was summer, but summer always felt better in Puerto Rico than in Florida. Gentler, more settled. People complained less about the heat, and so the heat didn't have a reason to gripe back.

Once I sat on Abuela's bed as she got ready for the nightly game. She added makeup on top of the makeup she was already wearing:

more pink on her cheeks, more brown on her eyelids, as though she were brushing the final details into a painting. I asked her how she had so many friends, and wondered if that sounded like I was insulting her. I wasn't meaning to.

"I stick around," was her reply.

"Can I help you tie your scarf?" I asked.

"Of course!"

I took the scarf by both ends, and folded it once, and then sort of rolled it up. I really had no idea how to tie a scarf, but I figured if she wore it messily this time, she could fool her friends into thinking she'd done that on purpose. Abuela was deliberate that way, and I liked being near her. I ran a hand along the bottom of her thick black hair.

"My hair is terrible compared to yours," I told her. "There was a girl in middle school who told me it looked like a rats' nest."

"That's silly," Abuela said.

"I know. When she said that, I told her she must know that because she spent a lot of time around rats."

Abuela laughed. "That's perfect. You always look great, you know that. I'm sure that old boyfriend of yours spends every second of the day being sorry he dumped you."

"Oh my God, I've told you that story ten times. I dumped *him*."

"Well, then," she said, surprised at having her version of the story thrown off. "I'm sure you've already found someone better."

I leaned in and whispered, not to her ear, but more to the folds of her scarf. "I'm in love with someone. But I can't tell you who."

She studied both of us in her mirror: Abuela standing at attention, me all bent and wrapped around her. I was afraid she was going to press me for more details, to ask me how I knew this person, and if I happened to slip a "Vic" or a "she" in there, I wondered if Abuela would ever let me back into her house. I was so close to saying it, to testing her. The flowers of her scarf blurred into a watery garden, and my stomach dropped as though I was falling into the swamp of pink and purple.

And then Abuela said, "That's beautiful, Mercedes. Love is always perfect when it's a secret, isn't it?"

"I guess so," I said.

Abuela unwrapped me gently from around her neck and gave me a hug. "But how long do you keep it that way? That's the question. What's the cost for trying to keep it perfect?"

"I'll let you know if I find out," I told her.

Angela says, "Are you sure?"

It's my car and the Alabama minivan keeping each other company again.

"Well, not completely sure. But I have a sense that I can throw things off just enough for this to work."

She drags her overnight bag behind her across the parking lot instead of hoisting it over her shoulder. I walk ahead of her with a backpack. Well, not too far ahead of her. Okay, maybe not ahead of her at all.

"Mercy?" Angela stops next to me.

"I'm just nervous," I tell her, "but I'm going. It's probably best if you wait right by the doors."

We talked about this. We agreed it was a good idea. We did. And yet, the reality of it is hitting me like a glass wall. We could go home and go to sleep in our own beds and then wake up and have some orange juice and waffles and clean the house and be ready for Mom to get home, but no. Here we are, attempting to spend Friday and Saturday night in Lilia's studio, and for what? For what?

For these things that we like to do.

For the sake of burying ourselves in art and music.

Surely, that's all that is going to happen.

The lights in the lobby flicker on as I head inside and upstairs. In the white room, on the second floor, a summer-camp-style metal bed has been set up for me.

But I have to push it aside in order to paint.

I choose purple—a deep, dark purple like Abuela's New Year's Eve grapes—and start rolling it on. How much will be enough to throw off the needs of the Estate? There's a shade of arrogance to all of this—why do *I* think I have the power to shift the Estate's needs? Why do I think I have the power to get Angela invited? But, no. I can't talk myself out of this. I've come so far already. I can take this next step.

Paint splatters on my arms and my gray T-shirt, drops that will be gone the moment I step back outside to see Angela.

One wall. No rumblings.

Ah. But there's a wall that's different. A wall with a secret.

The Victoria wall.

This painting of her is my best work ever, no doubt. If I were trying to critique it in studio art, I'd probably sit in front of it for a while, trying to find a single detail that wasn't filled in quite right. But there's nothing like that—it's got all the right lines and layers. All of which I have to slather in purple.

And so I do it. Piece by piece, Vic disappears under a blanket of purple paint. I'd like to tell myself that I can re-create this picture someday, in a place outside these strange walls, but I don't think that's true. What's within the walls is becoming my truth: I understand how to be in this place now, and how to throw it off just enough.

The lights in the half-purple room dim, then go out completely. I think I have done it. I lay the paintbrush across the top of the paint can, softly, so as to disturb nothing. And just as quietly, I walk backward out of the room, the lights still out, the Estate still holding its breath, and I head downstairs to get my sister.

nineteen

A LIVING ROOM again, but this time with a piano in one corner and a keyboard in another. There's a handful of us in the audience—me, Lilia, two older women, and a couple of people I remember from the party. Mae dims the lights and then takes to the keyboard. Angela appears, still wearing the Wonder Woman T-shirt and gray shorts she came here in, and sits at the piano. The guys wander in from the hallway and grab their instruments. Brad nods to Nelson, and then all five of them share a look. And the music starts.

Angela is playing with Firing Squad.

It's not a song I know—I guess it's not a song at all. Brad thumbs the bass but doesn't sing. If anything, it's Angela on piano who seems to be leading the group, pulling a melody out of the sound and letting the other instruments press themselves against it, one by one. Her cheeks are pink with energy, and her hands dance up and down the keyboard. She's fantastic. Who the hell needs sheet music when you can improvise like that? I sort of wish I could jump in front of the band and let everyone here know that she's my sister—but no. This is her moment. I'm in the audience of yet another Firing Squad concert, and that's perfectly fine with me.

Someone taps me on the shoulder from behind. I turn around. Edie.

"I heard you were here for a while," she says.

"Just for the weekend," I tell her. "I have something to finish."

"I knew it. Well, if you want to grab a drink after the show, let me know."

"You should stay and watch. That's my sister up there on piano."

"Oh yeah?" She nods her head to the music—well, a little out of rhythm.

They play for a long time. Maybe an hour, maybe less or more. Who knows? No one seems to have much use for time around here, and I'm slipping into the habit of only glancing at clocks when I'm confronted with them. Who cares if it's two in the morning if I feel like I could stay awake and paint all night?

Not that I'm feeling like that right now. After I give Angela a hug, I let her hang out with the other band members. "I'll meet you in the purple room later, okay?" I say, waving, leaving her there. She nods, and Mae gives me a salute, and I feel weird about walking away, but we've already escaped what we thought was going to be our biggest danger here. In my gut, I know this is a safe place. Still, I'll be back to check on her after my drink with Edie.

She makes me the amplified orange juice.

"It's delicious, yet again," I tell her.

"Pouring is an art, like everything else," Edie says. "I do it exceptionally well."

She runs a towel over the bar and watches me have another sip. There's one other person in the bar tonight—a guy about Tall Jon's age, wearing a fedora—and he's getting terrible service, but he's off in his own world, meditating or something while he drinks a beer. Edie's holding back questions, I can tell. She wants to ask me where I go to school, what I did for Christmas, do I even celebrate Christmas, how did my sister learn to play like that (never mind, she's probably figured that out), what do I dream about, and do I ever date girls?

"Have you ever been to New York?" I ask her.

"Like, the city? Yeah, I've been once. A school trip, though. Nothing fun. It was cold and the only museum we went to was the natural history one." She stops cleaning the counter. "Oh, let me guess. You're thinking of going. You think you can't be a real artist until you've roughed it up there. Lived in an apartment with four roommates and one bathroom. Look, it's not true. Do you realize you've got everything you need right here?"

I stare down into my drink. "Hmm, I guess."

"Hey. I can take a break in a minute. Let me show you what I've done since I've been here."

Maybe Edie's real art is evolution—her photos are arranged in matching black frames in a line marching around her place. The whole thing is hers, living room and kitchen and two bedrooms, all to herself. One bedroom is to sleep, and the other isn't quite a studio, but more like a catch-all for everything related to her photography. Despite the fact that there's no room for me to walk into it, the line of photos marches around all four walls and out again. The early photos are everyday things in everyday places: lonely umbrellas on the beach, a broken-down car on the street in front of the Estate, a cracked window.

The photos in the next room, Edie's bedroom, are different— stranger, and more arranged, and sometimes involving people. This one wall in her bedroom is a series of portraits of people (some including Edie herself) wearing identical bright pink feathered masks, Lilia among them. I recognize her long hair.

"She *agreed* to this?" I ask Edie.

"She was really supportive of my project," Edie says.

The ones on the wall by her closet are the hardest of all to look at. The same people from the mask pictures are now dressed as though dead and lying at a wake: mask off, eyes closed, face muscles relaxed and dark makeup filling in lips and eyelids and wrinkles. Edie looks the creepiest: white-faced and surrounded by flowers.

"So what inspired these?" I ask her, trying to keep my voice steady.

"My grandmother and my dad died," she says, "like, within two weeks of each other. That's too much for a girl to take at once. If I could have surgically removed the grief, I would have. This was my way of trying to let it out into the world."

"To make those feelings beautiful?" I ask.

"Eh, maybe," she says. "Or just, you know, to disperse them. To split my feelings among a hundred people who might see the photos."

I take a few steps out of her bedroom and back into the hallway. Edie's place is so strange—the pictures of death existing in these spaces where she lives her life. There's a smell of garlicky pasta in the air, and she's got old books and magazines on shelves in the hallway. It's settled and unsettled, just like me.

"My abuela's in the hospital." The words fall out, but I'm okay with them. "We don't know if she's going to make it."

"Ugh, I'm sorry," Edie says. "I shouldn't have shown you all this. We can head back to the bar."

"No, it's fine," I say.

And Edie smiles. She gets me a glass of water from her tiny kitchen. I wander around her rooms, looking at all her art supplies and the few bits and pieces I can gather of her pre-Estate life: a worn paperback of *Fun Home*, a T-shirt from some summer camp in Kissimmee, a couple of family photos taped next to the window. Outside, the gulf is all kicked up, steady in its thrashing. I look away, only to find Edie watching me.

"Your place is great," I tell her.

"Yup." She stretches out her arms. "I love it here. And, you know, you could have a place like this too, but you've gotta go finish your project first."

"Is that seriously it?"

"That's all I can tell you."

She shrugs, and I can't help it. I run to her and let her put her arms around me in a tentative hug. I like her. *I like her.* She's clearly one of those people who can pick through the wasted bits of another and find something they never knew they had.

But I'm scared. And, oh shit—did I just *say* that? I whispered it into Edie's shoulder, because this is the Red Mangrove Estate and nothing I feel so strongly is going to stay inside my head for very long. I'm scared because Edie kind of wants me, and because I know I could take away the "kind of" and still be thinking a true thought. I'm scared because I don't know how many and which of my feelings I could beam onto her without myself becoming dimmed. I put my lips on her cheek for the quickest of seconds, and she leans forward, then pulls back.

"Oh, girl," she says, breathing on me. "I know, I know. But we don't want to ruin this."

"Ruin?" I say. I mean for it to be a question, but it flattens itself into a statement. As though I'm agreeing with her. Am I?

She untangles herself from me and lets me go.

The door to Lilia's apartment on the second floor opens easily to reveal the homiest version of the front room I could imagine. She has decked the place out with a little couch, a floral easy chair, a floor lamp, and a coffee table. The lamp burns politely over the whole situation, annoyed that I took so long to get here.

And in the purple room, there are now two single beds. Angela is sleeping, her breaths slow and satisfied, because I suspect you probably sleep really well after you've had the best night of your life.

Me, I think I still have some work to do.

At some point, there is nothing to do but draw.

I begin in a dusty corner of the eighth-floor room by brushing away the cobweb tent that has formed and then wiping part of the surface clean. I take a sharpened drawing pencil I found in the kitchen and try to set myself free on this massive, imperfect canvas.

I doodle on the wall. This is the only sort of thing I can stand to assign the stupid word *doodling* to—crooked lines and asymmetrical ocean waves and drunken circles I draw when I am trying to make sure I'm not drawing anything. *Ruin.* Edie's word keeps coming back to me, a parade of *ruin-ruin-ruin* tromping through my head, and it's the last thing I want to do to anything here. Maybe I've found the way to actually ruin a piece of art within the Estate—to have absolutely no vision for what it should be.

Except that the lines of my doodle remind me of the Naples house, which was built in a "modern" style twenty years before I was born, and never aged well. When we lived there, I called it a cubist house out of love, but I haven't thought of it in that way in a long time. I think Gris and Picasso and their pals wouldn't have found anything particularly artistic about it.

Wait, no, that can't be true. I have to believe, if I am ever going to finish anything, that there's art to be had anywhere, whether it's New York or Savannah or that ugly old house that was probably glad to see us go. And it's a part of me more than almost any other place I can think of.

So onto the wall it goes: the house, or my memory of it. Its proportions are those of my elementary-school mind, when the living room was mostly ignored and the thick, crunchy grass of the front yard seemed to go on forever. It is now seven inches tall, tucked into this corner, its street lost to the cracked baseboard of this room. But it is here, and already I feel much less lonely.

I keep going. I draw Angela the way I remember seeing her the first time, tiny dark eyes opening within a bundle of pink blanket knitted by Abuela, and a wordless thought forming in my head that I would know this girl forever. I draw my parents, standing next to each other, not touching, stuck in different years—my dad looks like he did when I knew him best, when he would give in to my begging every middle-school morning to save me from the social jungle of the school bus, and my mom looks the way she did when she left the house a few weeks ago, pained expression and floppy hat and all.

There's no color to any of this yet. That will come later. For now, the outlines are enough.

I clean out another corner and sketch the first girl I ever drew, maybe the first nonimaginary person I ever drew. It was this girl from summer camp, Mia Cortelyou, and I covered a whole drawing tablet with this girl's face before I spoke a word to her. She was the first person I was fascinated with, the first person whose life I wanted to know, and since I thought I was never going to know it, I spent hours making it up with a set of colored pencils. Mia Cortelyou was the friendliest girl, the most adventurous girl, with a house full of ponies and puppies and exotic reptiles. And when she and I were the only ones from the old group who returned the next summer, and when she acknowledged this and said we should be friends, I was shocked. Did I *want* to know Mia, and her true history? I thought I did, but I resisted keeping in touch with her when the summer was over, so that I'd never be invited to her house, so that I'd never have to become part of her terribly normal life.

In this picture, there are two Mia Cortelyous: Mia the adventurer, riding bareback across a long landscape, and summer-camp Mia, looking shy and pretty in shorts and a T-shirt and old sneakers.

Mia was my first crush. That is as starkly obvious to me now as the gaping hole in the door, but to admit it in those words, to have her on the wall in front of me—these things are new.

And there's so much wall space left.

This is going to be harder than I thought.

"Hello?"

Sun streams in through the single, uncovered window. Footsteps on the concrete. It's Lilia.

"Hey." I sit up and rub at my eyes. Lilia is dressed as though she has responsibilities somewhere other than the Estate today—she's wearing black pants and a floral button-down shirt. The flowers remind me of one of Abuela's scarves, and that's enough to shock me out of my sleepy state.

"I didn't mean to doze off here. I just wore myself out. And also, this rug is way too comfortable for a rug."

"Don't worry about it," Lilia says, walking around the perimeter of the room. "I wanted to make sure you were still around."

"Yeah. Until tomorrow, when my mom comes home."

She nods. "You're doing a good job here."

"It's the start of something. I don't know what I'm going to do with the color or with, you know, the whole rest of the room." One of the penciled-in Mia Cortelyous seems to peek over at me. Not only will I have to revisit her, to give her color and depth, but I'll have to do it again and again, with so many pieces of my life.

"It's the start of something. Keep going." Lilia smiles at me. "Feels like it's going to be a good day." She produces a set of keys from her pocket and hands them to me. "Take these. Keep them with you. In case you ever find one of these doors locked, you'll now be able to get in whenever you need."

"Sure."

"When you finish the work here, you'll be able to get up to the top floor," she says.

"Which key is that?" They're all pretty much the same.

"Ahh, the one with the green tape on it, I think. I haven't been up there in a while. Once I finish a piece, I try not to look at it again."

"Your work is up there?"

She is turning to go. "Yes. And yours could be too, if you like."

"What, is it some kind of museum?"

Lilia considers this. "I suppose that's it. It's for those of us who are making decisions here, about what kind of work we need."

"How long have you been here, Lilia?" I ask, looking up at her. Her long hair. Her strange but familiar face.

She turns away, comes to a stop in front of the biggest blank patch of wall, runs her hands over it as though testing its strength. "I don't really know. Feels like a long time."

She leaves me with myself, and with the keys.

Oh man. It's almost nine. Victoria is for sure on her way to the audition right now, if she's not already warming up. I type out a text to her, wrists and palms and fingernails aching as I do: *I am breaking both of my legs for you at this very moment!*

She says nothing back.

It's weird how we got to be here—the one decision after another that led to us knowing each other. My parents getting divorced and my mother thinking she could "start over" up the coast from our old home, Vic's parents deciding to ditch their previous careers in corporate real estate to sell medical equipment in Florida, the school deciding to put us both in Ms. Donohue's third-period English class in sophomore year (although I like to think that even if we hadn't had any classes together, we would have spotted each other in the hallway and detected our Friend Chemistry, would have walked toward each other while working out the least awkward way to ask the other to hang out at Starbucks sometime). And I like to think that I'm more to her than someone she knows on her way to going somewhere else, but I'm not sure. I don't want this to be the end of us.

How does she fit into my self-portrait?

What is the first thing about her that comes to mind?

Lilia dropped off some newly sharpened drawing pencils, so I grab one and take to a clean space of wall. Pointe shoes. The stern face of Martha Graham. The sleek field of pink comforter I have woken up to at her house. Maybe I could draw the whole city of New York to represent her. Anything but her kissing me. I've already given that to the Estate once—no way am I leaving it here again.

I wonder how long I can keep this pencil raised, poised at the wall, unmoving.

"Hello in there!" comes a voice from the doorway. Angela.

"Come on in," I call back.

She bounds into the room and sits on the floor without even noticing its state of filth. "Oh my God, Mercy, can you believe it?"

"No." I really can't. Every time I think about Angela onstage with Firing Squad, I have to stop and be sure that I didn't dream it. It's exactly the type of thing I would dream up.

"We kept playing." The grin on her face is as wide as the gulf. "They showed me how to play some of their songs. They said I was really good."

"So, what's next? Are you all going on tour?"

"Don't be silly." Angela's old shyness brushes her face. "They said they'll be here for a little while, and they asked me to keep practicing with them. Oh, and they asked about *you*, too."

"What about me?"

"How long you were staying."

"Ange, sit on this lovely rug with me, please." I scoot over and she takes the side farther away from the big blank space where all the important things are supposed to go. "They want me to stay here, don't they? Just like Lilia and Edie and apparently everyone else."

"Who's Edie?"

"Another artist. She lives here."

"That could be us!" The grin again. "We could live here, in our own apartment, and you could work on your projects and I could keep playing piano and Mom could come visit us here and we wouldn't have to bother with anything else."

"You would like that?"

"I think so." She looks around. "Lilia told me you were working up here now. This is your assignment?"

"Yes. It's a self-portrait. I mean, that's what it will be."

"I can hardly see it."

"You have to get right up next to the wall. It's all in pencil for now."

Angela gets up and walks around the room, kneeling down every so often to see the details of one picture or another. She stops in the corner nearest to the window. "Hey, is this supposed to be me?"

"Yup."

"Cool," she says. "In a band and immortalized on a wall, all in one day."

It's nice to see her happy, so nice that I wish I could have her sit cross-legged in the center of the room for the rest of the day, a humming little jar of joy. But I realize I can't ask that of her, not that she would accept even if I did. She finishes her tour of the room, checks the time, tells me I should take a nap eventually. And then she's gone, off to practice with my favorite band, which is still the weirdest thing in the world.

I keep drawing. I clean more areas of wall and stand on a folding chair to reach the higher parts and the corners of the room. I snap a pencil in two and fling it toward the doorway. I grab another pencil, and use it and sharpen it and use it some more until it is shorter than my pinkie finger. I've got shiny gray pencil stains on both hands and elbows, and my wrists feel tired and heavy. I guess it's time to stop for a while.

Back in the second-floor studio, Lilia or Angela or someone has left a plate of cheese and crackers out on the counter, and there's a pot of warmish soup on the stove. I have some of both, and then I collapse in the purple room, on the untouched bed next to Angela's bed. If I were to take Angela and Edie and Firing Squad's suggestion, I wonder which apartment would become mine. Would I have to wake up in this purple room every morning (or afternoon, if I was left to figure out my own schedule)? Would Mom come to visit, or even be able to visit? Would Vic laugh at me and completely blow me off for planting myself here in Sarasota?

* * *

Angela shakes me awake. "She's got a flight. She's definitely coming home."

The purple room, still.

I stretch out my arms. My wrists have stopped groaning at me—it's time to start working again. "When? What time?"

"Monday afternoon," Angela says. "We don't have to pick her up. She's going to take a shuttle from the airport."

Angela saying that has a strange way of bringing Mom closer already, as though her plane ticket has brought a ghostly presence of her into the room. She's the type who asks questions after missing five minutes of a TV show—I can't imagine how much she'd flail around in the unfamiliar context of the purple room if she was able to see us now.

I stand up, put my shoes back on, and grab my phone from my back pocket.

It's actually here. A text from Vic:

I made it through all the dance parts of the audition.

I made it to the interview!

That's amazing, I text back. And because she's probably busy getting hugged by her mom or congratulated by various random passersby who detect her awesomeness, I add in: When you get back, we have to celebrate.

"She's leaving," I say, to my phone or to the walls.

"What?" Angela says.

"Nothing," I say. "Vic. Why are you still wearing that Wonder Woman shirt?"

"I just like it. It smells fine."

"Next thing you're going to tell me that if we live here, we don't have to wash our clothes, right?"

"I'm not sure yet," Angela says. "It's entirely possible."

I keep working. It's Saturday night, maybe early Sunday morning. Music bounces in and out of the air, and I am filling the walls. There are some of my friends from Naples, and some general compadres from the Smoking Corner, and Tall Jon, and even Bill, because why the hell not. The art room from school comes out as sort of a cubist version of the real thing, with Mrs. Pagonis looking more like a geometric scarecrow than a human being, and Gretchen Grayson as a lost figure from one of Picasso's paintings about the bathers. But not too much like Picasso. Actually, do I even *like* Picasso, or have I spent a lot of time convincing myself that I do?

I scrub at the triangular hands of Gretchen with the pink pencil eraser, but the lines stay as though I've carved them into the wall.

If Lilia was around, I'd ask her—are everyone's projects like this, or is it just a trick of *my* project that the secrets I put on the wall are apparently stuck here forever? If Lilia was around, would I have the courage to ask her that? Would she ask what I'm afraid to commit to the wall, and would I be able to tell her? Because there's so much. There are all the crushes on boys and girls, the ones I felt so strongly and the ones that pricked at the backs of my knees and then faded away. There's the thought that I'm glad my parents divorced, and that it was a relief when Dad moved away and we didn't have to know each other's day-to-day selves anymore. There are all the times I have lain in my bed at night and considered Victoria, and how, after everything that's happened between us, I wonder if my feelings are going to stay there, trapped under blankets, for the rest of my life.

I drop the pencil and roll it over to the corner where I'm keeping all my supplies.

The girl sitting here right now, dejected and guarded and covered in dust—how can this be the best version of me?

I will have to come back here and figure it out. But right now, both Mom and Victoria are on their way home.

twenty

IT'LL BE GOOD to see her. That's what I'm telling myself. That's what I told myself this morning when Angela and I were on our way to pick up Victoria, even though she and her dad had already left for school when we arrived at her house. After second period I walked by her locker, which was closed and kinda lonely looking, as though its current occupant hadn't bothered to come by to grab her English and trig books. I don't know why I keep thinking she's avoiding me, or that I'm avoiding her. She's not, I'm not. It's lunchtime. She is across the courtyard, approaching the Dead Guy from the opposite direction that I am.

She stops.

So do I.

The sun is insistent today, and with Vic standing in the shade of the school building and me standing in a bright, treeless patch of grass and dirt and lunch trash, we can barely see each other. The courtyard kids, Connor and his latest girlfriend and all the others we used to know, turn around and look at us. None of this fazes Vic. She is, as Bill once put it, a High School Nihilist, well-versed in the ways of not giving a shit about being seen alone. Her dresses and heels and nice hair—those things are for her alone. That's part of why I love her.

"Mercedes!" she calls out. "I can't believe I didn't see you this morning!"

We come together at the Dead Guy, even though it's way too hot to be here for very long. This is our place. Could I really ever ruin this? Ruin us?

Mom's not here yet. Angela rushes into the house to straighten a few things, and I peek into her car (now abandoned for my old Pontiac) to be sure it gives off the impression of being neglected and stationary for the time its rightful owner has been gone. She'll know what happened when she looks at the odometer (*if* she looks at the odometer), but that first look is important. It passes the smell test.

I shut the door, and the airport shuttle pulls up.

I shift into Daughter mode as well as I can; actually, it's easier than I thought it would be. A big smile and a wave. Seeing that her face looks a little tanner but basically the same. Meeting her at the shuttle and asking to take her bag and realizing I need to hug and kiss her, too, and trying to do that with the bag in hand.

Okay, maybe not so easy. I'll leave it to Angela to get it absolutely right.

"Mom!" She bursts out of the house, barefoot, races down the driveway, and throws herself into our mother's arms. Mom kisses the top of Angela's head at least a dozen times before she lets her go. They link elbows and walk like that together as Mom tips the shuttle driver, and then Angela, clever girl that she is, somehow talks Mom into walking in through the back door. I'm left to bring in the suitcase.

We order pizza and eat it in my mother's bedroom, Angela and Mom sitting together on the bed and me in the easy chair that usually serves as a plump clothes hanger. Angela handily keeps the conversation going, stringing in one easy topic after another. The weather, the sartorial choices of Rex McBride, more about the weather, Vic's audition, and what Angela and I have been doing at school. I reach for the last two breadsticks. No one notices. Angela is crafty—we haven't been in the living room the whole evening. Angela got up and answered the door when the pizza arrived. Mom still hasn't seen the piano.

"My girls," Mom keeps saying. "My burbujas." It has been so long since she's called us her bubbles. I miss it. She motions to me to join them on the bed. I do, and she wraps one arm around me and one arm around Angela, tightly, which leaves us no physical choice but to look straight ahead, as though we're posing for a photo.

＊　＊　＊

Angela heads to bed at ten thirty, looking worn down but also seemingly sure that she knows where Mom will be for the rest of the night. I can't bring myself to get up yet—my arms are still sore from drawing on the walls, and this bed feels more right than my actual bed.

Mom rubs my shoulder. "I know you're still worried."

I have my eyes closed, which helps to mute the strange experience of having my mother in the same room with me. "I'm sure you are too."

"I am," she says. "But I missed you girls. It was so hard to have our family divided."

"We did fine here," I say. "Did you see how the laundry hamper's totally empty?"

"I did, and I know. But oh, mijita, I felt so torn. I started thinking about sending you girls up to Ohio until I got back. I was thinking about this as I was sitting with Abuela. It felt like I could never put my energy in the right place."

I love hearing her voice beside me. It reminds me of when I would fall asleep listening to her read to me. I loved that so much that I almost wish I could fill that space with my story now—the Estate and how I got myself there.

"I missed you," is all I manage to say. "And I miss Abuela too."

"I know." Mom gets up from the bed. I recognize the sound of her moving her perfume bottles aside and plugging in her electric toothbrush. "But, well, back to the real world for now. They wouldn't let me take leave from work any longer, and I can't afford to lose my job, especially with you graduating this year."

"Yep."

"Did you hear anything from your colleges?" she says.

I knew she would ask this. And the way she says it, quiet and languid, slipping it out of her subconscious where it's been rolling around for weeks, makes me think I don't have to answer it right now. I know she's proud of herself for going to college. I know she wants everything to go right for me and Angela. And every time I consider that there's so much about me she doesn't know, I have to consider the same thing about her. Her childhood was in Spanish; her dreams and thoughts still are. I want us to understand each other.

She comes back to the bed and rubs my shoulder again. It feels amazing.

"I drove your car while you were gone," I tell her sleepily. "Like, a lot. Every day."

"Oh, Mercedes." She laughs quietly. "If I was so worried about you driving it, I would have locked it up at the Tampa airport the whole time. And you probably still would have found a way to get it."

"I appreciate that you appreciate my ingenuity."

"Always have," she says.

Sometime overnight, Angela has gotten rid of the piano. It's just gone. And the living room looks how Mom probably thought it looked the whole time she was gone—cluttered with our stuff, not hers.

It turns out Mom changed up her sleeping habits when she was in Puerto Rico. It's eleven p.m. on Tuesday and she's baking bread for tomorrow's dinner. I wander in and wait until she offers me a taste of her first finished loaf. I probably look convincingly like someone who is going to sleep soon, pajamas on and my hair pulled back in an elastic headband. She doesn't know that we are engaged in a silent game of physical endurance called "Who Will Sleep First?" I glance at her face, at her eyes, without her taking too much notice, and I am pretty sure I am going to lose this round.

Twelve thirty, and she's out in the living room, in the bare spot by the window, doing one yoga pose after another. I'm going to have to change my plans.

It's Wednesday and the fifth-period English girls are suspicious of my presence. We're sitting inside for lunch today, me on the periphery of their table beside the front windows as rain pounds against the school building. I used to imagine these days: the last quarter of senior year, when, as my mom always told me, everyone in the class becomes friendlier as they realize they're going to miss one another. I think secretly I was waiting for that, maybe more as an exercise in performance art than anything else. I wanted to witness that moment when a kindly ambassador from the Smoking Corner residents visits the AP kids' lunch tables, and bonds are formed on the basis of rebellion against the ruling class of Forever 21–clad statues to socially acceptable amounts of partying. But I have yet to see it happen. When I said hey and sat down next to the fifth-period English girls (Lizzy, always writing poems; Gianna, recently dumped after two years with the same guy; Em, queen of the swim team and *possibly* into girls), they looked at me like I was indeed a visitor from another place, and not one arriving out of goodwill. I think I regret not turning these girls from acquaintances to friends. I can't blame them for how they're looking at me.

"Hi, ladies. Can I join you all?"

A milk shake appears in the space on the table across from me. And then the familiar hands of Victoria Caballini.

I let the other girls officially invite her to sit. They want to know about her Juilliard audition, and so she holds court for a few minutes, telling them about each increasingly difficult dance section of the audition, and how dancers were sent packing after each part, with only a few making it all the way to the interview at the end.

"And so I finally got to sit down!" Vic says, which gets the expected laugh.

When she's not talking, she's been alternately sipping on and marveling at her milk shake, and I think she's going to start reciting a poem about it any minute now. But whatever it is, it'll have the rhythm that's behind everything she says: *I'm leaving, I'm leaving.*

My fingers tremble against my water bottle. Shit. I hold one hand down with the other.

Vic glances at me.

She's leaving.

The other girls are talking about the FSU party scene. Dorms and bars and how to start meeting people when you land in a place as big as the Tallahassee campus. I wouldn't know. I nod along. An ache starts in my back, tugging its way up from my tailbone to my spine and into my shoulder and upper-arm muscles. Painting muscles, I sometimes call them.

I shift in my chair. My hand shudders against my water bottle, and I barely catch it before it falls over. The other girls look at me.

Vic says something about how Tallahassee isn't as big as New York, which doesn't land with the same success as her Juilliard story.

I want to thank her for being socially awkward. But my shoulders ache and the backs of my knees sweat. "Girls," I say, standing up, "I'd like to announce that I have no idea where I'm going to college, and also that it's been nice chatting with you."

"Are you okay?" Vic says.

I'm not sure how to answer. The rain has stopped pummeling the windows, has moved aside for a minute to let me go. I hurry out of the cafeteria.

The Estate is silent and I feel like it has been waiting for me. Maybe. There's nothing about my new studio that makes the work easy. It's all dust and concrete and terrible lighting, with Lilia's rug being the one soft, quiet island in the middle of all the chaos I both inherited and created. I'm on my own now. The nonerasable pencils taunt me, to the point that I can't bring myself to pick one up today. Fine, if they want to be that way, then I'll deal with the permanence of what I'm creating, and I'll start painting inside the outlines I already have. I dig through the kitchen in the new studio and find enough paint to help me get started. Acrylics—not my favorite, but they'll do.

I remember my first paint set. It was the Crayola watercolors in a box, which is probably everyone's first paint set. And it wasn't a gift or anything—I picked up the set when Mom and I were out shopping at Target, and I stuck it on the bottom rack of the cart, where people usually put their dog food and diapers. I figured I would tell Mom about it when we got to the checkout, and at that point she'd wind up buying the paints for me rather than going through the whole mess of telling me no and putting them back. Except when we got to the front, when I was supposed to put this plan into action, I forgot, and the checkout guy wasn't looking for stray watercolors at the bottom of the cart, and so they went unnoticed. I was six years old, and a paint thief.

If I was going to be coexisting with these stolen paints, I figured I should use them, and use them well. I set myself up with the paints, and a cup of water, and a stack of paper from the recycling box, and I painted and painted, creating frightening new colors and eroding holes into each little thumbnail of paint in the box. It was freeing— a mess of guilt and creativity and dirty water. The pictures weren't anything interesting, but the watercolors were gone before I got into trouble, and before I knew how to stop myself.

Painting my new studio is like that. It's easier not to stop.

It's not finished yet, but so much is here. My life, surrounding me in brilliant colors on the wall. And for everything I have accomplished here, this self-portrait still doesn't really feel like me. It's the best thing I've ever done, the same way the Abuela and Victoria portraits were once the best things I've ever done, but there's something dishonest about it, in the way it only captures my best self.

I flop down onto the concrete. My jeans are dusty, my arms are sore. It is two thirty in the afternoon, maybe. Or it could be later or earlier, if the Estate decides it. I need to head back to school soon to pick up Angela, but I have time to do a few more things here.

First things first. I put a wide streak of black across several of the parts of the self-portrait. The house in Naples. My first day of middle school. A scene with my dad and me in his old Jeep, and me smiling as we listen to the Rolling Stones' "Shattered" for probably the eighth time in a row.

Ah, ridiculous "Shattered." I really had myself convinced that I liked that song.

The black streak is thick and shiny, like the shell of a beetle. It's certainly not the greatest thing I've ever painted, but it might be the most satisfying. I put the brushes to sleep in the dusty kitchen of the new studio and walk out, hoping the door locks behind me.

Several floors down, Lilia isn't in her studio, but it's clear that she's been here recently. Wet paintbrushes rest on the side of the sink. Empty glue bottles litter the countertops. She has been working hard, and it shows: the ceiling is nearly covered with recyclables now. But the other canvases, the abstract paintings I noticed the first time I came, are gone.

I walk down the hall and poke my head into the purple room. It's nearly the same as it was over the weekend, although someone has straightened up the place, with nicely made beds as though it's a hotel room that's expecting a whole different set of guests tonight.

There's one room here I've never been inside, and that's the first bedroom on the left. The corresponding one to Anna's creepy dark room in the condo unit down the hall. I lean on the doorknob, and just as in Anna's room, it sticks at first, then gives to let the door fly open.

And I should not be surprised. The piano, Angela's piano, is right here. It's polished and gorgeous, outfitted with a new music stand and an actual bench. I touch a few of the keys, as though, just because it's here in the Estate, I could possibly get a different musical result. But no—as usual, the piano doesn't want me, doesn't call out anything besides a clamor of off-key notes. It's waiting for Angela, maybe the one person who can play it right.

I let the piano be. Lilia's canvases are turned around and leaning up against the opposite wall. I flip one over.

And I am face-to-face with myself.

It's not even one of her abstract paintings. It's a completely realistic portrait. She has me down, from the wisps of hair at the top of my head that never lie flat, to the indent in my chin.

I turn over the next one. Angela.

And the next. My mother?

It really is her. Even though I have no idea when Lilia came face-to-face with Mom long enough to know the tiny mole between her eyebrows and the shape of her ears. For the first time in a while, I stand and listen to the endless back-and-forth of the waves, because it is a simple thing to concentrate on. *Swish-boom, swish-boom.*

Again and again. Around me, the Estate is silent, waiting.

I run out of the room. "Lilia?" I shout through the kitchen, through the living room, my voice echoing off the Goya cans and plastic bottles. "Lilia, where are you? What are you doing?"

And I don't really expect her to come running, but she does. She appears from the stairwell and meets me in the doorway.

"Why are you spying on my family?" is the first thing that comes to mind to say. Lilia looks perplexed at this—well, tired and perplexed. Her eyes are bloodshot, and her whole face is worn down.

"You saw the paintings." She tries to untangle a knot in the ends of her long hair. "I'm sorry, I didn't mean to scare you." Lilia leans toward me and whispers, "I've been trying to get them out. It would help everyone here if I could. But I can't seem to do it."

"Can I try it?" I ask.

And we stack the paintings and take them down the stairs. But as soon as we get out the front door, the canvases are blank.

twenty-one

DEJECTED, LILIA TAKES the canvases and turns to go back inside.

"Lilia, wait," I say.

It has stopped raining, but everything around us drips, and behind us, the gulf churns gray and white. I take to one of the old plant beds on the side of the building—it seems like a neutral location, not yet out in the real world, but also free of the Estate's power. A dead bush scrapes against my jeans, and a faded Fritos bag crunches under my feet.

Lilia joins me around the corner, her whole face and body in the middle of a long sigh.

"Is this who you want to be?" I ask her.

"What do you mean?" she says, staring off at the water.

"I mean, you told me that this place will give us the best versions of ourselves. But if you can figure out who that is, and take that idea outside the building with you, then . . . you know, you get to keep on being that person. Right?"

She brushes at a bit of dust on her pants. "Look at that. That's all I was able to bring with me this time." She shakes her head. "Mercedes. What did I tell you about everyone's art? I have to help keep it there. I have to help keep everyone else's secrets safe."

"Fuck all those secrets." I don't know where this comes from, but the words strike the building and bounce back at me. "If everyone else who's been here doesn't know what to do with them, then why should you have to take that responsibility? Fuck it."

Lilia meets my gaze. "Did you ever tell your dancer friend how you feel about her?"

"I should have known you'd remember that," I say, kicking at the Fritos bag.

"Of course," Lilia says.

I watch her as she's walking away. Her long black hair. Her strange stride that goes from slumped over to confident within seconds. I remember back when Rex introduced her to me, how I was wondering if she was going to be like Frida Kahlo. That's such a weird thought now. She's not Frida at all, but she's got a sense about her that reminds me of Frida's portraits, how you look at them and want to know the subject.

And I know her now. Sort of.

A green minivan rumbles into the parking lot. Firing Squad.

They park at the front of the lot, the sliding door opens, and none other than Angela Moreno pops out.

The rest of the band is right behind her. I duck around the corner of the building again and let them go in as a group. Angela doesn't say anything, but she smiles in that comfortable way I know, the way that says she belongs, that she's not afraid to show how happy she is to be with these people.

I wait a few minutes for them to be well into the building, and then I enter.

The music is clear even from the lobby. Angela is playing with Firing Squad again. The one comforting thing about having the keys Lilia gave me (wait, do I still have them? Yes, they've sunk to the bottom of my bag, hanging around with my lighter and my actual non-art-related key ring) is that I know I can find Angela, no matter where she is in the building. I can get to her.

They ramble through the first part of "City That Does Not Wake" (track one on the album) and then make it connect with "At Four in the Afternoon" (track six) and now they're playing something I've never heard, and all the while I'm climbing stairs. My steps occasionally sync with the beat of the music, but not often. Not when it keeps changing this much. How can Angela keep up with them?

It's exactly what the Estate needs right now. It's not enough to move the clouds or anything, but it's what will keep this place humming.

The eighth-floor landing. I'm parallel with the music now, for sure. I pass the door to my new studio, and a few more doors, and I stop at 815, at the end of the hall. No keys needed this time—the door opens with a gentle push.

"I found it in my heart to give you the strip of myself that says 'always,'" Brad sings, and he waves to me as I take a few steps into the living room. They're all right here, Angela and everyone, along with a very familiar piano.

I smile at everyone as though I've popped in to chill out and hear the music. Brad and Mae nod at me as I saunter across the room (nodding along to the music—*enjoy it, enjoy it*).

The music comes to a close, and Angela wipes the sweat from her cheeks and underneath her bangs. She lays the wooden cover over the piano keys and runs her hand over the piano. She's stalling, clearly. It's like when she used to put her Lego blocks away brick by single brick, to avoid having to get ready for bed.

"Hey, Ange." I lean against the wall by the front door. "I was about to go to school to wait for you."

"Sorry," she says, not looking at me. "I was in sixth period and I couldn't concentrate. I had the urge to come here and play."

There are a whole bunch of things I could say to this, things that would make me sound maybe not so much like *our* mom, but like *a* mom. *You could have been patient. You could have kept on being like the Angela I have always known, rather than this girl who sneaks out and plays with my favorite band. That would be easier.*

"Are you finished?" I ask her.

She glances around at the rest of Firing Squad (is she officially a part of the band now? Are they going to add her name and picture to their website?), notes that they are packing up too, notes that no one is stopping her from leaving, and says, "Yeah, I guess so."

I got so into the habit of cooking that it's weird not to have to. I offer to help Mom, but she insists that only she can make her famous chicken soup. So I put the clean dishes away and watch her chop the carrots and onion, her fingers soft machines making precise movements. It is a nice evening—Mom opens the door to the back porch and the breeze breathes in and out through the dining room and kitchen.

"I haven't seen you painting since I got back," she says.

"Yeah. I've been doing most of my work in art class lately," I tell her. "I had kind of a breakthrough."

"That sounds promising." She scoops the chopped vegetables into the big soup pot.

"Maybe."

"I took your advice about Abuela." Chili powder into the soup pot. "I whispered to her everything I could think of that I had never told her. And I hope you don't mind, I whispered all sorts of things about you and Angela, too."

"Oh yeah? I don't mind."

"I told her I sensed something was happening back at home, but I didn't know what. I almost felt like she would wake up and tell me, but she didn't."

"Hmm," I say. "Well, everything's fine here."

Except that when we sit down to dinner, Angela is silent and pale, and her soup spoon never moves from the bowl.

"I'm sorry, I'm just not feeling that great," she says when Mom notices that she hasn't eaten anything.

Mom sets some crackers by Angela's bowl. "Have these, then try the soup again." She says to me, "I bet you remember. When Angela was two, she had a terrible stomach bug, and I gave her this soup for the first time. It was like magic, the way she ate a whole bowl and then asked for more."

But I don't think it's going to work this time.

Angela lies on the couch all evening, not eating crackers or soup, not watching TV, but just staring at the ceiling with her headphones on. Mom, as usual, has no plans for going to sleep anytime soon, and she sits at the dining room table, drinking tea and reading one of her thriller novels, this one in Spanish. Should I say something—to either of them—or should I retreat to my room and sink into myself?

"Hey, Mom," I say. "I'm gonna pop next door for a minute. The girl renting Rex's room has a bunch of natural remedies."

"Oh?" Mom looks up from her book.

"Yeah, I thought, you know, it might be worth a shot."

"The soup always worked before," she says.

"I know."

"Who is that girl?" Mom asks. "I saw her getting into a car

this morning, but that was it. I said hello and she didn't even turn around."

I say, "Her name is Lilia. She works odd hours. I think she's tired a lot."

Mom says, "Hmm," like she wants to ask more, but also doesn't really want the whole story.

"Hi, Mercedes."

Lilia's wrapped in her purple bathrobe (but at ten p.m., this makes sense) and she looks strange to me, sort of like it was to see my mom after all those weeks away.

"Angela's not feeling well," I tell her in Rex's living room. "Do you . . . do you know—"

Lilia sighs. "Come in here."

Rex's bedroom door is closed, and the thudding soundtrack of some suspenseful movie leaks through. Lilia leads me into her bedroom, leaves the door open a crack, and turns on a small stereo. Thank God she doesn't start playing Firing Squad, but rather some quiet jazz. I never thought it would happen, but I may be fully sick of "The Getting Is Good."

"She needs to be there," Lilia says. "You understood that before I did, and you did it brilliantly, I have to say. Angela's really ready."

"What about me?"

"You? You've been ready, maybe even for longer than I thought."

"Then why haven't I gotten sick?"

"You'd probably have the same thing happen, if you stay away

280

long enough. I bet you've been feeling some weird things. Aches and itches, things like that. Right?"

"Uh-huh."

I sink onto the antique ottoman next to the antique bed. She has moved the Estate series and stacked all the canvases into a single tower in the corner of the room, tall enough that she might as well be creating a 3D model of the damn place. I imagine how she'd represent me and Angela and Edie and Firing Squad and the rest of them with a bunch of Lego people, a few of us trapped within each layer of canvas.

The red suitcase is right where it was before. Lilia doesn't seem bothered that I'm seeing her room—maybe she would have let me see her work all along.

"I don't understand," I say, and then nothing comes after this, nothing, still nothing, because where am I going to begin, and what if she doesn't understand either? I rub my hands on the knees of my jeans. I love these damn jeans. If I do what Lilia and Edie and apparently Angela all want me to do, will I be stuck wearing a rotation of floral dresses for the rest of my life?

"I don't either, sometimes," Lilia says. "I saw your mom is back. How is your abuela doing?"

"Not very well," I say.

Lilia leans against the bed. "I'm so sorry." Where, I wonder, are Lilia's grandmothers? If they've died, how lonely were they when it happened?

"But seriously," I say, "I don't understand. If I take over what you do, then what's your part in all of this going to be?"

"I told you before, I'm pretty sure I have to go. And I'm trying to do it in a way that doesn't mess everything up. It's an experiment, and it's so fragile." Lilia rummages in her suitcase for a minute and produces a hair tie. She gathers her long hair into a low ponytail, which she flings around to her front. "Every day, I try to get a little farther away, and every day, I wind up right back there, or back here, with you and your sister."

"Nothing wrong with being here," I tell her.

"I know," she says, turning away from me and opening one of the creaky wooden drawers of the antique dresser. "I know that. But it's been wonderful to live at a place where I feel like I don't have to worry. Where our art and music are perfect. Where we don't get hurt." She finds what she's been looking for in the drawer: a pair of red-handled scissors. "That's what you want too, right? I mean, it has to be, or you wouldn't have been able to get in so easily."

"I don't know anymore," I tell her.

Lilia looks down and clips off her entire ponytail.

"Damn," I say.

"What do you think?" she says. The ponytail in her hand flops over like a dead fish.

"Short hair, don't care, Lilia," I say, fluffing my curls with my fingertips. "But seriously, you've got the face for it."

"Thanks." She puts the scissors back in the drawer and lays the ponytail on the dresser. I'll have to come back later and tell her to donate it, or maybe donate it myself, since she's getting ready to go.

"Hey, before you go." My voice catches in my breath. "Tell me about how you got my picture out of the Estate. The one with the house. I thought I'd never see it again."

"You make it sound easy," she says, "like I just had to walk out with it one day. It took me ages to figure it out. And it had to do with the picture itself. The connection it has to the person who drew it."

I think of my mom, sitting a few walls away with Angela, knowing nothing about any of this. I could bring Lilia and the house picture to her right now and blow her mind.

"Why are you leaving all this to me?"

"Because you understand what the Estate can do for people," she says. "You understand how some things need to stay perfect. You understand how we want to hold on to the best moment of our whole lives, and the person we were in that moment."

I do.

Lilia runs her hand along the strange new ends of her hair. "But anyway, you haven't finished your self-portrait."

"Okay, but how am I supposed to know when it's done?"

"You'll know," she says. "I promise you'll know the second it's done, dear."

"You don't get to call me that," I snap.

I want to grab the red suitcase and hurl it out the window. To make her stay a few days longer to clean up her shit. *We* are her shit—my sister and me, left behind to take care of the things she couldn't. All the potential for beauty and tragedy in the world—it's all there, swimming around in one place, like the colors in my eyeball.

And I have let her lead us there.

My foot grazes the red suitcase as I get up from the ottoman. I give it another shove for good measure. "Look, sorry. I'll figure out how to finish the damn thing. But right now, is there anything you can do for Angela?"

Lilia's mouth slants. She opens one of the creaky drawers in the massive antique dresser and pulls out a bottle of antacid tablets.

"You think that's actually going to help?" I say.

"They won't hurt," Lilia says. "You'll figure out what you need to do."

I tell Mom that if Angela doesn't get better soon, then maybe I'm going to take her to urgent care? Or maybe I don't let a question mark hang in the air when I say this. We sit on the floor in front of the couch, drinking tea and staring at the opposite wall, where Mom hung my and Angela's school portraits up too high. That's my last-summer self, she who was still high on the victory of *Food Poisoning #1*, and who had just been blown away by the realization that she loved Vic. I can see it in her eyes, as she's holding it, her one big shining secret. And I've never noticed how stressed she looks—there's a certain anxiety to love, the way your mind and body wear down to make up for your heart beating so furiously all the time.

And I feel like that again now, but it's for all these other things. For Angela. For Abuela and my mother. For my huge painting sitting alone at the building, waiting for me to return and be sure I still want it to look the way it does. For Lilia, and hoping she's okay, and wondering what the hell her secrets are and what she's going to do. For all the other artists at the building, working away, but never able to have everything they want.

"Mom, you can go to bed," I say. "I'll take her."

"Ay, bendito, you've got school in the morning."

"Yeah, I know. But we got in sort of a pattern when you were away, staying up late and doing things together. This is just, you know, another one of those things." I nudge Angela's shoulder. "Hey, let's go."

She sits up.

Mom stares at her. "What kind of medicine did that girl give to you?"

Angela's eyes get teary. "She taught me how to play the piano."

"She's kind of delirious," I say. "Come on, Ange."

We don't waste any time getting to the Estate, which is all lit up again. She seems to gain some energy as we park and head inside. Going up to the second floor, there's color returning to her face, and opening the door to Lilia's studio, she's looking a lot more like herself. The floor lamp hums in the corner, waiting for us, and Angela heads straight back to the piano room. I check the fridge for some water, and not only is there one of those fancy water filters, but there's also an unopened carton of orange juice.

I figure we have maybe an hour or an hour and a half, max, before Mom starts freaking out and calling us. *Yes, of course we're at the urgent care place,* I'll tell her. Maybe an hour is all Angela needs.

Maybe that'll take her through the end of the week, or even just through tomorrow after school.

Angela's playing is quick and insistent, like she's a mad scientist at the piano. On another floor, someone is dancing to her music, and someone is drawing to it, and someone is tuning up their saxophone before starting to play along. Everything goes on here, and on and on.

---

twenty-two

THE DOOR TO Mrs. Pagonis's room is shut even after the late bell rings. We hang around outside, a bunch of studio art misfits with our supply boxes and portfolios, forced away from our color-coded tables for the first time in ages. It's Thursday, it's spring, and people are appropriately restless. I make eye contact with some of the Yellow Table people I've hardly spoken to all year. And I feel a particular allegiance with Rider, for once, who keeps taking glances through the door's thin window.

"She's in there with Gretchen," he whispers to me.

"Oh man." I scrape at a slick of dried glue on my art toolbox. It reminds me of Lilia and the ceiling art. I figured I was going to spend most of today silently willing Angela to make it through seventh period, but now, this worry about Gretchen is lumped on top of it. "Maybe it's nothing bad. I heard Gretchen got into SCAD, you know."

Rider nods. "I know. Good for her."

Mrs. Pagonis opens the door without a word, and all of us flood in. Gretchen's situated in her usual spot at the Orange Table, setting her supplies out neatly just as she would on any other day. But as I sit across from her, it's clear that she's been crying.

"What's going on?" I ask her, trying to weave my voice under the morning announcements.

Gretchen shakes her head, grips a drawing pencil, and slaps a fresh, blank piece of paper in front of her on the table. "Just starting my piece for the county show."

"What happened to the lizards?"

"Mrs. Pagonis said it was too much. Too confessional. She couldn't have that representing her class." She snakes a line across the paper, sort of like the traditional "here's the ground" line I used to draw as a kid. "She recommended me to a counselor. I told her I already see one. I just—I don't even know what to make now. Maybe I won't enter."

"No." I fling my sketchbook open. "I don't have anything either. Let's do this together."

Gretchen smiles. "Is it time for some more food poisoning art?"

"Nah. I never knew what that was about, anyway."

The blank sketchbook page looks like a door or a window to me this morning, an opening to a world of possibility that could be treacherous, but could be great all the same. I don't know what I'll find there, but at least it's a clearer path than the scuffed-up white walls of my studio in the Estate. Rider joins in, and the three of us are off, in our separate worlds, but with the scratches of our drawing pencils whispering to one another. I draw some lemurs, one napping, one with her tail wrapped over her shoulder, and one sort of jumping. Do lemurs actually jump? I don't care. It's my truth, and I'm happy to be living with it, at least for a little while.

I have so much energy from the lemur drawing that I go up to Victoria after lunch, after the fifth-period English girls are out of earshot, and tell her that I'm going to drive her to her dance class today.

"Sure," she says, as though this was a totally natural thing between us again. She doesn't ask if Angela's going to come with us, and I'm glad, because I have no good way to explain why an old minivan's going to show up and take her to the Estate. Vic, in her blue-and-white-striped dress and yellow sandals, standing with easy poise in front of the notoriously toxic front-hall girls' bathroom, looks exactly like someone who has always known what she wants to do with her life. She doesn't look like someone who has occasionally had that balance thrown off, or like someone who's about to have it thrown off again.

It's raining when Victoria and I head out. I have to do the thing Mom taught me where I turn the AC and the defroster on full blast to get the windows to stay unfogged.

Vic doesn't say anything about her playlist. I don't put on Firing Squad.

"It might be warm enough to swim this weekend," Vic says. "I mean, if you're up for that."

"Yeah, maybe."

"Have you talked to Tall Jon since his party?"

We're at a red light, and Vic starts twisting her hair into a bun.

"Nope," I tell her.

"Dearie." Vic faces me, or tries to, but the light turns green and I'm straight ahead again, pretending not to be side-watching her as she looks away from me and grabs her usual tangle of bobby pins from her dance bag. One, two, three, four, in they go. Good Lord, I think even I could do her hair in the dark at this point.

"Dearie." A little louder this time. "If there's something going on . . . with your new project, with Lilia, with anything, you know that you can tell me about it. Actually, let me rephrase that, you *better* tell me about it, because I don't want to see your picture on the news in a few weeks just because I didn't bug you for details."

"I'm not in danger."

"Yeah, but you keep trying to break into an abandoned building," Vic says. "Something tells me that's not going to work for very long, not in the land of fancy condos over there."

"My project is there. And Lilia is too. And a bunch of other artists and musicians." We are almost to Vic's studio. One more block down the street, past a funeral home and a plastic surgery place. Both too much and too little time and space to bring that weekend crashing back into this car. "And so were you."

"Oh, here we go. I told you what happened." She stares out the window. The plastic surgery place is busy, the funeral home isn't. "I don't understand why you thought it was something different."

"Look, I know that night was weird. There was definitely something in the building, about the building, that changed us. And that's what's terrifying about that place, and what's amazing, too. That's why I keep going back, I guess. Because I never know what's going to happen, but usually, it's something perfect. And beautiful."

I pull up in front of the Sarasota Dance Academy, Vic's poor, imperfect company, these people who are doing the Gershwin show again. She reaches down for her bag, then lets go of the handles and looks at me. Several hairs didn't make it into her bun this time. "So why didn't I get to see it?"

"Vic." I tug at my neck. I wish I could pick up my cigarettes right now and see how much smoke and ash I'd fidget away before I felt comfortable telling her the whole story. "Okay, tell me this. Think of a moment you'd want to live in for longer than a moment."

"Why would I want to do that?"

"Or think of a feeling you had once that you'd like to have again."

She's ready to go to dance, ready to move through that wordless world where she reigns. I wonder if anything has come back to her about that Saturday night at the Estate—a flash of a red-and-white wall, a tug on her hand that reminds her of me, a feeling that washes over her of trembling and comfort.

"Wait, so you're saying that your favorite abandoned building can give you those feelings?"

"That's not what I—"

"And wouldn't it feel weird and fake if you were only experiencing that because the building gave it to you?" Vic puts her dance bag on her lap.

"It's still *you,* though. It has to be."

"Okay." She turns to the side window and waves at a girl heading into the studio. The girl waves back and offers a big, openmouthed smile. I bet it is a lot easier to be best friends with that girl than with me. "Okay. I thought of something that happened during the Gershwin show two years ago. We were about to go out and do *Rhapsody in Blue* for the first time, and I was waiting a few steps offstage. I wanted to bust out of there before the music started and do a series of turns and leaps across the stage. Just me. The stage was so inviting—like, clean and black and shiny—and I wanted to jump in and experience it for myself before everyone else got there."

Every part of me aches when she looks at me again, and it cannot be Lilia and the Estate's powers prodding at me this time. It is Victoria. It is her near infallibility with the creation of her ballet hairstyle. It's the way she can let her perfectionism sag and sigh when she's with me. It's her playlists and her dresses and the way she says *dearie* and how she comes to Tall Jon parties with me and is, despite the abundance of cheerful dance girls in every corner of her life, the most loyal best friend I've ever had. It's the way she puts the right angle and weight and feeling into every step she takes, except perhaps for the ones she needs to take most.

"And I couldn't do it," she says. "I couldn't move forward at all. Not before the dance started."

"Vic, I kissed you. That Saturday night, in the studio. I know you don't remember. But you kissed me back."

The world gets louder in this second, I swear—the rain hastens from a steady shower to a pour, and the cars passing on Honore Avenue behind us seem to rev their engines at once, and all of it becomes a churn of sound in my ears.

The crack, the canyon, between our realities is filling up now. Victoria's cheeks flush. Mine probably do, too.

"I kissed you back?" she says. "What—what was it like?"

"It was perfect."

Vic sinks back against the seat, puts her hands on her face as though she's comforting herself, and I wish I could reach across and make the same gesture. "What else happened there?" she asks.

"I told you about it the next morning. I painted, there was some music, and we danced."

"Okay, okay. Enough about this for now." And she opens the door. It's the ultimate commitment to leaving, as the rain immediately dumps on her hair and her dance bag and everything. "I can't talk about this. I have to go."

It's the worst sort of Victoria exit—slow and graceless. Unbalanced and unshowy. And it's my fault. I've given her the information and left her to slink away with it—rather, to stumble away with it, as she's doing now, angling around puddles in her bright yellow sandals. The moment is gone. She has slammed the door behind her and

I can't even smell her makeup or her dance clothes or whatever it is that makes her smell like her. Instead, the rain hangs heavy in the air, its weight and scent clinging to me, and to this car whose windows are fogging again, obscuring my view of Victoria walking away.

She has to go, yes, but so do I.

twenty-three

WHEN I'M BACK in the Estate, standing in the center of the dusty lobby, the music from upstairs is going at full blast, with the sound of the piano front and center. I consider going up to the eighth floor to talk to Angela, or possibly to collapse into the piano, to wonder why it came clanging into our lives. I don't even know what I would say to Angela—I just want to see someone familiar, someone who might not run away into the rain.

But, ugh, the music is so joyful that I don't dare go upstairs and douse it with my sadness. Up the stairs I go, stopping at the second-floor landing. I sit on the top step and lay my head against my knees. It's something I've done enough times in my life to know how it feels, but this time I want it to feel different. My knees should be knobbier, my hair should be coarser . . . something to reflect this version of me who has tried to jump the Mercedes-Victoria Memorial Canyon of Awkwardness and missed the other side.

In our unending game of "How Many People?," now playing out quietly in my head instead of cheerfully at the Dead Guy, I'm asking her, *Hey, Vic, how many people who you've kissed before would you want to kiss again?*

And she would not even respond. She would put on her modern dance shoes, these strange half shoes that look like unfinished ballet slippers, and twirl herself back into the rhythm of the Gershwin show practice.

My jeans have a big wet spot on each knee, crowned with a smudge of black because I actually wore mascara today.

I get to my feet and trudge to the studio, even though I don't have any kind of solid plan for what I'm going to work on today.

Lilia is there.

And it's weird, but it's such a relief to see her. She's sitting on the floor, staring up at her damn ceiling art, and I go and do the same. Goya cans, Tide bottles, Dial soap dispensers. It's dizzying to look at—the different colors and shapes and heights of the elements of the work. My eyes keep adjusting and readjusting to it. I wonder if that's all the piece is meant to do.

"Hey, Lilia?"

I feel like I can finally ask her these things.

"Hmm?" Lilia turns to me. She's wearing plain dark jeans and a white T-shirt.

"Am I ever going to be able to figure out what you're doing with this, I don't know, this collage? Why do the rest of us have to give our secrets while you get to keep on being so mysterious?"

Lilia takes in a long breath at my question, my outburst. "But this *is* one of my secrets," she says quietly. "That I'm any kind of artist at all. No one ever knew. You never knew."

"Oh, come on. I'm here right now, surrounded by your art. I've seen your weird Estate series and your portraits and your abstract art. I've seen you work some sort of musical magic on Angela. You're totally a Renaissance woman. Give us both some credit, you know?"

She looks over at me with watery eyes. "You'll remember all that?"

"Hell, I don't know if I *like* this ceiling art, but I'm definitely not going to forget it."

"Okay," she says, stumbling to her feet. "Okay, I hope you're right."

I follow her lead in getting up, and I go over to the kitchen and pour some orange juice for both of us. "You know what my sister told me once?" I say, handing Lilia the glass. "That the orange juice you buy in the carton isn't what you'd think it is at all. It's, like, old juice that was squeezed, stored in huge pasteurization tanks, and then eventually reflavored to taste like oranges again. Angela called it 'orangified sipping water' for a year before I told her to stop."

Lilia looks even sadder than before.

"I mean, I didn't mean to disappoint you if you love orange juice or something, Lilia. You can try to forget about it. That's what I usually do."

She takes a couple of gulps. And then she says, "I'm leaving soon, Mercedes."

"I know," I tell her. "Are you still going to be at Rex's for a while?"

"No. I think I've exhausted his generosity."

"Well, fine." I finish my orange juice and put the glass by the sink. "Before you go, can you tell me what you think of my work?"

"Anything you create here is fabulous." Lilia wanders around the living room, toeing the weird zigzag black lines on the floor. "You know that."

"I know. But what's the point? Are you fulfilled by coming here and always creating your best work, every single time?"

"I used to be," she says.

"And now?"

"I'm not sure," she says. "I think I want to be a part of something permanent. Or potentially permanent, at least. I want to have a chance to mess things up and have to deal with them. I hardly even know what that's like."

"You totally do," I tell her. "You know me."

She kind of shakes her head at me. The short hair really does suit her. "Ciao, Mercedes."

I study her for a second as she traces the black lines on the carpet with her feet, and then I turn and leave the room. On the eighth floor, I'll be able to work. I'll be able to look honestly at my self-portrait and figure out what else I should do.

As I arrive, I grab all my supplies and go to sit on the floor. I study the whole painting—the pencil lines, the parts that have been filled in with color, and the big black streak. And I start to sense what else I need to do here.

Confession. Awkward confession. Here goes everything, onto the wall. The watercolors I didn't mean to steal. The rejection from SCAD I haven't told anyone about, and the acceptance from the University of South Florida that I've also kept secret. A picture of me being relieved at my dad leaving. All the girls and guys I've had crushes on. And the picture, again, of Victoria dancing and catching my eye in the audience, as well as I can re-create it.

And even after all that, the most honest thing is the black streak of paint. It juts in, announces itself, and doesn't care that it's wrecking my damn memories.

I streak another shot of black across the wall. And another and another. All the way across until I reach the one blank, white space that remains.

I draw all the people I fear losing: Tall Jon and Angela and my mom and of course, Abuela.

But when I draw Abuela, something different happens. The face I try to draw, the face of the Abuela I know, is not the face that appears on the wall. It's younger and softer. Longer hair. Abuela who loves nicknames and flowers. Abuela who left Puerto Rico as a teenager to spend a few years in Florida, to live on her own and perfect her English and discover herself.

And to discover, apparently, her love for art.

And how to keep this girl, this best version of herself, in an old building on the coast of Sarasota.

Hot and cold rush to my head and feet at the same time. I step back, dropping my pencil and then falling on the rug that she brought me. Lilia. Abuela. She has been here all along, guiding me to this moment, as though thinking that I wanted the same thing she did. This place to be perfect, to preserve my art and my best days.

But who's to say that the girl she preserved here is her best self?

And who's to say that the girl I would be here would be my best self?

I scramble to my feet and run down, down, down, from the eighth floor to the fifth and then to the second, the music with me all the way. The door to Lilia's studio is open wide, showcasing her ceiling artwork to anyone who walks by.

"Lilia!" I call through the rooms. "Lilia! I know who you are. I know I can help you. Will you come out and talk to me?"

And all at once, everything stops. The music. The lights in the living room and my and Angela's purple room dim. The pleasant hum that emanates through the building goes silent. It's just me and the gulf now.

Lilia, my abuela's perfect self, is gone.

But I still have the keys she gave me.

Wiping at my eyes, I climb as far as the stairs go, past the eighth and ninth floors, to where the stairs come to a stop at a landing. It's the penthouse apartment, a single white door, flanked by little white light fixtures without bulbs in them.

My hands are cold and shaking, not unlike Angela's were before she could get them on her piano. I unlock the door and just about fall into the penthouse room. No lights flicker on. I fumble for a light switch and find one next to the front door. Only one of the overhead lights comes to life, but it's enough to see what's there.

My self-portrait from two floors below. It has appeared here, at the top of the Estate.

I stand at the window and yank it open. The sea breeze rushing in makes it bearable to stay here longer. I can't go back downstairs right now, and risk running into Edie or the members of Firing Squad. Even Angela, with her physical enthusiasm for this place, is too much for me today. She's playing the piano, so she's fine for the time being.

I call on the only person alive who might be able to help me make sense of all this. Abuela. *I stick around,* she told me that time, and yes, she does. She has been here, in the form of her supposed perfect self, watching me, helping me. I realize I never saw Lilia in a place that wasn't our house or the Estate, both places where she seemed to carry her magic. She was with me. The breeze blows me back from the window, and, turning, I see her. Abuela, projected into this room. Abuela, still hanging on in the hospital room in San Juan. I want to whisper to her in Spanish, but the words don't come. But they're not there in English, either. *Please* or *por favor* is not even close to what I want her to hear from me.

Abuela's perfect black hair has grown out, slashed at the top with a thick line of silver-gray. Her face is relaxed and her eyes look so small without eye makeup. And her hands . . . ah, if only I could have the same moment my mom had, thinking she saw a flicker of movement from Abuela's fingers.

It's okay if you need to go.

This is what I'm trying to tell her.

It's okay if you need to move on.

It's a huddle of words, but it's also a feeling, a shove away from the window and toward the door of the room.

It's okay if you can't stay here anymore.

She's trying to tell me the same thing.

Across the gulp of air that separates the Estate from its nearest neighboring apartment building, there's a single light on—a woman sitting in bed, trying to finish reading a novel before she wears out for the night.

"Hey!" Did I just yell that out to her? Shit. I really did.

No sound comes back.

"Hey! Somebody over there!"

Nothing.

It doesn't matter if the woman across the way ever notices me. What matters is that Lilia doesn't belong to the Red Mangrove Estate anymore. Lilia is nowhere.

* * *

Angela falls asleep in the car on the drive home. She looks normal and calm again, but how long will this last? She could wake up screaming in the middle of the night, or disappear from school again. I'm going to be worried about her every second of the day until I figure this out. Figure out what I'm going to do.

twenty-four

OF COURSE I don't have any finished work for Mrs. Pagonis on Friday. Of course. She drops by the Orange Table and smiles understandingly at me, like she knows she's going to have to give me a low C (in art! The last semester of senior year!) and that I'm not going to have anything for the county show and that I'm definitely not going to SCAD and that I'm going to be one of those people who puts down my paintbrush after graduation and doesn't pick it up again until I'm, like, Abuela's age and taking a class down at Ringling on Wednesday mornings. That's really what she thinks.

I can explain, I want to tell her. She moves past the table, and I want to explain to someone, to Gretchen or even Rider, about Angela and the piano and everything else. Or I could pull out one of the big rolls of brown stock paper that Mrs. Pagonis keeps on a shelf at the back of the room, stretch it out from one end of the room to another, and paint everything, starting with the arrival of the piano and Lilia's and my red room.

Maybe I will.

I raise my hand. "Mrs. Pagonis?"

She lets me have the paper. I start with a small section, stretched across my territory of the Orange Table. But now, with the opportunity to draw everything out, to do a different sort of self-portrait, I don't even know where to begin.

Maybe with the red room.

It's going to be tricky, getting this painting the way I want it to look. I'm envisioning a whole swath of dark red, with two abstract figures, unpainted, approaching each other from opposite sides of the paper. And this time, these elements will be here for good reasons: for instance, Vic and I will be abstract because everything has been strange between us lately. With every brushstroke of red I make, I want her to know more and more about my life. I could seek her out after this class, take the still-wet paper from here to the hallway junction she crosses through on the way to second period, and hold it in front of my face as a way to say, *Hey, I miss you, learn about me again.*

Gretchen leans in toward my work. "What's that?"

"It's something that happened to me recently," I say, and Gretchen seems to accept this. There's an alternate first-period studio art today in which I stop drawing and tell her the whole story. She doesn't believe me at first, but when I get to the part about my self-portrait and where it could end up, I dig in my pocket and show her the keys, and she gasps—"Ah!" But then the surprise slides off her face as she nods and smiles, because even Alternate Morning Gretchen knows better than I do what I should do about all of this.

In this actual morning, Mrs. Pagonis says, "Mercedes?" and she motions to the door of the classroom, and I think I already know what this is about.

Angela is in the nurse's office, lying flat on her back on a cot. Temperature of 103. I sit by her while the nurse tries to get in touch with Mom. "Shit, Ange," I whisper. "We haven't even been here an hour."

"I know, I know." Angela has both hands over her face. "I feel awful."

"Your mom said she can come to get you," the nurse says.

"No!" Angela's hands fly out to her sides, and her eyes are wide open. "She doesn't know where to take me. Only Mercedes does!"

The nurse looks to me for an answer about that one. "She's very particular about doctors. It's a thing she has."

"Well, your mom's on her way," the nurse says. "Only she can check Angela out for the day."

"Can I sit with her?" I ask.

"Sure."

When Mom arrives, I corner her in the hall outside the nurse's office. "Look, you can't take her to urgent care—I mean, back to urgent care. They can't do anything."

"I wasn't planning on it," Mom says. "I'm sure it's just a virus. She needs to stay at home and rest."

"No, it's not that, either. She needs to go to a specific place. Can you check me out, too? I can take her."

"Damn it, Mercedes. Are you both on drugs? Is this what happens when I go away? Rex's renter was a drug dealer, wasn't she? Rex says she disappeared last night. Well, good riddance. She can wreck somebody else's family."

"That's not it. Just check me out of school. Say I have the same bug, or I'm the only one who can take care of Angela, or something like that. I know exactly what she needs."

"Fine," she says, "but I'm following you. And if that girl's there, I don't know what I'm going to do to her."

There's nothing to do but let her follow.

I let her tail me through a McDonald's drive-through first. I get Angela and myself hash browns and orange juice, and Mom goes through and gets something for herself, and waves at me from behind, as if she is relieved, as if this was the big secret.

Angela sips on her orange juice. She smiles at me, but she doesn't look any better.

We keep going. Mom stays behind us the whole time.

I pull into the parking lot. The green minivan is here.

"Just get out. Just run. I'll deal with Mom."

Angela leaves the rest of her breakfast behind, and she disappears into the building.

Mom parks and gets out of her car and taps on the window of

my Pontiac with a hand that is not holding an Egg McMuffin. "Did Angela go in there?"

My throat goes dry. My whole face. My body, down to my toes. Everything is dry and cold. "I don't think so."

Mom glares at me with the same look she's had each time she's talked about Lilia—anger at her own lack of control. Her lack of balance. "Well, I'm going to find out. Stay here."

There's an alternate version of this moment playing in my head, one in which Mom walks right into the Estate, hears the sounds of Firing Squad, follows the music to where Angela is, and requests no explanation for any of this. She'd smile, bop along to the sound while finishing her breakfast, and then go back to work.

Or Mom could go up to the glass doors and turn right back.

Because, in reality, there's no way for her to get in.

She sees me watching her, and she shrugs, and she keeps walking to the other side of the parking lot, the one overlooking the beach.

Everything gets very quiet. I roll down all the windows in the Pontiac because maybe, maybe, I'll be able to hear Angela and Firing Squad playing from here. But no—even the waves aren't that loud from here. This is what Victoria saw when she was here on the night of the bossa nova. Just closed doors and waves and their own kind of silence. And even though I suppose that's not the worst alternate reality to be in, I hate that she was in it. I hate that I wasn't able to track her down after first period today, and that she knows nothing about any of this.

My mother returns, having finished her sandwich and, apparently, started beaming.

"I get it," she says, nodding. "I understand now. Angela needs the ocean to be rejuvenated, right? I swear I read about this somewhere, how the presence of salt water can cure a person."

I attempt a smile from behind my orange juice cup. "Well, it's good we live here, isn't it?"

It's afternoon now. Mom went back to work after taking Angela's temperature seventeen times, looking behind her as she left the house, seemingly dazed at what happened. On our phones in the Estate parking lot, only three minutes passed before Angela appeared again, but whether the time in the Estate was the same, I never knew. We're sitting on the floor of my bedroom doing homework, and she looks normal. But here in non-Estate time, I know she doesn't have much longer until she descends again.

"So, probably tonight," Angela says, not looking up from her biology book.

"Probably tonight what?"

"When I'm moving in."

"The hell you are," I say, and throw down my English notebook, where I eventually need to draft an outline for my paper on *Slaughterhouse-Five*. "You're going to leave home at fourteen years old to play with a band that may not even exist in another year? Yeah, that's a grand plan."

"Oh, you sound like Mom, when she used to tell you not to throw your life away on art," Angela says.

"I suspect she's not done saying that," I say. "But this is different. You don't know what you're getting into there."

"I will if you go, too," Angela says. "Come on. Everyone knows that Lilia left everything there to you."

"Everyone? So they're all waiting for me?"

"Well, yeah."

"I didn't ask for this."

"Maybe you don't realize you did," Angela says.

"You don't know what you're talking about."

"Where are you going?"

"I don't know. Probably to have a smoke and some orange juice."

Except I haven't gotten any cigarettes from Tall Jon lately, so that's out. I'm on the porch with a glass of orange juice, but it's the sludgy end of the bottle. Orange-flavored motor oil.

Rex comes out on the other side of the porch. He's wearing a T-shirt that reads *You Don't Know Me* at the top, and in small letters at the bottom, *Federal Witness Protection Program*. It was funny the first ten times I saw it. Now it's comforting, because it is so Rex.

"Hey there, Mercedes," Rex says. "I feel like I haven't seen you around in a while."

"Yeah. My days have been kind of mixed up."

"I'm feeling a bit off myself. You know Lilia left? No warning whatsoever from that girl. I saw her in the morning, and then in the afternoon, she and her stuff had completely cleared out."

"Wow." I down some orange juice.

"Oh, and I wanted you to know, she took that painting of yours that I had hanging up. The blue-and-orange one you sold me right after I met you."

I smile. "I can paint a better one for you now. Free of charge."

But there's nothing I can do right now to change Angela's mind. I pass her room and she's putting clothes in a bag, even pulling the Wonder Woman T-shirt out of her dirty laundry.

Angela has everything timed right. Mom goes to bed at one a.m., and at one thirty, the green minivan pulls up. Seen from the living room window, Angela looks poised and confident as she heads down the driveway, but I wonder if she's trembling on the outside or the inside. She was always too scared of the woods and other people to go to summer camp. I could count on getting an existential-sounding text or two every time she went to a slumber party in middle school. She hates having dirty clothes. She doesn't even turn fifteen until July. But she is leaving.

twenty-five

IT'S QUIET ON the roads at this time on Saturday, and I am driving too fast and changing lanes all over the place. And I don't even hit a red light until I get stuck at the longest one ever, here at Honore Avenue, about five minutes from Victoria's house. The red seems to blink at me while I wait, daring me to blink back. I remember when I was learning to drive two years ago, and I finally figured out why people ever so slightly let up on the brake when they're sitting at a long-ass stoplight like this one. It's not that they think moving up seven inches is going to help them; it's just that it's damn hard to keep your foot mashed down on the brake for so long.

The light changes, and I head on to Vic's without another stop. The sky brightens from white to blue as I go. I have texted Mom, telling her that Angela and I are supposedly going to tell Victoria to break a leg before her matinee performance of the Gershwin show today. I have time. *We* have time. Vic and me.

"I promise you'll be back way before your show," I tell her. "Please, just come with me."

Vic leans against the door frame, looking so much like herself today. Like someone who is going to be at the theater by noon with her hair pulled tight and her eyeliner darkened and her routines practiced. Her American Ballet Theatre T-shirt looks new, but somehow exactly like all the others. She's got warm-up leggings. Socks. And about ten *Congratulations* balloons bobbing in the hallway behind her head.

Ah, that's exactly who she looks like. Someone who has gotten into Juilliard.

"Really?" I point toward the helium bouquet.

She kind of shrugs.

Vic's parents pop out from the kitchen and wave at me. "Mercedes!" Vic's mom splashes coffee on the white floor as she rushes my way. "Did you hear the good news?"

"I did! Congratulations!" I say it to the Caballinis, to the house, to the balloons. And I suppose I say it to Victoria, as long as she wants to hear it.

She asks where we're going, and I don't know.

It feels good to be in the Pontiac, which has been running like a dream ever since I traded Mom's car for it. I like the Pontiac's voice a lot better than the Ford's—a low roar as opposed to the Ford's nasal hum. *Ahhhh*—brake—*ahhhh.* It makes me want to sing along.

Vic says, "I knew I was right to be worried. All that time you were spending at that building. I thought about finding Lilia and asking her to stop letting you in, stop messing with your life."

"There's nothing you can do," I tell her. "It's all on me now."

"Lilia?"

"She left."

For all the ways that Vic could be relieved by this news, I think it terrifies her in just as many. Lilia is gone. My heart and mind are living somewhere in the spaces between those words. Gone. It's all up to me. Angela and the other artists and the Estate and whatever I choose to believe about the balance of secrets and the origin of beauty itself—they are in my ridiculous little paint-stained hands.

At least I can make this Pontiac fly. *Ahhhhhh.*

"Mercedes," Vic says. "Dearie. Please, just stop."

Fine.

I pull into the parking lot of a buffet restaurant. "Have you ever been here?" I ask.

"Nope."

"Me neither. It's perfect."

They're serving breakfast. Even Vic, with her show in four hours, cannot resist eggs and fruit and one small pancake. The place is packed and noisy, with families and seniors everywhere, and not even enough chairs for Vic and me. We're seated side by side in a pink padded booth in the far corner of the restaurant.

"Remember this moment," I tell her. "This may be the most Florida breakfast of your life."

Vic smiles, but her mouth is full of pancake.

"So you're going, huh?"

She nods. Chews. "June," she finally says. "I'm going to stay with my aunt and uncle until the semester starts."

Of course. I can already see it. She will live in a corner of their Brooklyn apartment, behind makeshift bedroom walls made of Broadway cast albums, used-up pointe shoes, and American Ballet Theatre T-shirts.

"That's, like, two months from now. What are we going to do?"

"What do you mean?" Vic says. She stares at her orange juice. She has actually *gotten* orange juice. That's about as weird as her wearing jeans. Orange juice is delicious but also kind of unforgiving. I should know. That glass is not going to let itself out of her sight.

"I mean, we've admitted that we're scared. We've accused each other of shit. We've gone silent. Now we're even more scared." I grab the orange juice and take a big gulp. "But we can't go on like this. How long are we gonna do this, Vic? I'm supposed to come visit you and play an epic game of 'How Many People?' in front of *The Starry Night* at MoMA. You're supposed to let me make you cocktails on grad night. We're supposed to know each other."

"We do know each other." Vic looks straight at me for the first time all morning. "I was going to say that the only thing we can do is move on, and then I was going to wonder aloud how to do that, but you've already done it."

"Really?"

She has made a smiley face with the remaining pieces of her pancake. I don't know if that's something her parents used to do for her when she was little, or if that is all Vic herself, but it is ridiculously charming and I still love her.

"Yeah," she says. "You committed to it. To our friendship. You weren't too scared to knock on my door this morning. I was just, like, terrified of you after a while. But, good Lord, it's *you*, dearie. I had to stop myself from laughing when I saw that you're wearing your purple sandals this morning."

Wait, what was I saying? *Still* love her? As if I had taken the matter of whether or not I loved her, hung it as a little cloud over my head, and waited to see if it would rain down on me. No. I shouldn't assume that love is as temperamental as the weather.

"These shoes are classic," I tell her.

"Indeed they are," Victoria says.

She eats through every bit of the smiley face, and I finish my eggs and her orange juice.

And then she says, "I keep thinking about what you told me at the dance studio."

"What's that?"

"That when you kissed me, it was perfect."

It was.

And I keep thinking about what Lilia/Abuela said about the

Estate's magic: *It's the best version of you.* That's maybe too much to live under for the rest of my life, but for a moment? Sure, yes, absolutely. The best version of me kissed Vic. I can live with that forever.

"Yeah?" I say.

"I wish I knew . . . I wish I remembered what that was like."

"We'll never re-create it." Around us, the restaurant hums, remaking itself every few minutes as people go in and out. Coffee refills. Buffet refills. Servers taking breaks. Vic and I haven't even been here for an hour, and I think we're about the closest thing to a constant in this place right now.

I lean toward her, nudge her shoulder. "But I can show you a little bit."

This is the most imperfect place. This is a place and a time and a motion that could wreck everything. Vic trembles, and so do I. Her rough T-shirt brushes my arm, and one of my purple sandals falls off. It's cold in here, and there's soft rock music pumping from the ceiling speakers. She's not my girlfriend, and she may never be, but in this one bright moment, I am enough for her, and she is enough for me.

It is just one kiss. Light and breathy. I'm sure I taste like orange juice. I don't know where to put my hands, if she'd want them in hers or on her knees, so I keep them in my lap. But it is the dot that completes a painting. Maybe not quite the signature in the right-hand corner, but close. So very close.

We return to the Pontiac. I drop her off at home so she can finish getting ready for the Gershwin show matinee. And I know where

I need to go next. But my hands sweat against the steering wheel, and I can't bring myself to go there yet.

"Moreno?" Tall Jon says, rubbing his eyes against the midday light hitting him through the doorway. "Everything okay?"

"Sort of. Can I come in and hang out for a while?"

We sit on the balcony, where he tosses me a pack of Parliament Lights and I don't hesitate to smack it open and take one out. Maybe this is how it should be. Instead of going to school or taking over for Lilia, I could become Tall Jon's roommate. I don't know what kind of roommate I would be—I guess sort of the strange one who's always at home and prompts people to wonder about her and what she does all day. That wouldn't be so bad, would it? This is a place where nothing seems to change, where I'd never have to worry about making a mistake or saying too much or too little. And there'd be no risk of running into various cute blond bartenders.

Actually, besides the point about the bartenders, Tall Jon's place would be a lot like the Estate, after all.

So maybe that's not going to work.

I cannot be stuck in the beginnings of things. I cannot hide forever. Look what happened when I took a chance with Victoria. The result wasn't everything I wanted, but it was more than I ever thought possible. It was more than I would have gotten if I hadn't begun. And I haven't been able to take it further since then. Is that okay? Will I ever? The only chance I have is to get myself out of there. To break down whatever barriers were set. And that means getting Angela out, too.

"Hey, do you want to see something wild?" I ask Tall Jon.

"Sure, I guess. What is it?"

"A midday Firing Squad concert."

I mean, as long as he's able to get in.

"Wait, so this is your studio?" Tall Jon asks. We're standing at the glass doors. "I imagined it'd be swankier. It looks pretty broken-down in there."

"It's a practice space. So, you know, it doesn't have to be perfect." The sunlight strikes the glass doors and beats back at us, as though it's trying to push us toward the parking lot, toward Tall Jon's Mazda, maybe all the way back to Tall Jon's apartment. *It doesn't have to be perfect,* I just told him, but it isn't true. Everything inside these walls has to be exactly right for the Red Mangrove Estate's magic to keep humming along. A green room at the top of the stairs on the ninth floor. Light and airy music and dance on the floor below the penthouse. My head aches at all this, and Tall Jon looks like he doesn't believe anything I've told him about the Estate so far. He takes his cigarettes from his back pocket and lights one.

"Hang on," I tell him. "Put that out, and come into the lobby with me. You're going to hear a song, and when it's over, I need you to go back to your car. Seriously."

"Moreno, you're telling me I have to deal with hearing a Firing Squad concert from some crappy lobby?"

"Yes," I tell him. "And I guarantee you'll love it."

It is strange and heady to be in charge, to be able to bend the rules just as much as I need to. I use my keys to get inside, and Tall Jon steps into the lobby, taking it all in. The air infused with salt and dust, the hiss of the vents, the years of solitude clinging to the gray walls. It must have been an amazing place back when people were really living here. But not everything is worth preserving.

I take the stairs to the eighth floor, where Angela is practicing with the rest of the band. She gets excited when she sees me, and oh please, don't let her make any grand proclamations about how I've decided to stay.

"Hey, guys?" I say. "Can I make a request?"

They all snap to attention.

"Can you play 'The Getting Is Good' just once? I have a friend downstairs who would love to hear it. He's actually the one who introduced me to your music."

Brad says, "Sure thing, Mercedes."

Angela readies her hands at the keys. The view through the window of this room is perfect, in some ways—nothing but blue, blue sky. I'd have to get closer, to put myself at a certain angle, to see the gulf and the road and the other buildings from here. You could trick yourself into thinking that only you exist.

"Oh, and wait! He'd love to meet you. He's a DJ at the USF radio station, so he could give you some more exposure."

"Mercy," Angela says, "we don't need that. We're fine."

"Ange, come on. Go see Tall Jon at the end of the song. He's downstairs, being all weirded out, and he'd love to see a familiar face."

They begin. *The getting is good, so let's get going.* I know what Tall Jon's hearing in the lobby isn't exactly like what I'm hearing on the eighth floor, but it's still Firing Squad, and it's perfect for him right now, just like it's perfect for me in here. Angela plays with everything she has, her fingers flying over the keys, head bowed in religious concentration. This is who she's becoming. But there's no reason it has to only take place here.

The sense comes again, starting in the soles of my feet and then prickling at my scalp. The sense of what the building needs. A soft, sad song on the third floor. A shocking photograph on the second floor. Somewhere, a splash of yellow. It is exhilarating to feel this power. But maybe I don't need it.

Except for perhaps one thing.

In the penthouse, in the blank space in the corner, I concentrate as hard as I can on the tiny hospital room in San Juan where Abuela Dolores is. Yes. She is there, silent and unmoving, her life represented by the green waves on her monitor.

My self-portrait in its original, uncovered state flashes on the walls. Angela in the blanket, Victoria's ballet shoes, my mother and my father and Abuela and the houses of San Juan. Lilia and my red room and my purple room.

It's here. I can stay. But I don't need to. I duck out into the hallway and pull the fire alarm.

Then, I sit down and start playing on Angela's piano. The notes stream out like a tantrum. They thrash against one another and break into pieces. I may as well be playing all of the piano parts from all the Firing Squad songs at once, the way my fingers are flying across the keys. It's music. It's noise. It's every confession I have, bursting out of me in the world's most mixed-up song, one that no one else will hear. The floors rumble beneath me. The walls shake and crack and I have only a few minutes to get out of here myself. In a minute, I will race down the stairs for the last time. I'm leaving; I'm leaving, just like Victoria. There's no time to stop and rescue a single thing, no time to smash my fist through the wall on the eighth floor and attempt to steal a piece of my self-portrait.

After heading downstairs, I pause on the second floor and look out the window of the purple room for the final time. A crowd has gathered outside, by Tall Jon's Mazda and the green minivan. I'm the only one left in here, and my head aches as though a thousand needles were pricking at it—*more, more,* the Red Mangrove Estate says. *We need more of everything. More art, more music, more feeling.*

Lilia said that we needed to sense the needs of the Estate, preserve everyone's secrets.

But Lilia was willing to risk that to head off on her own.

A terrible crack from the purple room walls, from the side of them visible to me and from the structure within them. And in the hallway and the living room, Lilia's ceiling art trembles, a great metallic-plastic clatter from all the bottles and cans. A soap bottle and a Goya can are the first to fall, and I'm sure the others will follow soon. But I won't be here to see them.

I believed Lilia when she told me about the secrets and the needs of the Estate, maybe in the same way I believed my mother when she told me to pray to St. Fiacre for good grades (St. Fiacre, it turned out, was the patron saint of taxi drivers), or the same way I believed Victoria when she thought the spirit of Martha Graham wouldn't help her through life.

I won't say that I know, but I will say that I believe. I believe that imperfection and tragedy are going to find me whether I stay here or not, because some of those tragedies will be from my own choices: I will hurt people, and they will hurt me. I believe in my mother's yoga, in Angela's fevered sessions at the piano, and in the New York version of Victoria and how she'll feel the first time her pointe shoe thumps against a Juilliard practice floor. I believe that Duchamp was alternately brilliant and fucking cheeky to try to bottle the air. I believe in giving the world my portrait, however that may happen, and then walking away. It could be a picture the size of a room or a fingernail. It could be a bottle of breath, a laugh, a song, a sigh, or even a mood piece.

I believe in the people who've been here and the secrets they've left behind. But I believe they've been keeping me standing all along.

The Estate will fall. The artists will scatter, except for those who are nothing but a version of someone else, someone living a beautiful wreck of a life elsewhere in the world. Angela might not forgive me for a long time. Alone in the lobby now, I spot her, standing in the parking lot, her face creased in terror and anger, but also complete and utter certainty. She knows exactly what has happened, and exactly who did it.

I push through the glass doors for the last time and toss my keys inside as they close.

Edie and some of the others turn and run farther inland.

Tall Jon yells from his car, "Moreno! Why are you still standing there?"

Angela motions for me to *come here, come here*, and I do, and she doesn't touch me and she says nothing. Finally, she takes a step backward, toward Tall Jon's car.

The women in the neighboring buildings have their curtains open.

The windows and walls in the Estate's penthouse succumb to their cracks.

In a theater across town, Victoria Caballini waits offstage to begin a sequence in the Gershwin show. She sees the stage laid out in front of her, scratched yet smooth, a face of perfection and imperfection, terror and potential. And she leaps into it. Before the music starts, she tears past her fellow dancers, and she leaps and twirls across the expanse of black.

And at the same time, in a hospital room in San Juan, Dolores Camila Hernandez Acosta takes her final breath.

twenty-six

I KEEP THINKING about Abuela.

About how I knew her and loved her my whole life but never suspected she was an artist. About why she was so sure that the nineteen-year-old version of herself that she kept at the Estate was the perfect way to be. About how many of the other people at the Estate were versions of an older self.

I bet she'd prefer me not to wonder. But how can I not?

Gretchen is working on a collage of some black-and-white photographs of people's faces. She has ripped them apart and is now figuring out how to piece them together: an eye, a hairy nostril, one smiling side of a mouth, a forehead with bangs.

She catches me looking at her project. "This was a better idea in my head than it is on paper."

"Nah, I think you can turn it into something cool," I tell her.

We leave class at the same time, both of us awkward with our portfolios and toolboxes. I stumble three paces behind her down the hallway, until I catch up to her at the stairwell.

"Are you going to be at the show this weekend?" I mean, the answer's obvious, but what else do I say to the person I've spent almost four hundred school days not becoming friends with? What do I say when I want to wish her well?

"Yeah. My whole family's coming. Grandparents and everybody. You?"

"Sure. I mean, I guess. We had a death in the family a couple of weeks ago, and everything's kind of a mess. I'll probably just come by myself." I let her ahead of me on the stairs so that she doesn't have to see my face. "But I finally came up with something to enter. That red painting with the two figures."

"Well, then, you won't be completely alone, will you?" Gretchen says.

People shove by us. Some of them say hello to Gretchen and sort of nod at me. Our portfolios hang out into the walking space, disturbing the universe. "You mean, because I've got the people in the picture?"

"Yep." She moves to head up the stairs.

"I'll see you there," I tell her.

✳   ✳   ✳

The house is quiet at night now. Mom has finally settled back into normal sleeping patterns, and Angela seems to be catching up on all the rest she missed when she was the newest member of Firing Squad. I think they're both kind of suspicious of me right now, and I think Mom's got Rex in on it too. He's waiting for me to run after Lilia.

I head out to the front steps with my sketchbook and a pencil. Once the point gets dull I'll go inside, but until then, it's nice out. The air sticks to me like it's trying to keep me here, and so I sit on the concrete and let the night fall all over me.

I owe Rex a picture, to replace the blue-and-orange one that disappeared with Lilia. (The question of where the painting is now and who it's with have kept me up a lot of nights. That's fine—those are nights I would have otherwise been awake missing Abuela.) A few things have been taking shape in my head, and I want them to start taking up actual space on the paper. It needs to be something to represent what happened at the Estate without actually depicting it—something sneaky, so that when Rex or my mom or anyone else sees it, they'll get a feeling about it like a burst of light or a dream in color. The whole story will be there for them, but they'll have to piece it together, moment by moment.

Okay, that could be too much for one painting. Maybe I have a new series to create.

All I know is I'm not drawing any buildings.

If I can wait here long enough tonight, I might see one of them.

The other night, it was the guy I saw at the bar that one time, the one who wore the fedora. He'd lost his hat somewhere along the way, so when he looked at me and waved, I didn't know who he was at first. And then his face came back to me, and the bar, and the photographs in the room, and Edie. I was going to wave at my hatless friend, but he was already gone.

And then again, the next night: it was one of the women from the party, on the night I almost finished the red room.

I was prepared with a wave and a whole tide of questions for her. *Where are you now? Do you know where Edie went? Do you all hate me?* But she didn't stop. She smiled at me, friendly as could be, and then went on walking down the street, striding around the corner as though she was one of the standard-issue dog walkers or stroller-wielding parents. I guess I could have followed her, but I didn't think I needed to be anywhere that she could take me.

Tonight, though, has the feeling that I'm alone. Just me and the lizards. Me and the pencil point that's wearing down. Me and this gray sketch of an empty room—I think I'll be able to fill it in.

"You need to get up."

Angela doesn't look any more prepared for the day than I do. Wonder Woman shirt and Tweety Bird pajama pants. She looked tired this whole week at school, in a way that could fool anyone else into thinking she was plain old last-month-of-school tired, but to me it's something much grayer than that.

She sits at the foot of my bed, gazes around at all the crap I've got on my walls that seems irrelevant now. A sagging poster I got at the Dalí museum. An article I printed out describing a play about Mark Rothko. A small print of one of Frida Kahlo's self-portraits. Well, maybe I'll keep that one.

Angela says, "Mom's made the travel plans."

Mom sits cross-legged on the edge of the living room recliner. When she smiles up at Angela and me, I can't help but think of how she looked when picking me up from summer camp a couple of years ago—like I'd been picturing her face for weeks, and now here she was, looking happier than I'd imagined. That's how she looks today: like someone who has all her energy here in the room with us, rather than split between us and a hospital room in San Juan.

"Okay," she says, "I've got this worked out."

Angela and I wait.

"Looks like there's not going to be time for you to work at the deli this summer, Mercedes," Mom says.

I attempt a smile.

We are leaving. After school's out, Angela and I are flying to San Juan, and then we'll see Mom a few weeks later when she can take five days' vacation. Angela and I are going to be in Puerto Rico most of the summer, helping clean out Abuela's apartment, staying with our San Juan family, and trying to convince them to let us have Abuela's dogs. And when we get back, it'll be almost time for Angela to start tenth grade, and for me to start classes at USF. Victoria will have already left for New York.

We agreed to this. I agreed to this. But it seems a lot different now, with all the arrangements made.

"I think this will be good for both of you," Mom says.

My knees shake. I don't think I have looked at my knees in a long time. I mumble something about needing to get some orange juice, but there's none in the fridge, so I wind up back in my room, on the floor, with a stained palette and some colored pencils and about half of my pencil sharpener collection surrounding me. Maybe this is the right time to work on my painting for Rex, when I'm feeling all weird and conflicted. I grab my sketchbook, and it falls open not to last night's pencil drawing but to a few words scrawled in bright blue Sharpie marker. *If you still want to work here, come see me. I need you to do a self-portrait.* Lilia's directions to me from a few weeks ago. It is the only permanent thing she left behind.

The pieces are arranged in a circle in the Sarasota Central High School courtyard, which creates either a nice communal experience of art appreciation, or an exercise in creative claustrophobia. The judges are circling, literally, and Gretchen and I hang back behind the pieces—specifically, behind Rider's monstrous *A Study in Chickens*. It's a massive canvas dotted with orange triangles and starlike patterns. Chicken beaks and feet, I guess.

"I don't know if he was inspired by you," Gretchen muses, "or if he completely ripped you off."

"Eh, I wouldn't care if he did." I poke my head around to see the piece close up again. The beaks and feet create a dizzying effect, pulling the viewer into their pointy web. "But I think even if he got the idea from me, he came up with something totally new."

Rider is in the middle of the circle with a bunch of girls, all of whom are pretty hot in that white-but-tan Florida-girl kind of way.

It's noon and we're due to hear the announcement of the winners anytime now. The heat is blazing, radiating at us from the sky and the ground, and we've all probably got about twenty more minutes out here before it gets to be too much. Other people are streaming in now: the underclassmen slouching around with their resigned, maybe-next-year looks on their faces, the kids from other schools, wandering around and probably wondering why our courtyard features a plaque and bench for one random kid, and the families and friends, all shiny and loud, talking about where to go to lunch after this whole mess is over.

Actually, some of those people belong to me.

Mom and Angela and Tall Jon and Victoria are all coming my way, waving, and Tall Jon points with both hands to my picture, which cowers between a metal sculpture and a watercolor portrait. Mom looks where Tall Jon is pointing. "Oh, is that it?" she says. Well, it's better than a frown.

Angela is excited to see my latest painting out in the world. Victoria stands there looking amazing in a blue floral dress, tan sandals, and sunglasses. I saw her just yesterday, for lunch at the Dead Guy, but she seems different now, now that I know I'm leaving first. Some of our infinite possibilities are gone, plucked out of the air as they flew by.

"Well, hey, everybody," I say.

Gretchen's entourage moves toward mine, and the woman I remember from last year, the head of the county schools' art departments, comes to the top step of the school and talks about how art is important, how we mustn't shut down the schools' art departments, how all we need to do is look around us at the talent in this courtyard. She's right about that, but there's more than this circle—there's art being poured out into the world right now, in ways she can't even imagine, and ways I can't either. Everyone from the Red Mangrove Estate is out there now, somewhere, learning how to be themselves, learning how to bring their creations to the world.

And one of them is closer than I expected.

Edie is wandering around the back of the crowd, poking her head in here and there, looking at the art but mostly looking for me.

I duck around Mom and through Gretchen's family and train my eyes on Edie until she spots me.

"Let's go over to that bench," I whisper.

And so we sit together on the Dead Guy's bench, and the woman on the steps goes on about the art program, and I have so many questions for Edie and I figure she has the same for me. She's wearing jeans and a red T-shirt. I'm wearing a long orange dress that Mom picked out for me. I stare at both of our shoes.

Edie takes a breath. "I know you had your reasons for doing what you did."

"Yeah."

"But this . . . whatever it is you're doing here . . . it doesn't seem like you."

"It *is* me, though." I look out over the crowd. "It's not everything about me, but it's part of me. My piece very possibly sucks, but I'm glad that everyone here gets to see it, as weird at that sounds. I'm glad that *you* can come here to see it, too."

"I wasn't planning on staying," Edie says.

"You can, though."

The names start. Four honorable mentions, and Rider is among them.

"Chickens."

"Chickens?" Edie looks at me sideways.

"You have no idea of the artistic potential of chickens," I say.

She smiles.

"And third place goes to Mercedes Moreno, a senior at Sarasota Central, for her painting *A Moment in Red.*"

Edie nudges me off the bench. "Red, huh?"

"You just never know," I say.

Angela, Vic, Mom, and Tall Jon didn't see that I'd slipped away, and now they're watching me make what looks to be a grand entrance from the other side of the courtyard, my orange dress swinging all the way. *A Moment in Red*—was that the right thing to call it? Is everyone narrowing their eyes at me because, yes, they understand that the two figures in the painting are girls moving toward each other? Is this the peak of my work, and is everything going to be downhill from here?

I reach the steps where Mrs. Pagonis and the judges and the honorable mentions are standing.

Enjoy it, enjoy it.

For once, it works.

I claim my certificate and smile, and Vic's hand pops up from the middle of the crowd, waving—saying, in a way, *Yes, everyone here, I know her.* And for now, that is perfect.

But it's weird when she and Edie come up to congratulate me at the same time, and I say, "Hey, Vic, this is my friend Edie," and a realization crosses Vic's face—quickly, like a page turning—that there's a whole part of my life she knows nothing about.

"I think we're going out to lunch." Never mind the tuna sandwich and two helpings of potato salad I ate at the senior reception. "If you want to come with us." I guess I'm saying this to both of them. As there are other people poring over the Dead Guy's plaque and taking up the shade by the bench, we're stuck out in the sun, all of us barely able to see one another.

"Thanks, but no," Edie says. "I've gotta get home."

The word sounds perfectly normal coming from her, and yet to imagine her anywhere but between the borders of black-and-white photos is like trying to imagine Victoria taking up woodworking.

"Where do you live?" Victoria says politely.

"Downtown," Edie says, "with some friends."

Now I'm the one narrowing my eyes.

"It's probably a temporary spot. I don't know what I'm doing right now. I might try to get a photography business started. I might travel for a while and then come back. I don't know." Edie looks from me to Victoria and then back to me. "It's good sometimes, not to know."

"I'm going to Puerto Rico right after graduation," I tell her, "but I'll be back in August."

"Cool. I guess I may see you then," Edie says.

And she wanders off, through the courtyard and off school grounds and past the Smoking Corner and on down the street. I wonder if she was lying about living downtown. There are so many things that could be true about her: she might have had a comfy room at her mom's house waiting for her all along, or she could have had a secret girlfriend the entire time I've known her. Or it could be worse: she could be transient, going from couch to couch, maybe searching out another half-abandoned building to make her own.

But I don't think so. I think she's found a happy medium.

Vic grapples for nonexistent pockets in her dress. "Wait, dearie. Right after graduation?"

After lunch, Vic and Angela and I head down to the beach. I haven't been here since Tall Jon's very windy birthday party in the winter, and everything's different now. Transitional. The locals are starting to hate the weather and the summer vacationers haven't made their way down here yet. Angela slips out of her shoes and walks into the wet sand, but Vic and I make things hard on ourselves, trudging through the soft, dry sand in our heeled sandals.

"Think of a place," she says.

"Um. New York City," I say.

"I knew it. Okay, you need to narrow down. As you'll see one day, New York's a massive place."

"Fine. Your future dorm room."

"Okay. Easy way to start—how many people total have lived in my future dorm room?"

"Easy one to follow up. How many people have *died* in your future dorm room?"

"Morbid. Excellent. How many people who have lived or died in my future dorm room have been convinced that the spirit of Martha Graham visited them?"

We walk past a couple baking themselves faceup on beach towels. The guy turns his head toward us at the sound of Victoria's question.

"Okay. How many people who have lived or died in your future dorm room, and who have been visited by the spirit of Martha Graham, have also been involved in the strange but necessary destruction of a beachfront property?"

"Umm," Vic says, looking at me over her sunglasses, "I'd venture to say . . . none?"

"Oh shit, did I break the game?"

Vic laughs. "Not entirely. I think you trampled on a couple of our infinite possibilities, though."

Here's the thing: New York is massive. I'm sure I will be able to take note of that one day. It has mass—it is huge and heavy and somehow does not manage to sink the land it stands on. It has stretched itself into the sky and yawned into a couple of different states. But the coast down here doesn't need to assert itself in the same way. It takes creation and destruction in stride, the tides sweeping in and out with the thump of time, under the hand of the moon. How many people have stood in the same place on this beach, this tiny place in the universe where I have chosen to sink my weight, and been so afraid and so comforted all at once? It's getting late in the afternoon, and the water is rising. Vic takes off her shoes and goes to join Angela in the shallow surf. I wait at the place where the water just meets the sand.

It looks pretty good in the living room. I mean, black and red don't match any of the decor in the house, so it stands out more than it should, but it's a bold statement: red! dancers! Abstract, square-headed people framed on the wall above my school photo! It wasn't even my idea—it was Mom's.

"I still have no idea what this is," she says, "but it'll remind me of you until I see you again."

She smiles from the recliner. She's back to wearing her beachy clothes again: long floral skirts and sleeveless tops, capped off with a straw hat when she leaves the house.

"Can you do a small favor for me when we're gone?" I ask, stepping into the bare spot by the window.

"In theory, yes."

"Okay, well, I need you to get Angela a piano."

"A piano? You do realize how much we've been spending on plane tickets, don't you?"

"Seriously, people give them away for free. Nobody likes pianos, apparently. Except Angela—she needs one. I've made a few calls already. There are some people nearby who have orphan pianos. All you'd need to do is arrange for pickup."

"For this orphan piano. To go where?"

"Right here." I sit in the spot. "It'll fit, I promise."

"You've been strange since I got home. Both of you. I can't even say if you or your sister has been weirder."

"Yeah. That's a toss-up, isn't it?"

"Mercedes, hijita. Can you tell me? Can you tell me anything?"

Anything. For the first time, I wish I could show her my self-portrait room, because I think the reaction she'd give me is fairly close to the one I'd want. She would know everything from how I hated my bedroom in Naples, to the strange days of summer camp and Mia Cortelyou, to how Lilia, damn it, is not a drug pusher. All that, and more. For a minute, I think the carpet under me feels like that rug Lilia got me to work on the room. My perfect painting rug, which got cleared away by the bulldozers last week, with the walls of the purple room and the self-portrait room and the penthouse and the rest of it.

But I know I can re-create it. Maybe it won't be as huge and grand as the original, but it'll say exactly what I want it to. Maybe I can start it at Abuela's house and then assemble it at the end of the summer, piece by piece.

"Mom," I say, "Victoria's leaving."

"I know," Mom says.

"But she's *leaving*." Maybe there's another way to say this. "But *she's* leaving."

Mom gets up from the chair and sits with me in the old piano spot. Her arm wraps around my shoulders. Her hair falls against my cheek. She's looking at me sort of like she looked at my painting a few minutes ago, with an expression that says, *I know these shapes, I know these colors, and I think I know how you've put them together.* Sort of like that. Maybe. I mean, I know I'm not a painting. Ah, damn it, I'm crying now.

Mom rubs my shoulder. "I know. I know," she says.

It's strange how long a single lizard can keep our attention.

He's on the outside of the porch screen, darting up and then down, stopping to breathe in his little lizardy way, and then racing up to the top of the screen, seemingly to grab a different spot of sun.

"How long do lizards live, do you think?" Vic says.

"A couple years, I'm pretty sure," I say.

"I wonder if that's the right idea." Vic goes to press her face against the screen to get a better look at the little guy. "Spending your life going from place to place, sunning yourself along the way."

"This is the sort of philosopher graduation turns you into, huh?" Because we're done with school, technically. We're caught in a strange appendix of time when everyone who's not a senior is taking finals and we're waiting for Friday night to walk across the stage in our goofy gowns. I have to say, I'm looking forward to it in a weird way, like I'm getting pre-sentimental about hearing "Pomp and

Circumstance" played five hundred times.

I go to the kitchen to refill my orange juice, and when I return Victoria is still pressed against the screen, and I could start into a cheesy metaphor with her that we'd both laugh about: *Vic, I think you're already a lizard. You've lived around the whole perimeter of this country and you've probably sunned yourself from time to time.* But instead, I put the orange juice on the table and I wrap my arms around her from behind.

"Hi," she says.

She turns toward me and we are holding each other and that's all we are doing. She leans her head on my shoulder and her breath collides with my neck. And I think a part of me will always want that in the same way I did last summer, but it doesn't ache at me like it once did. We are making the possibilities wait for us. We are Florida and New York, an artist and a dancer. We are best friends and we are leaving. We aren't stuck in beginnings anymore—we're in the confusing, strange middle, and right now that has got to be the best place to be.

Acknowledgments

I'VE BEEN WRITING about Mercedes, Victoria, and Angela since I was a young teen. They've evolved from the characters they were in those early stories, but the heart of why I loved those girls at age thirteen has remained intact. It feels like both a beginning and an ending to be giving their story to you.

So, after many years writing about these characters, in stories I often kept to myself, let me tell you how strange it was to talk about them with an Actual Literary Agent, in a We Are Going to Sell This Book! kind of way. Yes, very strange. And wonderful. That agent is Victoria Marini, and I'm so lucky to be working with her. She's strong and kind, wise and funny, a great advocate for my book and for the greatness of books in general. My thanks to her, and to the teams at Gelfman Schneider and Irene Goodman Literary Agency.

Victoria found my book a home at HarperTeen, where I began working with my editor Emilia Rhodes, a storybuilding genius who knew just the right questions to ask to make my book better. I'm so thankful for her guidance through this weird and wonderful publishing world. Thank you also to Alice Jerman, Michelle Taormina, Renée Cafiero, Valerie Shea, Gina Rizzo, and the rest of the Harper team.

The beta readers and critique partners who worked with me at various stages in the drafting and editing process have been invaluable. Thank you to Alexis Allen, Kara Bietz, Ashley Blake, Jenn Woodruff, Maryann Dabkowski, Natasha Garcia, Ashleigh Hally, Liz Lang, Dana Lee, Terra McVoy, Cathi O'Tyson, Margaret Robbins, and Ricki Schultz. A special mention to the ladies of my two fabulous writing groups, the DSDs and the WIHGs. I would never have written "the end" if not for you. Thank you for sharing chapters and conversation, despair and inspiration, and the sense that part of the answer to "why are we even *doing* this writing thing?" is to spend time together.

Joanna Farrow saved my plot half a dozen times. She's brilliant, and I can't wait for her own novels to be out in the world. Ash Parsons once told me to get out of my way, and a couple years later, I finally took her advice. Jocelyn McFarlane gave me a single word of inspiration in 2009 that eventually unspooled itself into this story. Adi Alsaid gifted this book with a gorgeous blurb. I am so thankful for all of these fine folks.

Going way back here: In the seventh grade, my friend Melanie Garrick Hill read every novel-ish thing I wrote, including some of the early Mercedes and Victoria stories. Whenever I needed a deadline or some fangirling, she was there.

Also, thanks to my high school English teachers: Jane Davis, Jim Wade, Don Perryman, and Ross Friedman. English class was always the challenging, comforting, bright spot of my school day.

I've got the best day job an author could ask for. Thanks to my ALTA family, particularly Annette and Rob, for the years of support, and the quiet place to write on Saturdays. Jenn Steele has shared either an office or a wall with me for years, and yet she still wants to take coffee walks with me and hear about the publishing world.

To everyone else in my various communities—the 2017 debuts, the 11/11 moms, the CPA trivia team, and the Atlanta YA crew—thank you, and I'm glad you're in my life.

My sister Tricia and I spent years creating characters together, and Tricia, however kindly or recklessly, ceded them all to me. Our parents, John and Karen, encouraged our cottage industry of character-related stuff (posters! maps! board games!) and introduced us to books, art, and theater. Thank you for the love and support. Many thanks to the rest of my family—the Hopkinses, Karczes, Hotzes, Coppels, and DeVivos—with special mention to my grandparents the late Charles and Millie Hotze, for always encouraging me to keep writing.

To Adam and Gavin—thank you for loving me and loving books, and for always making me laugh.